WHEN EDGEWOOD MET ELM STREET

MEET.LOVE.MISSING.MURDER.REPEAT.

BREE KELLER

First Edition: February 2026

ISBN:9781971779010 (ebook)

ISBN: 978-1-971779-02-7 (paperback)

Published by Scarfnay Press Publishing LLC

❀ Formatted with Vellum

To anyone who ever had someone make them feel like they were hard to love. Fight for the ones you love, and the love you deserve.

TIGGER WARNING

This story depicts difficult and sensitive topics, including domestic physical abuse, emotional abuse, sexual assault, violence, and mental health struggles. Please take care while reading.

WHEN EDGEWOOD MET ELM STREET

MEET.LOVE.MISSING.MURDER.REPEAT.

By
Bree Keller

INTRODUCTION

Love.

I was in *love*. I only use that word because it was a feeling I never felt before. I mean, sure, I knew what it felt like to be loved. But *in* love? That was different, but so was this. It was painful, but I didn't know any better. The pain made the peace so addictive. Enthralling, overwhelming, underwhelming, and at times, frankly, horrific. But one thing was for sure: if anyone was going to find out what happened to Rosie, it was going to be me. She had been missing and forgotten for too long. And the realization that I would rather put myself in danger, be privy to the most gruesome insights in people's minds, and possibly go missing myself, than stay in this relationship for one second longer was all the confirmation I needed. One by one, somehow, I need to unhook the cat claws stuck to my soul.

ONE
DOT 1972

ROSIE

"Dotty! The Sheriff is finally here. Come on in and sit down."

I heard my dad yell from where I swung on our lone tree swing, about a quarter acre away from our back door. I had been sitting here all morning, waiting for someone to show up. Either Rosie or the Sheriff.

My prayer was that it would be Rosie.

Rosie is my older sister and my best friend. She just turned seventeen. About the same time, I turned sixteen. She has long dark brown hair, deep blue eyes, and fair skin. She's tall and thin. I am short and petite with long blonde hair, but the same deep blue eyes and fair skin. Almost like we are different copies of the same person.

It was a rare day in Sumner, Washington. The sun was shining, the mountain was out, and summer had just started.

How was it that my insides felt as dark and foggy

as the dead of winter? Guilt wrapped around my lungs, thick as overgrown ivy.

I slowly got up from my swing and made my way over to our small farmhouse on Elm Street. Already in my cutoff shorts and a t-shirt for the day. Barefoot as usual.

But my thoughts weren't on summer, they were on my sister.

I didn't know whether to cry, scream, or just hide. How could I let this happen? She was just with me. She was just here!

My mom and dad are sitting at our yellow Formica kitchen table, talking to Sheriff Jones, making this so much more real.

"Now, I wouldn't start to panic just yet. These things do tend to work themselves out eventually."

"What is that supposed to mean?!" I shout irrationally over the table at the Sheriff. My hands are gripping the sides of the plastic and metal of the matching yellow chair, knuckles flexed white.

"Well, now, no need to shout, girl." He puts up his hands like I might continue, or lunge across the space between us. His black mustache twitches.

"What I am saying is, girls of a certain age, a certain type of girl, if you will, do end up making their way home eventually."

My mother, in her worn, almost see-through apron and house dress, went rigid at his words. It was my broad-shouldered ex-marine dad who was the first to respond, though.

There was a sound of scraping metal on vinyl. Before any of us could blink, my dad had the Sheriff's shirt collar wound in his fist. His toes were barely grazing the floor. Mere inches from Sheriff Jones' face, my dad said low and very slow, "If you are insinuating that my daughter is anything more than a *child* who has gone missing, not of her own free will, then keep talking and I'll have you by your much too big nostrils and smear you around like butter." My dad's coveralls were dirty from the morning's work, but the Sheriff was too busy trying to find the ground to notice.

My dad's face was beet-red and angry, but not even close to the deep blotchy purple shade of embarrassment that had crept up the Sheriff's neck and all over his face.

I am always surprised at my dad's strength. His normal, gentle demeanor makes these moments stick out.

"Okay, that...that's enough, Mr. Luis. Now, all I was saying is sometimes they come home unharmed, and unbothered is all."

His hands are up in a *please don't smear me* kind of way. But my dad has already put him down and let go of the front of his shirt.

"No, we both know what you were saying. But hopefully, now you have a better understanding of our Rosie. And the level of professionalism I expect you to have when helping us locate her."

My dad's face wasn't red anymore, and his breathing had calmed as well. It seemed that the situation had somewhat dissipated. Leaving us all to sit there in an awkward silence.

We sat and waited for my mom to finish making us some herbal tea.

Once she joined us, we got right back to business.

"She has long dark hair, almost to her waist. Blue

eyes, like the sea. Her skin is really fair, except for the freckles on her nose and cheeks from the sun. Rosie was about five feet seven inches tall. And she was meaner than a striped snake when she felt cornered."

The way my mom talked about my sister felt so matter-of-fact. As if the Sheriff would plug in all these details somewhere, shake it up, and out would walk my older sister, Rosie.

She was only a year older than me. We did everything together. Well, most everything. I had been sitting on some information, too stunned when she didn't come home, to share it with anyone. We told each other everything. And it felt like I was tattling, but the guilt had taken over, and I couldn't hold it in any longer.

"She was with Harvey," I offered after the tea had us four almost all the way calmed down. I was taking even breaths and staring at my almost empty cup to keep from unraveling.

Everyone stayed silent. So, I went on.

"Night before last. She told me not to tell anyone, but she was supposed to meet Harvey up at the wall for some...star gazing." I looked sheepishly over my chipped cup at my mom. Her cheeks burned with anger.

"Harvey who?" The Sheriff takes out his pen and paper, finally ready to be useful, it seems.

"Harvey Green, her boyfriend." If Rosie ended up being alright, she was sure gunna kill me for this.

At the word boyfriend, my mom pursed her lips into one thin line.

"Dotty, is there anything else Rosie did that you didn't think to tell us?" My mom said with such steadiness, I had to double-check it was her who was speaking.

"No, mom." I shook my head and looked down at the kitchen floor.

I stayed quiet until the Sheriff again turned to me, "What and where is this *wall*?"

"It's just east, up the hill, past Salmon Creek. We all hang out there a lot. We bring picnics up there when it's nice out. It's a bit of a hike, though."

"And what? There's just a wall? I don't get it?" Scratching his chin he tilts his head to the side.

"Well, yeah. Rosie and I found it one day when we were just kids. It's like a big retaining wall of some kind, built right into the hillside."

"There weren't any private property signs or anything," I add quickly.

The Sheriff nods and looks to my parents.

"But I already checked there yesterday. When I woke up, she still wasn't home. I ran all the way there, and there was nothing and no one. I was pretty nervous, though. I could have missed something."

I had to be careful not to say *someone*. I look over at my parents again, my dad clenches his fists, and my mom's bottom lip quivers slightly.

"Anything else you folks can remember, just give me a holler."

All three of us watch in silence as he goes out the door, down the front porch stairs, and gets in his cruiser.

I slowly turn my head back to my parents and wait for the rapid-fire questioning to start.

"Dorothea Luis, your sister is missing. How on earth do you expect to find her if you keep secrets?"

"I'm so sorry, Mom, I just really thought she was coming back." I choke out the last few words. I'm not going to cry; if I do, I might as well admit that I'm afraid she's never coming back.

"I'll tell you all that I can remember." I form the words with determination, but I'm still worried about how much she will hate me when she comes home.

My dad, who has been silent since his threat to smear the Sheriff, puts a steady hand on my arm.

"Dotty, please, don't leave anything out."

I nod and spill my guts. My betrayal feels like mud. Thick and dark, I can hardly get through it. I ache from the inside out. There is nothing like a sister's pact. But Rosie not coming home the past two nights, with no note, no word, and no phone call, is bigger than our pact.

"Rosie has been seeing Harvey Green since the spring. So, going on a few months now. She seems really smitten, but she and I fought about him because he is older than us and has such a temper. She's been sneaking out almost every night to see him. They meet up at the wall. Or sometimes down by the creek. Two nights ago, it was just going to be like any other meet-up. When she wasn't home by morning, I didn't worry much until I went and checked at the wall. I had thought maybe she fell asleep. But last night when she still hadn't come home, I...felt like something might have happened."

My mom put her hand over her mouth, her eyes wide with shock.

"I even tried to track down Harvey, but his mom said he was working a long shift at the slaughterhouse and wouldn't be done till this evening. But I swear, Mom, Dad, that's all I know."

Last night, my parents asked me where Rosie was. When I told them I hadn't seen her since the previous night, my parents realized Rosie hadn't been home all day either. They were worried and had called the police. The police said they wouldn't be around till the next day.

Apparently, if you're poor and over the age of fifteen, they assume it is a runaway situation. I told my mom I was worried too, and we spent all the previous night calling around to see if anyone had seen her.

Everyone was shocked to hear she hadn't come home. No one has gone missing in this town that I can remember.

I don't know how long the three of us stayed at the table listening to the beats of three fractured hearts.

There's emptiness in both their eyes, reflecting the emptiness inside of me.

TWO

RAY 2007
ELM STREET

"Rayel! Where are we going?" Winnie tries shouting over the music.

"I told you, we are going ghost hunting!" I tell her again, in the most dramatic way possible.

There were no streetlights in my town. But luckily, it wasn't fully dark yet. Edgewood is a small suburb outside of Seattle. Used to be mostly farms, now there are more houses. But still, the neighbors are pretty spread apart. We turned off my street and started heading down towards Sumner.

"Yeah, I understand that. I mean, *where* are we going ghost hunting?"

"The slaughterhouse. Where else?" I give Winnie, my best friend, a big, *trust me* smile.

"That's what I was afraid of." I heard her growl over the radio.

"Winnie, trust me." I reach over and turn down the music and pivot slightly to face her. "You're going to love it!"

"I'm going to *love* an abandoned slaughterhouse?" Winnie's voice drips with skepticism.

I turn the radio back up as we wind our way down North Hill.

It's still somewhat light out and around seventy degrees. The first day of Summer, and we just finished our freshman year of community college.

Winnie was my closest friend in the world, besides my mom. It's been that way ever since I can remember.

I rolled my windows down and let my long, dirty blonde hair blow in the breeze. I looked in my rear-view mirror and saw the blue eyes I inherited from my mom staring back at me. I had medium tan skin, most likely from my dad, whom I never met, and a petite frame. I was soft but definitely had some muscle. I think a lot about what I look like, wondering what my dad left behind and what he didn't. My mom and I, for starters, but what I really meant was traits. The stuff he couldn't slink away with in the night. What parts of me were his? What wasn't?

My eyes go back to the road just as we turn the corner and see the tip of a white flat-roofed building, poking out from dense foliage. Something I had gotten used to growing up in the Pacific Northwest, never seeing too far in front of or behind you, on account of the thriving acres of forests in all directions.

"Okay, but if we don't find anything, you promise we can go to Ashley's party?" Winnie looks at me expectantly.

"Cross my heart and hope to die." I make a hand motion of an X over my heart for emphasis. "I mean, I didn't wear my party boots for nothing." I do a little dance to remind Winnie that I wore my patchwork cowgirl boots out tonight.

I had found them in our garage a couple of years ago. I remember my mom had gasped when I came into the house. They were a perfect fit.

Apparently, they were her older sisters; there's just a lot to unpack for my mom with that. But she told me my aunt would have loved for me to wear them. Aunt Rosie was crazy about the boots. They were real, legitimate leather boots, made out of squares of different animal skins, and they were atrocious, and I loved them.

"Yeah, your mom actually gave me five bucks to somehow get them off you and throw them in a dumpster at some point tonight." We both roared with laughter. Even though I know my mom would have never had me do such a thing.

We were still laughing as we made our way down the narrow, dimly lit street. Both of us clutched each other's arms to keep steady as we were walking and laughing.

Winnie's long, red curly hair bounced as we went. She was quite a bit taller than me and very slim. I think I only came up to her shoulder. But in my boots, maybe a little higher.

She was very pretty and very shy. I guess that's why we made a great pair. I was loud enough for both of us.

We were starting to shiver in our t-shirts and cut-off, way-too-short shorts. But we were almost to the side of the building that had a busted-out window. Everyone knew that's where you could get in easily without having to break anything to enter.

"Why do you want to go to Ashley's anyway? We don't even know half the people that will be there." I try to sound casual, but it's coming off pretty whiny.

"Well, Ray, I think it would do both of us good if we could make some new friends this summer. You are the one who's been getting on me about not pining after Ryan. And when Ashley mentioned she was having an end-of-school-year party, I thought *Hey, why not?*"

"*Hey? Why not?* Winnie, you sound like a grandmother." We dissolved into laughter at that, but we kept on our way.

It wasn't that I didn't like parties. I loved parties, but I just wasn't sure how much I liked Ashley and anyone she was friends with. Besides Winnie, obviously. They knew each other from a physics class I didn't take, and apparently, they became fast friends. I had only met her once, briefly, and wasn't too impressed. Besides, she lived in the next town over, which meant different social circles.

"Well, I am proud of you for ditching Ryan. And I am thankful to Ashley for helping you *move on*. So, I suppose I can give this party a chance."

"That's all I'm asking!" Winnie gives me a thankful squeeze.

Winnie's ex, if you can even call him that, went out of state for school last year and hasn't called, texted, or bothered to visit her since he left. I didn't like him in the first place, but his not even bothering to break up with her puts the rest of the nails in his coffin. He told her he was leaving, then never talked to her again. Who does that?! She had taken it very hard, and since I had never been in a very serious relationship, it was hard for me to empathize with why in the world she was wasting tears on Ryan.

We both looked ahead and saw the broken window. We take a few steps closer. I suck in a breath.

I am smacked with this sudden feeling of impending doom. It creeps down my neck, spreading, and gurgling until it settles in the deepest pits of my stomach.

When Winnie takes a step forward, I stay in the same place.

"Um, are you coming?"

"Yeah...I just...there's...something..." before I can finish stuttering my sentence, a figure appears in the window. I see it just before Winnie. But she looks at my wide eyes and whips around to face the window. And there. A figure dressed in dark loose clothes, a gray hood draped over their head. I know they're real because I can see their chest moving up and down with every breath they take. We are only about eight feet apart from one another, but the hood plus the setting sun makes the face harder to see. But I'm afraid of what I think I see. I know this has to be some mistake. I can feel it staring. Winnie looks from the figure to me and back again. Her movement shakes me from my trance, and in one motion, I grab her hand, and we both turn and run. Her in her white sneakers and me in my patched-work boots, clomping down the road. I fumble with my keys but manage to unlock my car as we approach it. Its dark interior lights up as we throw ourselves inside. I waste no time locking the doors and starting it up. I say a grateful prayer that my mom helped me buy this car. It was small and bright blue, but it had automatic locks and windows.

I step on the gas and make a U-turn so we don't have to drive past the slaughterhouse. After a few tense seconds, I turn to Winnie.

"So? Pretty spooky, huh?"

"Ray, what the hell was that?"

"I don't think it was a what. I think it was a who." I turn on the radio quietly. The silence felt too heavy. "I could see it breathing, so I'm pretty certain that was no ghost."

I look at her smiling like my statement makes it better.

"Oh yeah, wow, my bad. That makes it so much better, Ray." Winnie has her arms crossed, and her thin eyebrows scrunched in concern.

"Look, I promised you scary, and I delivered. And now I'm going to take you to *Queen Ashley's* party, so I'd say this night is going swell for you."

As soon as I finish, Winnie gasps. "Wait, shit, Ray!"

"What?" I say, turning my head to see what she's pointing at. It's a street sign.

"This slaughterhouse is on Elm Street?!" Winnie's voice goes up an octave.

"Yeah, I thought you saw that when we drove up? What's the big deal?"

I knew the *big deal*, but if I played aloof, then I felt like I would get less of a tongue lashing from Winnie. So I casually throw out a few harmless facts.

"This is just the street my mom grew up on. And her sister, who went missing. You know, her boyfriend used to work at the meat factory? Plus, it's the same street that the party is on. Which is why I thought to come here..."

I wait to see if she falls for my feigned innocence.

"Oh! Now it's *the meat factory*? Ray, that shit was so messed up." Winnie is staring straight ahead with her arms tightly folded.

"What shit exactly?" I say sweetly, still playing dumb.

"All of it."

She really didn't like to get scared like I did. But she usually humors me with a good attitude. But for some reason, anytime I brought up my aunt Rosie or stories from when our moms were kids, she got really uncomfortable.

This street had always had a reputation for disappearances, accidents, and strange goings on. But that's what made it more fun, more real. Ghosts can't hurt you. And it's clear Winnie didn't think she saw what I think I saw under that hood. Because if she did, she would not have calmed down so fast.

I guess I was just used to it. My mom mostly won't talk about it, but I think the whole story is such an interesting mystery. And I loved a good mystery.

THREE
RAY 2007
HOUSE PARTY

We show up at Ashley's party fashionably late. I am hoping to go unnoticed until I get my bearings. However, unnoticed hasn't ever been my forte, per se. One-handed, I check my lip gloss in the visor mirror and run my hands through the length of my hair, as we near the end of the long driveway to *Queen Ashley's*.

Pulling up, we can see that there are about twenty cars here already. Perfect. I do see a few that I think look familiar.

Her house is massive. Old, but massive.

It's a farmhouse-style estate, probably built a long time ago. There seemed to be five or six roof peaks lined up in a straight row, making the house look at least half an acre long. In the dark, I can't see how far back it goes. The wrap-around porch is in okay shape, but it has a very worn look to it.

We decided to park in the circle of the driveway alongside some of the other cars. I was careful not to get blocked in. There is an old fountain with water still flowing in the middle of the roundabout.

The house is painted white and looks to be somewhat fresh. Black trim around the windows and edges of the residence. Man, I bet this house has a history. I stare up at it and shiver.

Apple orchards stretch far beyond in all directions of the estate.

Set back on a secluded farm, there are acres and acres out here. I see one barn off to the right, a little way back.

"This is her house?"

Winnie rolls her eyes and grabs my arm. We make our way to the front door. The music is loud, even from where we stand on the porch, so we don't bother to knock.

Winnie pushes the giant wooden door open, and the party is in full swing. There are bodies everywhere. Dancing, kissing, chatting. The smell of alcohol, vomit, mixed with old and new wood, washes over me.

Most houses have an entryway, a small hallway of sorts. This house has an entry room. With a vaulted ceiling and two staircases that create a balcony overlooking the party. The banister looks new, along with the stairs. But the floors are creaky and ancient. Along the sides of the room, there are tables with drinks and snacks. A couple of doorways leading to other parts of the house, and a beautiful chandelier that looks like it's from the *Titanic* hangs in the middle of the ceiling. I wonder what time the party started. From the looks of it, a while ago. But I pulled my phone out and see it's only 10:30.

"Man, Ashley's parents must either be really cool

or really out of town." I have to yell over the music, so Winnie just nods in agreement. Most of the kids here are probably over twenty-one. I'm not, but I've been to enough parties that the presence of alcohol has never surprised me, no matter what age we all were.

Still, I didn't know anyone who could afford their own house yet. Most of us had stuck around here after high school to go to one of the community colleges around here.

Winnie spots Ashley and goes to say hi to her. I look around and see a girl from my last semester's math class getting a drink. I wave and yell in her direction.

"Hey, Chelsea!" She turns and looks surprised to see me as I approach her.

"Hey! I can't believe it's you!" She is slurring her words, and I take an instinctive step back. I do not want to be the girl who gets puked on five seconds into a party. But she rushes to throw her arms around me anyway.

"Yeah, it's good to see you too!" Somehow, I peel away from her and turn towards some loud laughter.

I see some guy. No. A man. Holding court in the middle of a group of people. He is tall, very tall. He was wearing a white t-shirt, which clung to...everything. Jeans and skate shoes. His light brown hair was cut close to his head, and his laugh was easy. Everyone around him was in hysterics as he told a story, or a joke, maybe? Looking at him was like watching a movie, all his peers hanging on his every word. His laughter boomed above all the others. Girls were actually twirling their hair on their fingers, staring at him. I looked down in horror as my hand was in my own hair. I swiftly pinned it to my side. The movement reminded me that I was in a room full of people, and not watching a movie.

"He's really something."

I started; I hadn't noticed Ashley had walked up beside me. My face heated realizing she noticed me, noticing him.

"Yeah," I said, trying to sound indifferent.

"Be careful. And I don't mean that in a bitchy *keep your hands off my man* way. I mean that I have known girls who got involved with him and got really hurt way." She took a long drink from her red cup.

I tilted my head to the side and couldn't help but be curious. She did sound like she maybe had an experience or two with the guy.

"But I can tell you, it's one hell of a ride."

I liked her boldness; it reminded me of...well, me.

"That did sound like a pretty bitchy *don't go for my man,* thing," I said as cold as I could muster, but a smile tugged at my lips.

We both started to laugh awkwardly. It must have caused a scene, because once we stopped, the party had gone somewhat silent, and the giant specimen was looking right at me. As well as his cat-eyed subjects.

"Ashley." His voice carried right to us over the music. "Aren't you going to introduce me to your friend?" I had to do a double-take; his eyes were such a light brown they looked the color of glowing honey. I'm almost sure it's actually two microscopic suns instead of eyeballs.

Ashley points to me lazily with her thumb, "This is Rayel. She came with my school friend Winnie."

Winnie gave a small wave from the other side of

the room. She looked relieved to see me, but a little nervous at this display of attention. Her eyes kept darting from me to him.

Luckily, most people had lost interest and turned back to their cups and friends. But not the giant, he was starting to close the gap between us, and I panicked and held up both my hands. Shouting the first thing that came to mind. "Never have I ever!"

Without missing a beat, he took a deep breath and yelled, "Never have I ever!"

Everyone who wasn't passed out or paired off came and sat in a circle. On a big woven rug in the middle of the floor.

Winnie sat next to me with a nervous look, "Ray, I don't know how to play this."

"Okay, for anyone who hasn't ever played, here is the game." I held both my hands up.

"You say the phrase *Never have I ever* and then you say something, anything you have never done. And anyone who is in the circle who has done that thing has to put a finger down. The last person with a finger up wins."

"Well, actually, around here we play the first person out wins." The sun-eyed beast interjects.

This invokes new fits of laughter. I roll my eyes and start.

"Never have I ever made out with anyone in a moving car!" Every other person in the circle had to put a finger down, even Winnie.

"That's not fair!! Are you like a damn nun or something?" One of the boys shouted.

The circle erupted in laughter, and with a smile, I looked the giant dead in the eye. "What do you think?"

The tall stranger looked down at my full lips, freshly glossed, then at my patchwork boots. He had no idea who he had just met. Because for all intents and purposes, I was a nun. I mean, not really. But I would like to think of myself as careful. A flirt? Absolutely. A tease? No doubt. But there was something about this guy. He had arrogance dripping out of his ears. I could tell he saw me as a challenge. So, he liked to play games. What he didn't know was how much I liked games too.

His response was to extend his hand toward me.

"Hi, I'm Leto. Nice to meet you, Ray-el."

I know he knows my name, and I know he knows that I know that he knows, because Ashley had just told him two seconds ago. I was determined not to let my annoyance show.

"It's Rayel, said like rail. But everybody calls me Ray." I lean in and hold out my hand as sweet and unassuming as the honey in his eyes. I am surprised to find that his hand is rough with calluses. Not a lot of guys our age work any sort of manual labor jobs. It's mostly fast food and the mall in between college courses.

He must have sensed my question because, without prompting, he answers it.

"I work on a farm; I have my whole life."

I nod and go scooting back to my spot in the circle. He seems taken off guard that I didn't immediately demand we go somewhere quiet and *talk*.

Or I imagine that's what he's thinking when his eyes go wide for a split second. Clearing his throat, he moves the game along. "Never have I ever kissed a guy!"

"Boo! That's not fair!" the girls were protesting, having to put another finger down, while all the guys laughed. Leto never broke eye contact with me as I put one of my fingers down.

"Okay, so not quite a nun, I see." He smiled, but curiosity burned behind his eyes.

Someone tried to say something, but Leto cut them off.

"Never have I ever woken up in someone else's bed." He tips his head to the side, still staring straight at me.

I put another finger down as well as every single person besides Leto.

He must not be very bright; I've had hundreds of sleepovers with Winnie. Waking up in her bed is almost a daily occurrence. I am wondering, though, someone with his looks, attitude, and reputation, I would have bet money on him almost never waking up alone.

Just as we were about to hear another pointed question from *Leto the giant*, there was a loud and boisterous voice coming from the hallway.

"AND I TOLD THAT PIECE OF SHIT THAT HE WAS LUCKY MY COUSIN WASN'T THERE!" followed up by even louder laughter.

Leto must have known exactly who it was because he got up and walked over to the voices.

I saw right away whose cousin was whose. Leto stood next to a guy who could have been his much shorter brother.

"This is Damon, my cousin," Leto yelled to me over the party that had resumed. I nodded and raised an eyebrow at the guy next to Damon. I'm still wondering why he's acting like I'm his guest and it's his job to make sure everyone knows me. But I play along.

"And this is Miles. My best friend." Damon shrugged, but I could see Leto's comment annoyed him. Miles, on the other hand, beamed at me. He was also very tall, with dark hair, dark eyes, and tanned skin. Okay, where has he been hiding my whole life?

"Hi, I'm Ray." I close the gap between me and the three guys. I can't help but smile. Miles' dimples are even cuter up close.

Not wanting to be weird, I try to make conversation that will allow me to walk away before I say anything stupid.

"Well, it was nice to meet you three. I'd better go find the host; she promised me a tour." At that, all three men's eyebrows shot up.

But it was Leto who spoke.

"Well, you wouldn't want to keep her waiting, of course."

"Yeah..." I tried to sound casual as I turned around and went to find Ashley, but she was nowhere. And neither was Winnie. Purposefully walking away, not too fast and not too slow, I decided on a drink.

Pouring myself some pop, I rehearse my *Why are you not drinking* answer in my head. Good thing too, because about one second later, there is a person at my shoulder and a voice in my ear.

"Why aren't you drinking?" It's Leto, of course it is. I decided on a different answer than the one I just practiced.

"I am drinking, see." I take a long drink of the very nonalcoholic cola in my hand.

"You know what I mean." His gold eyes never leave my mouth.

"Why aren't you? I'm just a poor nun. What's your excuse?" I can't help but want to make him squirm.

"I'm not drinking because I don't like to be out of control. I like control, love it actually." I believed him. And realized he was the one making me squirm.

"And, if you're really good, I'll get the owner of the house to give you a VIP tour." He lightly flicked my nose with his index finger, and I couldn't decide if I liked his touch or not. I'm leaning towards...not.

"I'm pretty sure Ashley will show me around regardless."

"Well, she might get lost because she doesn't live here. I do."

Heat burned my cheeks as I realized how dumb I must have looked to him and his stupid friends just moments ago.

But before I could ask any follow-up questions, the song changed.

"Well, I'll see you around, *Ray*, I gotta dance." He pointed his thumb behind him and was gone before I could put my cup down. The way he made sure to say Ray and not Ray-el curled a smile to my lips.

Most of the partygoers were in the middle of the room dancing. It wasn't too long until I couldn't help it either. I scanned the room for Winnie, and when I found her coming down the hallway from where I assumed the bathroom must be, I pointed to her and nodded. She nodded back, and we both met on the dance floor, which was actually just that giant rug with the furniture pushed off of it. We started to dance like we always had. Like no one was watching, and like we had no cares in the world. We were dancing our hearts out, and I noticed Miles was watching me over the heads of some girls who had cornered him against the wall. A smile tugs at his mouth as he observes me make a damn fool of myself.

"Oh my gosh!" Winnie points and starts laughing uncontrollably. I turn to see what she's pointing at and can't help feeling amused myself.

In the middle of the crowd is giant Leto, dancing full out like no one is watching. Except I'm watching, and he knows it now because he's watching me too.

FOUR
DOT 1972
SCARECROW

S till nothing. Not one trace of Rosie has been found anywhere. It's as if she walked out the front door and disappeared into nothingness. Evaporated. I'm back out on the swing, looking out across the fields of farmland. So many of the people's farms around here have sold, I don't know what belongs to whom anymore.

The overcast sky gives everything a bluish green hue. Magnified by the many evergreens that fill in any empty spaces that surround the farmlands.

I am just about to go inside when I see Harvey in the flesh, making his way around our little blue house and over to my swing. He still has his work clothes on, and I see some suspicious dark stains on his apron.

"Heard about Rosie." He's about five feet away from me now with his hands in his denim pockets. "Figured your mom and dad would have some questions for me." He looks awful. Red puffy eyes, scratches on his neck. Where has this guy really been?

"You figured right." Glaring at him, I wonder if he would be truthful to me.

"My parents went up to Salmon Creek with the rest of the volunteers. If you heard about Rosie, how is it you aren't there?" I ask, narrowing my eyes even tighter at his neck.

"Stop looking at me like that. Last I saw Rosie, she was alive and well."

His athletic build did nothing for his professed innocence. Imaginary horrors are flashing across my mind, trying to picture what could have caused those scratches.

"And how is it you aren't there either, Dotty?"

"My mom wanted someone here in case Rosie came home." I know how hopeless my voice sounds. His presence is starting to make me feel panicked. "When was it that you last saw her then?" I turn my hopeless tone to accusatory.

"A couple of nights ago, we met up at the wall, as you well know, we hung out, then she left." He shrugged as if to say *it's as simple as that*.

"You walked her back home?"

"Well, no. I never do. When we cross back over the creek, we walk to Elm Street, and then we just go our separate ways. It was around 10:30 pm two nights ago."

"And did you already tell this to the Sheriff?"

"Yeah, Dot, just an hour or so ago. When I got off work, he was waiting at my door. He said I should lie low and not leave town."

"So, you just came over here to tell me, you don't know anything? Thanks, that's really helpful, Harvey."

Felling suddenly brave, I stand up and shout. "Just get the hell out of here, okay?!"

He starts backing up from the same direction in which he came, with his hands up in surrender.

Over his shoulder, he shouts, "Maybe you just didn't know your sister like you thought you did."

This really burns me up inside. Doubt it, I know her better than she even knows herself.

Just as the rain starts to fall, I am left alone once again.

I go back to staring out over the fields. Feeling the rain drenching the top of my head and my shoulders.

I look out across the land and spot the apple orchard in the distance. Iwasn't too familiar with the owners. Barely visible is the tallest peak of the sprawling farmhouse. Built way back in the 1800s. Their family had come into some money but fell on hard times during the depression. Sadly, they have been struggling ever since. You never want to see fellow farmers in a bind. You never know when you will be right along with them. I think they are the only family that hasn't had to sell off any parcels of land yet, though.

Our own farm is a very small wheat farm. My dad has a couple of farmhands to help run it and makes an okay living. I think he was pretty disappointed in only having daughters. Especially when Rosie took the job over at the Berry Farm instead of helping out around here.

The other fields belong to an assortment of farmers, but I can't remember which or what they are growing. The apples, though, those are hard to miss.

I'm squinting through the rain to look at what I

can see of the big farmhouse still when something big catches my eye. A very large Scarecrow. It looks like it was in the middle of all the properties. I could have sworn it hadn't been there before Harvey showed up. I kept my eye on it for at least ten minutes. Watching it, making sure it wasn't a person. Couldn't have been. Who would stand there just staring for so long?

The Scarecrow is still there when the sun starts to set. Making my way inside, soaking wet. I grab a drink of milk and a slice of bread. My parents haven't made it back yet. But it's starting to get dark, hiking down the hill can be dangerous. Especially for old people, and especially in the rain.

Just as I'm thinking I should probably meet them over there, I hear a knock at the front door. Takes me all but a few seconds to down the rest of my milk and put my plate and cup in the sink. Walking through the kitchen doorway into the entry, I can see a figure at the front door.

There, standing in front of the storm screen, is a very young, tall, and skinny farmer. He's got his work coveralls on and dirty work boots. He takes his hat off and is wringing it in his hands.

"Yes? Can I help you?" I call through the screen because there is no way I am opening the door for this guy.

"Well, how you doin, little miss Dotty?" he nods to me, and I nod back. He looks vaguely familiar, but I am sure he shouldn't know my name.

"I have been better." I hold his uncomfortable stare and refuse to be the next one to speak.

"I suppose that would be the case, yes." He looks really nervous; his throat is bobbing with every word.

"Are you that apple farmer?" That must be it. I should ask him about that creepy scarecrow.

"I am, that's right. In any case, I was over at Nicholson's pharmacy and overheard the clerk telling a lady that your sister had gone missing. And... I... I don't know, I thought maybe I could get my dogs involved and help somehow."

"Okay... What's your name?" My eyes go to his hat, still twisting in his hands.

"Dale. Dale Lee."

He looks too young to have a farm of his own. Barely older than me, even.

"You got a wife?" I prod.

"I do. Pamela Lee. We have been married for three years. We inherited the estate and orchards from my late uncle. They didn't have any children, so I guess we were it. The house needs a lot of work. But it's quite a house."

His words feel rehearsed to me.

"Do you have any kids?" I don't bother to sound polite.

"No, we don't. The Lord hasn't seen fit to bless us with any yet."

"Why do you have a scarecrow out there in no man's land?" I couldn't help but ask him; it had been so unsettling for me earlier.

He scrunches his face up in confusion, "Miss, I don't have a scarecrow anywhere near my land or anyone else's."

The hairs on the back of my neck stand up, and I swing around to look out the back door window. Sure enough. Nothing but open fields out there. For miles. I stand there staring for a few seconds, not believing my eyes. Surely, even if it were a person, I would be seeing them walking away in the direction of their home?

I turn back to the screen door, and the nervous farmer is gone.

My parents shuffled in not thirty minutes after my visit with Dale Lee. They were soaking wet and muddy from head to toe. I asked them how it went, even though I could already see it on their faces. Disappointment flooded through me.

"Harvey stopped by, he said the last he saw her was around ten-thirty two nights ago." My dad just nodded in my direction.

To give them some space, I made my way up the stairs into Rosie's and my shared room. It was across the hall from my parents' room and right beside our shared bathroom. Our house was built in the 1940's, but my mom never missed a chance to clean, wallpaper, and paint, whatever surface she could get her hands on. We lived a big life in this small home.

Our tiny room had just a double bed, which we shared, a nightstand, a small dresser, and our closet.

I opened our window and let the cool night breeze in. My mom had sewn little laced curtains that swayed in the cool night breeze. Lying there on top of the covers in my pajamas, it felt like hours. Staring at the ceiling, and then staring into the closet that had Rosie's two dresses hanging beside my own two dresses. One for school and one for church. All four hand sewn by our mom. On the floor, just below where our dresses hung, were my sister's prized possession, her patchwork cowboy boots. She had just come home with them one day, a couple of years ago. My mom always rolled her eyes at them, but I knew she secretly thought that they were endearing.

I don't know what made me get up and walk over to the closet, but there is no way I was going to be able to sleep tonight. As I was standing there touching the soft fabric of one of her dresses, I noticed something on the top shelf. Being just shy of five feet and two inches, I wasn't used to seeing... well, anything up there. Reaching for it, I pull it down and see that it's a notebook.

On the front, scribbled in marker, *Rosie's keep out.*

My heart starts beating, and I start to sweat. I don't remember Rosie having any sort of diary or journal. I wonder how old this is.

Plopping down on my bed, I open it to the first page. Seeing her handwriting brings moisture to my eyes. I keep my emotions from taking over by letting my curiosity outshine my sadness.

April- 1972

I really thought I was going to die tonight. I didn't. But I really thought I might.

FIVE
DOT 1972
RODGER

I never thought I would end up working at the Spartan Drive-in. I had wanted to work on the Berry Farm with Rosie, but she convinced me that the pay wasn't worth the trouble. So, when I saw that Spartan's was hiring, I filled out an application and was hired on the spot.

It could be really fun sometimes. After our high school's football games, everyone always seemed to end up here. My boss, Daryl, never minded if I took more frequent breaks to hang out with my friends. As long as I did some work in between.

Since it was really close to school, during lunch I could walk here and usually get something to eat for free. I pop a fry in my mouth and fan myself with one of our menus. Feeling glad I was in my short button-up, collared dress uniform. And not something stuffy. I missed the rain. I was used to the rain; no one expected this hot of a day in June.

Wiping the grease from my hands onto my canvas change apron, I inspect my coin dispenser. Rolling out there on my skates and discovering too late I was out of pennies had happened way too often. I was trying to keep my mind distracted from thoughts of Rosie. She was still gone. I was only able to read that first entry in her journal before I felt too much like the worst sister in the world.

Rosie would be so mad at me when she came back if she found out I was reading her private thoughts. I had hidden it under my pillow last night and had not opened it at all today. And now I wouldn't get another chance till after seven when my shift ended tonight.

"Earth to Dot!"

Jumping, I looked up from my change belt to see Daryl waving his hands at me.

"You've been requested to stall five."

I give Daryl a smile and a nod and roll out of the dining area and into the parking lot towards stall five. There's a red Ford Mustang hardtop with a single boy in it. I knew that familiar frame, the car, and the boy. Rodger. He had been trying his absolute hardest to court me. Not only was I not interested. I was down-right hacked.

"Hey there, Dotty." A wide smile spreads across his already summer-tanned face. Despite the heat and humidity, he is wearing his letterman's jacket. His perfect black hair and Dimples remind me of John Davidson. I couldn't help but find him handsome and relentless. Even after his efforts to ask me out were rejected during the school year. I guess he thought he might have better luck now that school's out. It's not that he was a bad person. It was that I didn't date. Not guys like him anyway. He was a jock, popular, rude, loud, and way too sure of himself.

"Welcome to Spartan's Drive-in, what can I get ya?" I figure the faster I get him his food, the faster he will leave. He sees my plan to get rid of him all over my face.

"You know? I have no idea; I think I need someone to help me go through the menu." He smiles and pats the passenger seat next to him.

It's out before I can stop it, "Not now, not when you asked me two months ago, and not ever, Rodger. I. Don't. Like. You." I point the end of my pen at him for emphasis. "Now, what can I get you?"

I throw in a smile, and he starts to laugh. Not a polite chuckle, but full-out laughter. I want to give him a real smile because I expected him to be cross with me, and instead, his laughter calms me.

"Wow, I don't think I have ever gotten such tongue from anyone, Dotty."

Trying to hide my smile, I shrug and tap the pen on my notepad.

"There are only four things on the menu, Rodger: burger, fries, a shake, and pop. Even you can't be that dense."

I don't bother to hide my smile this time. Clearing his throat, he says, "I'll take one of each, then I suppose."

"That will be $1.35." He hands me a bill and some change, and I slip it into one of my canvas apron pockets. Skating back inside to give one of the cooks his order, I feel somewhat relieved. This is the first time in a few days that no one has brought up Rosie. Something had felt normal; I hadn't been sure I would ever feel like that again. But as soon as I thought it, Rosie's journal came careening back into my mind. I wanted her to be okay, and resorting to this invasion of privacy most likely means I was giving up on her being gone by her own free will.

After a few minutes, I take Rodger's tray of food out to him, being careful not to fall on my skates. I hook the tray to his car, and with a wave and a small smile, I turn to leave. Until I hear him mumble something.

"I heard about Rosie."

My stomach sinks at the mention of her name. Slowly turning towards Rodger, I see there's pity in his much too blue eyes.

"It's a shame, she didn't seem at all like the type to just run away. She was smart, you know. Helped me out of a few sticky situations in school last year. Never asked me for anything in return either. Just helped a struggling guy out of the kindness of her heart."

I think for a moment before I decide to respond.

"I know what you're doing." I eye him suspiciously. He looks back at me, innocent as a baby.

"You think you can connect with me over my missing sister, and somehow it will make us close or something. Well, let me tell you something, I don't need you to say anything to me about Rosie. I *know* she was smart, and kind, and helpful. She is my best friend, and she's coming back."

Without another word or glance, I make my way back inside, slamming the door on my way. I had made another decision, to read Rosie's journal, all of it, tonight.

SIX

RAY 2007
EDGEWOOD

I t's almost midnight by the time I pull up my curving driveway. I couldn't help but notice how freaky it was at night with all the trees.

My mom loved Edgewood. She and her parents moved here back in the 70s. It had been an extremely tense time after my aunt Rosie's disappearance. My mom's family ended up not being able to stay in their house. The house where they had two daughters became unbearable when it became just one.

Dotty, my grandparents' only child, and my mom inherited the house when they died. I remember them vaguely as a kid. They used to talk about my dad sometimes, too; *he was such a nice boy, we never saw it coming.* That is, unless my mom was in the room. She wouldn't entertain any admirable thought of my dad.

The house itself was stunning. It was built in the late 60s. My grandparents kept it in amazing shape. I remember them having me help them paint the front porch white just about every summer. We had to power wash all the moss off after the wet falls, winters, and springs. The house had one tall peak in the middle. That's where my room was. Upstairs on the second floor. There was one other bedroom and a bathroom across from my room. The home was modest, but well-kept and in a craftsman farmhouse style. Everyone who saw it always commented on the lilac trees and roses that framed our porch. It was a sage green with white trim, which was tricky because of the moss. But my mom worked so hard to make it shine.

I always admired my grandparents. With their help, she got through college and became a nurse. When I was ten, she went ahead and finished more school to be a Nurse Practitioner.

Her shifts were a lot better, and so was the pay. There had been a little money left over when my grandparents sold the farm on Elm Street, which has helped us along the way, too. Now we are mostly comfortable.

My mom is letting me live here while I finish my associate's degree. Though she did enforce a curfew, even if I was twenty years old.

I walk in through the main level. The dining room, kitchen, and den are on this floor. And there, in the den, is my mom. A big leather couch against the wall faces our only TV. The fireplace is cold and dark underneath it. I don't blame her; the sticky hotness from outside is seeping through the walls. I look around to see that there are no windows cracked. But there's my mom, reading her book by lamplight.

She calls it *being at the crossroads*. I'm not going to

lie; it is both my favorite and least favorite habit of hers.

It can make it really difficult to get away with, well, anything.

"Ray, you're home a little early. Is everything alright?"

I scrunch my eyebrows when I see my mom tuck something beneath her on the couch, then fix her bathrobe over it.

"I thought I told you, you didn't have to be back before midnight? Did you not have a good time?"

Forgetting about the gesture, I turn and look at the cuckoo clock on the wall behind me. Just a hair before midnight. I was notorious for pushing my midnight curfew by at least ten to thirty minutes. Again, you'd think, since I was an adult, that I wouldn't have a curfew, but my mom insisted. She would say, *My house, my rules. If you want different rules, move into your own house.* I was too poor to argue with that.

I think for a moment, how do I explain to her that in order to create a mask of mystery, I needed to leave a party early? I decide those exact words will do.

"In order to create a mask of mystery, I needed to leave the party early."

My hands are behind my back as I rock back and forth on my toes.

"Oh, so you met a boy. I'm surprised the patch-work boots didn't already give you all the allure and mystery you needed." My mom giggles and rolls her eyes.

I can tell when she looks at me in these boots,

sometimes she's seeing another young, happy woman. The thought of it hurts my heart for her.

"I did meet a boy, yes, and he really thinks he's something. Didn't even mention my boots. So yeah, obviously, I had to leave early without saying good-bye." I sit down by her feet and start to take my boots off.

"Yes, quite obviously." My mom agrees quickly.

I sit there for a second and really look at my mom. In her bathrobe and no makeup on, she is still one of the prettiest people I have ever seen. The only flaw I have ever noticed is a scar that runs from the front of her earlobe to the top of her breast. From an accident in the woods years ago. She didn't like to talk about.

But tonight, I can tell she's been crying. There is a little red around her eyes, and she sounds a tad congested.

"Mom? Are you okay?"

I wait a few seconds for her response.

"Yes, sweetie, I just...Rosie went missing thirty-five years ago today. And as I was thinking about her...I just don't know. That's the worst part. I just don't know what happened."

I lean over the space between us and give my mom a hug and a kiss.

The weight of it all, I just couldn't imagine. Losing your best friend would be tragic. Not to mention if that best friend was also your sister, and you never learned what her fate was.

We spent a while just sitting there hugging. And a part of me wonders if she's hugging me or Rosie.

It's a while before I make it up the creaky wooden stairs to my room. I covered my mom up with a blanket after she dozed off to sleep. I don't know how long I lay there next to her, long enough that my arm fell asleep, and I became desperate to get out of these jean shorts immediately.

Upstairs, I turn left and go down a short hallway to go into my room that overlooks the front yard. The honey wood floors are a nice contrast to my black iron bed.

I opened my window and cursed this damned heat wave. My head hits the pillow after I change out of my clothes and put on a t-shirt and a pair of shorts for bed. People don't realize how humid it is here. Wet and miserable without AC, which hardly anyone has. Of all the renovations we have made, that was not one of them. My mom spent time getting all the wood floors put in and the leather furniture, big area rugs, but no AC.

It's almost impossible to sleep, and I feel okay about that because I need time to think about Leto.

Why did I like him? What was it about him that made me think I could, how did Ashley put it? Survive *one hell of a ride.*

As I'm lying there, I hear a voice, or is it music? Not my mom, not the TV. I go very still, trying to pinpoint its origin. We only have one TV in the den, and there's very little chance I can hear it from up here. Not to mention my mom is asleep on the couch, and not up watching it. I am still frozen trying to make sense of who and where it's coming from. Then I feel it. Someone is there. Waiting for me.

I jump up from my bed and cross the short distance to the window. I crouch below the windowsill until I pluck up the courage to peek out over the front yard. I slowly stand up and start to scan over the acres of dense woods in front of our house. There.

I don't know how it could have slipped my mind or why I didn't think of this upon first hearing a noise. The person at the slaughterhouse. It had to be. Standing there leaning up against an evergreen just beyond the tree line. There they were.

A hooded figure, looking right at my window. Dark loose clothes and no face that I could see. They were staring right at me. I quieted my breathing, and now I could hear it again. But it wasn't a voice exactly. It was a low five-note hum. The hairs on the back of my neck stood up, and where I was sweating before, I am now ice cold.

In one motion, I slam my window shut and lock it. Making quick work of running from my room, locking the rest of the doors in the house, and waking my mom up to go to her bed. Having her on the same level of the house felt a lot safer. I didn't tell her about what I saw. She had enough on her mind thinking about her sister.

But who was that? And did they follow me? Or was it two different people? What are the chances of there being two dark figures following me? Could they have been at the party? Or did they wait for me outside? After locking down the house, I chanced another look out my window. Nothing. They were gone.

By morning, it felt like I hadn't slept for even one minute. All night I tossed and turned, having nightmares about an old woman in my room crawling around and scratching at my bed.

Angry at myself for wasting an entire night, I snoozed my alarm and decided *to hell* with my summer *routine.* You know the one everyone makes at the beginning of summer?

Every day I'm going to wake up early, work out, and make money. Or some variation of that at least. I knew my mom wouldn't mind because she had the day off today and would already be starting her house chores; she wouldn't notice I wasn't up until she got to the upstairs bathroom. That was my chore.

Sure enough, I hear Shania Twain blasting on our kitchen radio an hour later. She really worked fast today.

Rolling over, I see my phone poking out of my jean shorts pocket. The light is blinking, which means I have a message. I open it to see a message from an unknown number. I'm not surprised. Texting is still a fairly new concept. I regularly got texts from people who had updated their plans to *unlimited texting* and wanted someone to try it out on. Sometimes it was people I knew well, and sometimes it was just acquaintances.

Hey

I text back.

Hey

There's a pinging noise and another text. My stomach does a little flip.

It's Leto, from last night. You forgot your VIP tour, and apparently, your manners.

I can't help myself.

Who?

I can feel his smirk through my phone.

You know exactly who I am. Be ready at 7 pm. I'll pick you up.

Forgetting all about the strangeness from last night, butterflies danced in my middle. My plan had worked perfectly.

SEVEN
DOT 1972
BREAK-IN

Walking home as fast as I could after my shift was harder than I anticipated. My roller skates felt like a ton of bricks in my hands. I hadn't realized how nervous I was to read the rest of Rosie's words until I was almost home, and my heart felt like it was going to beat out of my chest.

Running up the porch steps and throwing my skates on the single armchair in our sitting room, I take the stairs two at a time. Hurrying inside my bedroom and shutting the door behind me.

Not even bothering to change out of my work dress, I almost didn't notice it. Something was wrong.

I could feel it. A chill rolled down my back and arms. I slowly turned from the doorway to face the window, wide open. I didn't open my window, and neither would my parents.

I know my dad was out working the farm. It's getting closer to harvest, and my dad likes to make sure all the wheat is flowering as it should. He's been out since dawn and won't be back for another hour.

And my mom, bless her heart, had plans to meet up with all the businesses in town to see if they could display Rosie's missing poster. She still needed to have them made, and then she was going to visit the stores and shops. I wasn't expecting her till after eight tonight.

But someone had been in here. Even a different smell lingered...like an aftershave...or maybe a perfume...a different soap?

I was still frozen, but my eyes scanned the closet. The only space big enough for someone to hide. No chance anyone was getting under the bed; there was only about an inch of clearance under its painted white frame.

The closet is empty, save for our four dresses and Rosie's boots. Then I take a closer look at our bed. The white sheets were still pulled up and tucked in, our worn pale yellow quilt with tiny pink flowers on it, still folded on the top. But the pillows, they were askew. They shouldn't have been. I know I was meticulous in covering the journal before I left.

Finding my strength, I make my way to the head of the bed and lift the pillows. To my horror, Rosie's journal is gone. But a single piece of paper lies there in its place.

The paper looked like it had been ripped out of the same notebook. It was definitely in Rosie's handwriting, only there was no date on it.

Shaking, I picked up the piece of paper. Fearing what it might say, I utter a silent prayer in my head.

I just can't anymore.
It feels like I'm living two lives.
I just need a break from it all...

Who the hell left this? Because there is no way it was my sister. She was...my person.

I held back the tears that were ready to flow, as I set down the piece of paper and tore my room apart looking for the journal. This isn't happening, this can't be happening.

"Dotty? Is that...Dotty! What is going on in here?!" My mom had found me a short while later, sitting on the floor, my room torn apart around me, sobbing and clutching Rosie's note.

"Mom...Rosie." was all I could get out. She snatched the note, and I heard her gasp when her hand shot up to her mouth.

"Not our Rosie. NOT OUR ROSIE! Do you hear me, Dotty? I don't know who left this, but it was not our Rosie." Now my mom was shaking, trying to calm herself down.

But as soon as she sat down on the floor next to me, we couldn't hold back our emotions anymore.

We both sat there holding each other through our hysterics until my dad found us.

"What the hell is going on here?!"

He only looked at us for half a second before he took the note, read it, and demanded an explanation.

"I... I found Rosie's journal. I was too nervous to read it. So, I put it under my pillow. But while I was at work, I convinced myself it might be useful and planned to read it when I got home. But when I got here, my window was open, the journal was gone, and this was in its place." I wipe fresh moisture from my face while I get up, putting my arm out so my mom can stand too.

"What aren't you saying here, Dorothea?" My dad's words are slow and measured. In a very marine interrogation type of way. Out of instinct, I straighten my back and tell him.

"I read the first page last night. It said, *I really thought I was going to die tonight. I didn't. But I really thought I might.* It was dated all the way back in April. And it scared me, and then I worried she might be mad at me when she got back if I invaded her privacy. That's why I hid it."

My eyes cast down to the floor. Looking back, I should have taken it straight to my mom and dad. Full of regret, embarrassment, and guilt, I meet my dad's gaze. Moisture gathers there.

"Dad? I'm so sorry." My voice shakes, and before I can say more, I am scooped up into a bone-crushing hug.

"Dotty, it's going to be okay. We are going to face this as a family, whatever it might be."

After a few minutes, we made our way downstairs while Dad called the Sheriff.

He arrived shortly after in his squad car. My mom had been eerily silent and as white as a ghost since we came down to the sitting room.

"So, you think someone came in through the second-story window...took a diary, and left a forged note?"

"Yes, that's the gist of it." My dad looks uneasy, but I can tell he is trying to be calm and collected.

"My daughter would not have run away. There would not have been a single thing she wouldn't have been okay with bringing to us." Everyone sat, but my dad was standing. It was obvious who was in charge here.

"So, you knew she was sneaking out most nights?" The Sheriff countered, sitting up a little taller.

"Well, no but..."

"And you knew that she had a boyfriend?" He interjected, standing up from his seat.

"Well, no but..." I could tell my dad was deflating; heck, I was deflating.

With the Sheriff at his full height, he was still a little shorter than my dad. "Then it might not be the craziest idea in the world that she ran away, came back to get her diary, and left you a note so you wouldn't worry?"

"No, it *would* be the craziest idea." My dad says through a clenched jaw.

"She would never do that to us. Especially not to me." This time, it was me who interjected.

"You know, child, pretty much everyone would want to assume they mean something to someone. And the cold, hard truth of it is, they didn't, sometimes you just don't. Now I told you before, these things tend to work themselves out eventually. I'm sure she will be home safe and sound, tail between her legs, before you know it."

The shade of red my dad turned was alarming. Uh-oh.

One second, the Sheriff of Sumner was standing in our sitting room, and the next he was on his hind end in our front yard. My dad had grabbed him so fast that if you blinked, you would have missed it.

"Get off my damn property!" was all he said before

slamming the door, which I had no memory of him opening. He must have somehow opened it while holding the Sheriff.

A giggle escapes me, despite the worry, guilt, and horror that I feel. I look over to see a small smile on my mom's still ghostly pale face.

My dad looks at us, kneels down, and makes a promise.

"You girls listen to me. We will never stop looking, thinking, and praying for Rosie. Not until we know exactly what happened to her."

His words struck me, and right there and then, I promised I would do just that.

One thing bothered me about my dad's wording, though. I don't just want to know what happened to her. I want her to walk through that door. I want her to be home.

None of us says anything to each other the rest of the night. No one bothers to ask what's for dinner either. We all just go to bed. Wishing, hoping, praying to wake up from this nightmare.

EIGHT
RAY 2007
THE JUMP

I heard the cuckoo clock give out five chimes as I paced back and forth in my room. I had been wrestling with whether to tell my mom about my little visitor last night. We sang and cleaned, and the mood was so high in our little house that I didn't want to see her face turn in concern about anything because of me.

Ultimately, I think I won't. She has enough on her plate already. Her bringing up Rosie last night was the first time in years, *years!* My mom doesn't even keep pictures of Rosie around. She has been so traumatized by what happened to her sister that she tries to act like it never happened. And I can handle it myself. If there's someone out there who wants to hurt me, I pity them. I'm no dummy. *Street smarts* is my middle name.

I look down and remember I'm still in my pajamas. Okay, so I have about two hours to get ready. Perfect. Just enough time to get ready but not too ready. I mean, who is this guy anyway, right? Why should I go all out? I can't help but smile, because I know I'm gunna look good tonight.

About two hours later, I admire myself in the mirror. Makeup? Just enough to eccentuate my glowing skin. Hair? Long, dirty blonde, and flowing down my back. Outfit? A short floral red sleeveless summer dress and clean white Keds. Perfect. I looked perfect. Remembering my vow to be smart, I text Winnie.

Hey, I'm going out with Leto tonight! He is picking me up. If I don't text you at 10 o'clock tonight, saying I'm home... sound the alarm!

I only have to wait a fraction of a second for her to text me back.

What?!? Last I checked, we didn't like this cocky bastard? What changed?? I need details!

Just then, the doorbell rang, shit, I didn't even tell my mom yet. After our cleaning session, she shut herself in the den. She said she had loads of paperwork to catch up on.

When she told me that, I thought, man, if I'm her age, single, and doing paperwork on my day off? Kill me. I instantly felt like a brat for even thinking that. But...still. It seems lonely. But I know everything I have is because of her. I will be lucky to be half the woman she is.

I text Winnie back quickly.

Come over to my house at 10:30 pm, and I will debrief!

Flying down the stairs, I open the den's door and talk quickly.

"Hey, I am going on a date with a guy named Leto.

I'll be home at 10 o'clock. Winnie is staying the night. Bye!"

I give her a quick kiss on the cheek and shut the den door behind me. She hardly looked up from her papers; that was easier than I thought.

Making quick work of grabbing my purse that my mom hates, I shove my lip gloss and phone inside. In her defense, it does look like it was made from someone's grandma's curtains. I open the front door slowly, not too eagerly.

"Hi." He says, standing there, head almost touching the doorframe, in a black baseball t-shirt, jeans, and ripped-up skate shoes. His eyes find my shoes and slowly pan up to my head. I try not to smile at him, checking me out.

"How did you know where I lived?" I suddenly remembered that I had not given him my number or address.

"We have some mutual friends." Is all the information he gives me with a chuckle. Hands in his pockets, he stands there waiting for me to either invite him in or cross the threshold to him.

Lost in my suspicion, I don't hear the den door open. But I follow Leto's eyes to my mom standing behind me. Reaching out her hand over my shoulder, she introduces herself.

"Hi, I'm Dot, Ray's mom. Where will you be taking her tonight?"

Dammit, I forgot about the *crossroads*.

"Well, it is very nice to meet you, Dot. I am Leto Lee, and I am going to take your daughter for a burger and a swim."

My mom slowly pulls her hand away.

"Where?" she says, in a much less warm voice than before.

"I was going to let her pick..." His voice is a little quieter now, sensing the mood change.

"Burger, yes, swim no. Have her home by 10."

She turns to leave and gives me a big squeeze. "Be safe, call me if you need anything."

And with that, the den door closes, and we walk out to his car. Which is not a car at all. It's a big powder blue Chevy that looks like it's been around since cars were invented. I loved it.

The passenger door made a screech when he pulled it open for me. Oh, I liked that too. I had to find the door handle and climb in. Trucks, dresses, and very short people don't always mix well. He chuckled and waited until I had my seatbelt on before he shut the door.

"I put these seatbelts in myself, you know. This is a 1972 Chevy LUV. And boy has it seen some things." Rolling my eyes, I try not to picture Ashley's words from the party again.

"Do you like it?" He asks expectantly.

"Sure, it's got an engine and a seatbelt. What more could a girl ask for?"

He laughs at that. I notice his eyes keep darting over to me.

"What?" I finally say.

"Nothing, it's just...it's just you're like really pretty."

"Oh, umm...thank you." I guess this is the moment in my existence when all words escape me. For the life of me, I can't think of one thing to say.

"So, are you hungry?" He says.

Thank goodness, words I could respond to. "Yes! Starving! I eat everything."

He starts laughing again.

"Okay, that's good. There's a place I think you'll love."

"I thought I was choosing?" It didn't even take me any effort to be contrary, just in my DNA, I guess.

"You can choose next time, I promise. It's a little hole in the wall, a place I like to call Gorvey's." We both started laughing because this was a major chain restaurant in our area.

"Sounds lovely."

He must have added a little more than seatbelts to his Chevy because it was hauling on the freeway. And I won't lie, the fact that it was a manual was pretty hot too.

We arrived, and he opened my door for me again. And then the restaurant door as well. It's not that I hadn't dated before. I had dated and kissed a few guys. But nothing serious in the last six months. And I can't explain why, but this felt serious.

Meaningful. Different. The way every time he looked at me, his eyes darted from my eyes to my lips like he was trying his hardest not to kiss me or something. It made me nervous, excited, and terrified. I mean, we didn't even know each other, and somehow it felt so comfortable.

All through dinner, he was laser-focused on me. What were my favorites of everything? My childhood, my college plans, all of it.

So, I went into the short story of me. I'm short, just like my mom, obviously, whom he met. I love to laugh, my favorite color is red, I want to go to a better school to get out of town and see the sun, and I don't care what I study. My dad left when my mom was pregnant with me, and never spoke to us again. My mom had a sister, but she went missing in the 70's. My mom is pretty protective, but she and I are very close.

After an hour or so, I felt like I had touched on most everything I could think of in between bites of my burger.

"Why?" I finally said, after I felt like there was nothing else he could ask me.

"Why what?" He said, tilting his head to the side, furrowing his brow.

"Why do you care? Why are you being so... interested?"

"Honestly? Because I've never met someone who was so...indifferent to me before. Someone who like, hates me."

"Wait, back up. You think that anyone who isn't instantly obsessed with you hates you?"

"Don't you?" He counters, a smile tugging at his lips.

"I don't know, I'll let you know what I do if that ever happens to me." I smile at this, and so does he.

"Well, I think we're done here." He doesn't even wait for the check, just throws some cash down on the table and holds out his hand for me to take.

So, I do. When our fingers close around each other, heat snakes up my arm, and I swear, right into my heart. I had never been with someone so sure of me. I'm second-guessing myself, though. Was it the fact that every girl at the party seemed to want him? Or was it because I genuinely wanted him?

Boys were strange. If they were mean to you, that

meant they liked you. If they were nice to you, that meant they just wanted to be friends. It was a lot easier for me to just flirt and kiss and then go home to my mom every night. Not getting seriously involved with anyone was the surest way for me not to make the same mistakes as the women who came before me. The first man who was supposed to love me didn't even stick around for my birth. How could I expect any of these yahoos to do any better? If I got hurt, it would be entirely my fault here. So, it's in my best interest to just have fun. I could feel my own determination not to get hurt strengthen my resolve not to tell this guy too much about me or my mom, from here on out.

When we are back in his truck, I notice we are headed east. His house is just down in the valley from here. My house is north of here. The only place east of here is the lake. Sometimes my friends and I will sneak onto Snag Island and go bridge jumping after dark. Feeling like I knew exactly what his plan was, I blurted out, "My mom said no swimming." I crossed my arms and turned to him.

He thought for a moment, then turned to me, "Then we'd better hurry so your hair will dry before I take you home."

A jolt of nerves went through me. I knew I was going to swim even if I said I wouldn't. His only having to think for a minute about my hair needing to be dry impressed me.

"Listen, I know you've got a reputation for being..."

"A nun?" I interrupt so he can stop stumbling over the word.

"...Careful. I was going to say, careful."

Still pretending to be difficult, I spit, "But I don't even know you. And, I didn't bring a swimsuit."

"Well, it's dark outside, no one would see. And I didn't bring one either." He raises one eyebrow at me.

I scoff, "What in our very short time together makes you think that would work on me?"

Laughing, he reaches under the seat and pulls out a pair of basketball shorts and a t-shirt.

"Will this work?" He extends the folded clothes to me, absolutely already knowing they would work.

Taking them, I hid my smile.

"You don't have to be careful with me. We are a lot alike, you know. My mom and dad were out of the picture most of my life, too. I was raised by my grandparents. They did the best they could. But a lot of it was left up to me. And you know Damon? You met him last night. His parents were also deadbeats. He and I were raised like brothers on that farm. Miles and Damon might be the best friends I'll ever have, and the closest things to brothers."

Ignoring his vulnerability, I ask, "Tell me more about Miles?" I didn't want to keep Leto too happy. This was our first date after all.

"Miles? Man, he's a good guy. Real hard worker, his family does construction. He doesn't have real plans to go to a four-year college or anything...But I would guess him and his girlfriend get married sometime in the next year or so."

I know it shouldn't, but that disappointed me to hear.

"Oh, and what about you? Do you want to get out of here someday?" I ask.

"Oh yeah, I would love to. Travel around, have a brand-new house that isn't falling apart. The kind where you walk in and all the furniture matches."

"That sounds really nice." Is all I can think to say. I feel on edge. I wanted him to like me. But I didn't want to like him anymore than I already do.

The rest of the ride up is in silence, because of all the things he added to his truck, a working radio was not one of them.

It isn't long before the highway turns into a dark winding road lined with as many evergreens as my eye could see. I don't know if it was the darkness or the trees or being alone with a guy whom I didn't know very well, but my thoughts turned to what I saw last night. The person at the slaughterhouse and outside my bedroom. I still wasn't sure if it was the same person.

It's like he could sense my unease.

"Hey, Ray, are you alright?"

"Umm... yeah, I just... have you ever been to the old slaughterhouse?"

"Yeah...Of course I have. I live on Elm Street..." He shrugs like I should have known that.

"Right, well, last night before Ashley's...I mean, your party...Winnie and I went there. And I swear there was a person in there. Like, waiting for us or something. And then when I got home last night, I could have sworn the same person was in my front yard, watching my house."

Even in the dark, I could see Leto's knuckles whiten on the steering wheel.

"Ray. Don't. Ever. Go. There. Alone. Again. Do you hear me?"

His voice suddenly got so rough and serious that I couldn't help but flinch at his words. Recovering slowly, I asked.

"Why?"

"Ray, you don't know the kind of people that hang out there. Just please, promise me?"

"Dude, it was fine. Calm down. I was just wondering if you'd seen anything like that."

"I've seen a lot of things. And let's just leave it at that."

"Ooookay. Well, anyway, I guess we're here." Feeling very awkward and scolded like a child, I was glad when the lake came into view.

We had arrived on the island, and it only took us a few winding turns to find the shorter bridge to jump off of. The water was so dark it could have been a road.

Trying to lighten the mood, I picked up the bundle of clothes and waved them around.

"Can you get out so I can change?"

He nods, and when he gets out, I see him walking over to the bridge, taking his clothes off as he goes.

I start to change, but I can't help feeling exposed in here. Leaving my underwear on until I have the t-shirt and shorts securely on my body, I do a Houdini trick and pull both items out of the other clothes. Just in case anyone was watching.

Balling up all my clothes, I put them under the seat, and join Leto out on the bridge.

"Well, you're already swimming in my clothes, you might as well jump into the water." It's a lame joke, but I laugh anyway. And then I get a good look at him.

Leto is standing there slightly shivering, and I can't

help but admire his *I've worked on a farm my whole life* physique. He had ditched his shirt, shoes, and pants. And it was definitely not dark enough to hide him in only briefs. I don't know if anything was. Dude looked like a linebacker standing there in the dark.

We climb over the rail, and I'm trying not to open-mouth stare at him. Even though the sun is almost down, it was such a nice day today that you can see the outline of Mt. Rainier off in the distance. Its dark silhouette matches the dark water below. This was a man-made lake with little rivers that run off of it and connect back into the center of the lake. There are a few bridges around the island where the water is deep enough to jump into.

"If I didn't know any better, I would think we were jumping into a pit of nothing. With just each other to keep us company." He sounds intense, and far away at the same time when he stretches out his arm towards me.

"Now take my hand and gambol."

I roll my eyes at his pretentious word for *jump*, but lace my fingers through his and do just that.

NINE
DOT 1972
THE GIRL

In the morning, I am devastated to find out that nothing that has happened in the past week has been a nightmare that I could wake up from.

It has been real, all of it. I slowly lift my head from my pillow that has stuck to my face. Dried drool and tears crust to the side of my cheek and neck. I go wash up in the shared bathroom and see that my parents' bed is made, and they are already off working the farm.

Making quick work of the oatmeal breakfast my mom had on the stove, I brush my teeth, dress in my shorts and t-shirt, and run out of the house.

My bike needed a new chain, so I had been walking everywhere since it broke. Sumner is a small town, but since it was in the valley, walking to any other town would require a considerable amount of uphill walking.

That's okay, though. I wasn't leaving Sumner. Plus, I like the exercise, and since I didn't have to work until tonight, I had time to do what I intended. I headed east towards Salmon Creek. Just down the street and into the woods a tiny way.

Rain started to fall just as I was crossing the little bridge to the other side of the creek bed. The ground was still pretty dry because of all the tree cover. I was thankful because there had been times Rosie and I made this hike and were so covered in mud when we got home that Mom made us clean off in the pond in the freezing cold, at the edge of our property. I smiled at the memory of us laughing and swearing to each other, and my parents, that we were dying from pneumonia.

I make my way deeper into the woods. The incline is steady at first, but slowly becomes steeper and steeper.

The first time I had made the hike up to the wall, the day after Rosie didn't come home, I was in a hurry. I didn't look around like I should have.

I hadn't wanted to find anything then, besides my sister sleeping on a blanket with her stupid boyfriend. I wasn't looking for clues or anything.

But the way Harvey looked when he came and saw me was not sitting right with me at all. Why was he all scratched up? And why didn't I demand more answers out of him when I had him in my yard?

Despite what people have said, I do know Rosie best. My parents both love and adore her, but it's me who would recognize anything out of place here.

I'm slowly climbing up the last of the incline, having to use tree branches and roots to steady myself. The rain has gotten heavier, and the ground is starting to get slick. My flat tennis shoes were hardly hiking worthy. Their worn-down soles hardly counted as shoe-worthy.

Finally, pulling myself up and over the last part of

the climb, I give up trying not to get muddy. Lying on my back, I look up into the treetops, letting rain hit my face until a noise snaps my head up.

It's a man's voice. And it's mad.

Slowly, I start to crawl over to where the trees open up, and you can see the stone wall that's built into the side of the green hill.

There, on top of the wall, is a man with his back to me. Arguing with a girl. The man looks to be of average height and athletic build, while the girl is tall with long, dark red hair. Not Rosie. Disappointment floods through me. I can see that one of her palms is out towards the man, and the other is clutching onto a broken strap on her left shoulder. She is trying to keep the top of her long paisley-patterned dress from falling down. Immediately uneasy, I hold my breath and watch in silent horror.

But I have to clamp a hand over my mouth when, through the rain, I see the man backhand slap the redheaded girl in the face with such force that she is inches from falling off the wall. He doesn't even make a move to steady her. She falls on her hands and knees and turns to try to crawl back across the wall, away from the man. In one step, he is standing over her, pulling her up by her hair. He's behind her with her back to him. He holds her head close to his mouth so he can shout in her ear.

"YOU THINK YOU CAN WALK AWAY FROM ME?!"

I decide it's do or die. I'm not going to just sit here while this monster hurts this girl. And I feel I am running out of time because at any moment, he could decide to throw her over the wall, and onto the forest floor below.

It's about fifty feet on either side down a steep embankment.

I use his outburst as cover to crouch and run up the side of the hill to where I can look down onto the wall.

He's not hearing me crash through leaves and bushes because he is still yelling at her.

"AND NO ONE, I MEAN NO ONE, WOULD FIND YOU!"

Right as I am at the spot where I have the higher ground, I can see in her eyes that she's about to make a run for it. I reach down and grab the biggest rock I can find and throw it as hard as I can at the back of his head.

The rock goes sailing down, and with a *thwack,* it hits him square in the back. The girl teeters as he sways, but then she gets her footing and sprints to the other side of the wall. In a flash, she is falling, sprinting, and tumbling through the woods. And to my surprise and delight, he just watches her go.

When she is no longer visible, he slowly turns around and looks directly at where I am hiding behind a thick fern.

And I see a very familiar face. Harvey Green.

TEN
DOT 1972
BULLSEYE

Without a second thought, I wiggle another rock out of the mud and huck it down the hillside. Turning to run before I even know where it lands. It only takes me five steps for the ground beneath my feet to turn into a wet slide of mushy earth. As I am tumbling down the hill, I hear a man yell out.

I hope that means the rock found his big, stupid face.

I don't slow down, using the momentum of my descent, I keep myself going down the hill. Covering my eyes to protect them from any sticks and various pokey things, I finally hit somewhat level ground. Standing up, but very dizzy, I can hardly walk in a straight line, let alone run. But I do it anyway. The rain is so much heavier down here that it's getting hard to see, but from the looks of it, I'm only a few yards from where I should be able to cross back over the creek. Stumbling and tripping over air, I look down and am completely caked in mud and debris.

Still, I can't stop thinking about that redheaded girl. Who was she? Is she okay? Did she get away? Did I give her enough time to get to safety?

My thoughts are interrupted when I hear a thunderous noise coming from above. I look up to see the trees shaking just a few hundred yards up.

Oh, no. He's catching up. I start running towards the familiar creek and right through it. Not bothering to cross at the little bridge. My shoes are soaking wet, and it feels like I am running in sand. Every step, I am sure I am going to get jerked right off my feet from behind.

I push myself faster, past the slaughterhouse, down the street, up the front porch, and through the door.

I keep running until I come face-to-face with my mother. Oh no.

"Good Night, Nurse!", a phrase my mom used only when she was really at her wits' end. She shrieked as we met face to face.

I instinctively start walking backwards out of the house.

"What in the world is going on, Dotty?!" She is following me right out the door towards that icy pond in the corner of our yard. "What has gotten into you? Where have you been? I came inside and had no idea where you had gone, and now you come home looking like this?!"

She keeps yelling, but by now I am at the edge of the water. With my hands up, I feel a stinging around my ankles. Looking down, I let out a yelp-like scream.

Leeches covered my ankles, and blood trickled down onto my soaked shoes. It was rumored that they dump extra blood runoff from the slaughterhouse into the creek. But no one had ever proved it.

My mom put her hand over her mouth and pointed to the little vermin. And I turned and jumped right in. The chill of the water takes my breath away. Even though yesterday was sweltering, it had been raining all day, filling it with cool water. I stay under the surface, scrubbing the mud and fanged slugs off and out of everything, until I can't hear my mom yelling anymore.

I bob my eyes above the water and see her stalking back up to the house, shaking her head.

I don't linger outside for long. I have no idea if Harvey recognized me or if he followed me home. But two things are for sure. One, I have to find that girl with the red hair. And two, I'm not going to tell my mom just yet. If I can protect my parents from the horror of what might have happened to Rosie for a little longer, I will. I'm not going to put this idea in their heads without solid proof.

If what I saw and heard was any indication of how Harvey treated my sister, then there is a really good chance she won't be walking through that door. I feel gutted, but I am telling myself that unless I get a confession or we find her...body, I am not going to freak out.

My mom came into my room a few hours later. I was showered and in my work uniform. I had been staring at my ceiling, trying to think of a plan. I had a pretty good idea of what I was going to do tonight, but my mom interrupted my thoughts before I could come up with a solution for the most important detail.

"Dotty, would you like a ride to work tonight? I hate to think of you walking all the way there alone." I took my eyes off the ceiling and studied my mom for a second.

She was in her housecoat and had a book in her hand. Her eyes were puffy from crying, and she looked rail thin.

"Mom? Are you going to be okay? I mean, if Rosie's not. Will you be?"

My mom's blue eyes met mine, and they stared right through me. Blank. Dead inside already. Her stare answered my question, and it's a good thing because she turned around and left. She might have already accepted what I couldn't yet.

"I'd love a ride!" I call after her, trying to diffuse some of my guilt for asking her such a thing.

A few minutes later, we are in our old Ford and bumping down the road to the Drive-in.

My mom is silent the entire way. I, on the other hand, refused to stop talking.

"And I didn't even know that guy! Can you believe that? He's been trying to get me to go out with him for months, and he thinks that showing up to my work, even when I rejected him at school, is going to win me over?"

It worked, she finally asks, "And who is this boy?"

"Rodger. He thinks he's real hot stuff. But all he is is a letterman's jacket, and a nice car, and dimples, and dark hair."

"You know, Dot, you have always been really sharp when it comes to boys. You really have a good head on your shoulders." She smiles at me and pats my leg.

"Thanks, Mom." What I don't bring up is how bad Rosie was with guys and always has been.

I never had trouble seeing through to who they were deep down. I could feel their intentions like they were shouting them to me from across an empty room. I used to look at Rosie in those situations and think, *Can you believe this guy?* Only to see Rosie's eyes turning all starry at the sight of them. I used to have to drag her away from those creeps. Once she turned sixteen, though, she had really grown into herself. She became a beautiful girl with a lot of confidence. Her response to me was usually, *I can handle it.* Or something similar. I wonder if Harvey was the one man she couldn't handle. Had she finally met her match? I didn't want her to see him in the first place. She used to come back from meetups with him, and we would giggle at the hickeys on her neck. There were only a few times when she came home in tears, and I begged her to break it off. Obviously, she didn't listen.

There was one night she talked about how Harvey was joking around with her, and she almost fell off the wall. I have a very high suspicion that was the incident she was referring to in her journal.

My mom stops the car, and I give her a quick kiss before I jump out. Carrying my skates in one hand and my apron in the other, I look around to see that the place is packed.

Annoyance at the crowd suddenly became an answer to my prayers. There, parked in stall three, is Rodger. He has another girl I vaguely know from town in the passenger seat. She might have gone to school with me. I do feel kind of bad for not knowing a lot of the girls around here very well. When you have a built-in best friend, you don't branch out too often.

In the dining area of the restaurant, I cram my skates on and tie my apron on, and secure my change belt. I hear bits and pieces of about twenty side conversations going on in the restaurant. Either all the guests hadn't realized I work here, or worse, they all just saw me walk in.

"Did you know she was dating like half the basketball team?"

"I heard it was drugs."

"She told someone that she was hitchhiking all the way to California to become a model."

Okay, that's enough. Something like rage takes over me.

With extreme effort, I crawl onto the table closest to me. There are two customers there whispering and shouting that Rosie joined a tough-looking motorcycle gang. I grab on to the one closest to me. He yells, "Hey!" But I keep using his shoulder to pull myself up, so I'm standing on the table. I am trying my absolute hardest not to go flying off the table in my skates.

"Attention! Can I please have your attention?!" Everyone stops talking all at once.

"Hi, yes, that's right. It's me. Dotty Luis. Sister to the missing Rosie Luis. I'm here to clear some things up for you all. Rosie did not run away, she did not hitchhike, do drugs, run off with some boy, or join a gang. We don't know what happened to her or where she is. But we do know, she did not leave willingly. So please, if you aren't talking about ways to help find her, then you can get the hell out!" When I'm done, I look around to see everyone's shocked faces. I smile at my boldness. I start to get down when Daryl comes out of the kitchen.

"What she said!" He yells louder than my whole speech.

I really thought I was about to get fired. Gratitude flows through me as I, as carefully as I can, climb down. No one moves to leave or starts talking again until I turn to go outside and run right into a wall. Before I can hit the floor, the wall reaches out and steadies me. It's not a wall at all; it's Rodger and his date.

"Well, that was quite a show, Miss Dotty." Rodger grins while his brown-haired, somewhat familiar date hides a snicker behind her red, polished fingernails.

"Don't call me that. I don't like it, and I don't like you." I poke the end of my pen into his broad chest before I push past them both and go out to the lot.

I didn't stick around to see what look he had on his face. What a stupid face it was. Handsome, sure, but stupid. Still fuming, I try to distract myself by taking every person's order who is parked in the stalls. We have ten stalls total. It takes me a good while since I seem to be the only carhop working tonight. Plus, I have to run the order back to the kitchen after every car. Including Rodger and his date's order, they came back out to his car to wait for me to take their order. As I am methodically writing things down and taking notes, my mind goes back to what's really important about me coming out tonight. I need to find the redhead. I've been taking an extra good look inside every car. Not one redheaded girl to speak of. She would most likely be sporting a bruise on her left cheek as well.

The first part of my plan was to search the Drive-in. After a couple of hours, it's clear she isn't here. And most likely isn't just going to materialize out of thin air. The second part of my plan was to get a hold of a yearbook. Rosie and I never bought any. They were expensive, and I didn't really need reminding that my only real friend was my sister. We hung out with folks quite a bit, but they were all more like acquaintances. Rosie and I were both keen on getting out of here after high school. I mean, I guess we *were*. I push the thought away that she left without me. There's just no way I would believe that.

I could try and see if the city library is open; they usually stay open late, and I know they keep copies of the town's yearbooks. But it's already dark, and the library is all the way across town. I need a car, or at least someone with a car.

I roll back into the restaurant to grab the last order, it's Rodger's. Just as I am rolling up to his window, it hits me.

I clip the tray on the side of his car and watch him hand over his date's food. I stand there trying to decide how I'm going to word this.

"Hey." He looks up, half-startled, like he didn't see me standing there watching them. I lean a little into the car.

"What are you doing after you drop her off?" I point to the passenger seat.

His date's face immediately pinches into a scowl. Rodger looks up, amused.

"I suppose whatever it is you say, Dot."

I smile and touch his shoulder.

"Perfect, pick me up at closing." I can't help but wipe the hand I touched him with on my apron, as I roll back inside. Something about it felt strange, personal. But I had seen girls do that to flirt all the time.

And it had worked. When closing time came around, Rodger was out front, leaning up against his Mustang, waiting. His date, long gone. He opens the car door for me, and we are pulling out of the lot soon after.

"So Dotty, what are we really doing tonight?" He looks at me with that same amused look from earlier.

"What do you mean? You've been asking me out for ages?" I even throw in a little eyelash batting.

"Exactly, the Dotty Luis I know would never ask me out. Let alone while I was on a date with another girl. So, like I said, what are we really doing?"

I let out a light laugh. Huh, I guess he does know me a little.

"Okay, fine. We are going to the library to look at some yearbooks. Can you read? You can read, right?" I lift my eyebrows and keep my face stoic.

"Yes, *I can read*. Jeez, Dot."

"Great, then we will head there now." I gesture for him to take the next right, and instead, he takes the next left.

"Hey!" I start to protest, but he puts his hand up.

"We don't have to go all the way to the library, I have the yearbooks from freshman to junior year all at my house. Plus, it's two minutes down the road instead of ten."

Okay, I know this is probably not the smartest

idea, but it's Rodger. The guy seems harmless. I mull it over for a few seconds, and by the time I'm done, we are already out front of his very middle-class home. A white colonial-style home with columns framing the front porch, and perfectly little round bushes line the brick walkway up to the red door. The grass is cut in perfect lines all the way across the front lawn. Yeah, this seems fine.

"Well then, let's get to it." I open my door and rush up to the front door before Rodger decides he's going to do something gentlemanly and distract me.

"Alright then." I hear him mumble under his breath as he jogs to catch up.

"Umm, just a warning, I have like seven little sisters, so anything you see and hear...just ignore it."

My face is, I am sure, confused. What? Since when? It is apparent I know close to nothing about this guy. I nod and gesture for him to be the first to walk in.

He takes a deep breath and throws open the door. Instantly, I am struck with over-stimulation. The door must be made of soundproof titanium painted to look like wood. Because there was absolute chaos happening in every direction.

Girls spanning from the age of two to fifteen were everywhere. In the living room off the entry, there were two tween girls watching a television and singing and dancing to whatever was on the screen, at the top of their lungs. To the left in the dining room, there were a couple of girls having an extremely loud tea party with about nine stuffed animals between them.

I stood there gawking, just as two more sisters

came crashing down the staircase wrapped in blankets, laughing uncontrollably.

Rodger took my hand and, stepping over the two girls at the bottom, started leading me up the stairs to what I assume will be his bedroom and yearbooks. At the top of the stairs, there is a bathroom, and the last sister is lying on the counter while another girl irons her hair on a towel with a clothes iron. The sister sticks her tongue out just as her friend shuts the door.

"Almost there," Rodger says more to himself than to me.

Down a few doors to the left, he leads me to a perfectly clean room. Not a thing out of place. An expertly made twin bed, against the right wall, a desk pushed up below the window, and a closet and dresser to the left.

He goes to close the door, but leaves it a crack open. For some reason, that makes me like him, just a little. As well as his circus show family, I had never seen anything like it. It was so exciting and lovely.

Rodger walks over to his closet and pulls out all three yearbooks and puts them on his bed.

"I would ask what we are doing, but I have a feeling it has to do with your sister..."

I nod and grab the first yearbook.

"I need your help to find a girl, she has long red hair and is tall and skinny."

He stares at me for a moment with one eyebrow raised.

"You realize these are in black and white, right?"

Dammit, why didn't I think of that?

"Umm, yeah, but that is where you come in. You're going to help me decide which of these girls has red hair, or the closest to it. Haven't you dated like every-one?" I hold out the other yearbook to him.

"Right." He says as he takes the book from me.

I'm trying to keep focused, but I'm starting to feel a little exposed here in his room. The truth is, I've never been in a guy's room before. Sensing my discomfort, Rodger sighs and tells me, "Don't worry, I'm sure the cavalry will take turns showing up here in a few seconds." Before I get the chance to wonder what he means, I gasp as the door bangs open and two girls around seven and nine run in singing.

"K-I-S-S-I-N-G! First comes love, then comes marriage, then comes a baby in a baby carriage!" They giggle and run from the room.

"See, told ya." Who is this guy? Okay, back to the matter at hand. I am poring through the pages, tracing my finger along every single person's face that shows up in every picture. I break my focus for a second and look up to see Rodger watching me. His cheeks burn red, and he clears his throat.

"Umm, okay, what about her?" He points to a girl laughing with long hair and high cheekbones from the journalism club.

"Yeah, that could be her. Make a note of it and see if we can find out what class she is and what her name is."

"Well, that's Mia King, it's down here under the photo." He points below her picture, and there it is. Mia King.

"Okay, find out which class she's in." I put my head down again and keep looking. Everyone starts to look the same, except Mia King seems to stand out every time I come across her.

"She's in our class. I found her." There she is smiling in our class picture. That's so strange, I have no memory of her.

"How did you know she has red hair?" I ask Rodger as he is writing down her name on a piece of paper.

"Well, funny enough, I took her to a dance last year. Her hair is really only red in the light, though. It looks mostly brown, usually." He shrugs, and I look back down at the book. That's a good way to describe the hair I saw on the wall. And she looks to be the same build.

"Let's keep going through them, and make sure there isn't anyone who fits better." He nods, and we keep going; every single page is studied.

"Okay, now what?"

After an hour or so, Rodger stands up and sits down next to me on the floor.

"Now, we go find her."

ELEVEN

RAY 2007
WET

Climbing out of the water was like pulling myself out of a pit of frozen tar. I was not ready for how freezing and thick the cold was. Or for how much Leto's clothes weighed. I had touched the bottom of the lake; I had never done that before. The slime of the bottom sent a dreadful chill that didn't have anything to do with the temperature through my body. Just as I think I can pull myself up onto the rocky shore, I slip back into the water. I feel strong hands grab me under the arms and throw me onto the shore. Oh jeez. I barely catch myself from falling back in.

"Alright, let's go." Leto is shivering from head to toe and already jogging back up the embankment to his parked truck. I take a step to follow, but something stops me in my hunched-over tracks. The hairs on the back of my neck stand up, and my gaze goes up to the top of the bridge where we had just been standing before we jumped. There, in a dark colored dress, is a person. No hood on their head. They were illuminated under the streetlamp, but the features were blurred by the distance. They look down at me and give me a slow, wide, toothy smile, I think. I gasp and scramble up the rocky hill after Leto. I shout from just below him.

"Hey! Leto! Do you see that?" He turns to look at me, and apparently, he didn't hear me cause he cups a hand over his ear.

"Look over there!" I point and look over. They're gone. What. The. Hell.

I'm gasping and shivering when I reach the truck. Leto is putting on his jeans and shirt.

"What were you saying?" He slips his shoes on, then grabs my pile of clothes from the front seat.

"I saw someone on the bridge. Did you see them?"

He looks at me, then over at the bridge.

"Uhh...no. Who did you see?" His eyebrows are pulled together, and he looks over his shoulder again.

"Umm, a person. Like a really, really creepy figure. And I know how this sounds, but I think it was the same person who was at the slaughterhouse, and also... my house. Standing in my yard."

Leto just stands there looking at me, then hands me my clothes.

"Well, that sounds scary as shit. You'd better hurry and change, or I'm climbing in there with you."

I nod and climb into the truck. I don't think I have ever taken clothes off or put clothes on faster than I did just then. I knock on the window, and Leto jumps in and starts the truck up. He locks his door and leans over me to lock mine. I notice he lingers as he fumbles for the lock. I didn't hate it. Despite the lake water, he still smelled good.

"Okay, let's get the hell out of here." I click my seatbelt on in agreement, and before I know it, we are coasting back down to the valley. Water still clung to Leto's hair, and droplets slid down his neck. He notices me watching him and puts his hand on my leg, just above my knee. What was I getting into? I had always been guarded, my walls built up so thick, Winnie was the only one allowed in. She was safe, she was my friend. Leto is not safe, or so I hear. But so far he's kept me safe. Why do I want to trust him?

"You know, you're not the only person to see that thing," Leto speaks in a low rumble of a voice. Is that fear in his voice I hear?

"What do you mean?" I turn in my seat and notice we are pulling into the old Spartan Drive-in. Leto doesn't answer until he tells the speaker in our stall that we will take two chocolate milkshakes.

"I've seen them before. Or felt them. I camp a lot in the woods around here. With friends mostly. And I never remember a time when I don't feel like someone is out there. Watching me."

His eyes bore into mine, like he was trying to figure out if I believed him. I do.

"Here." He turns his heat on full blast and points it towards my hair. "I do not need a reason for your mom to hate me on our first date." I make quick work of drying my long hair. Just in time for our dessert to arrive.

We sit there for a while in comfortable silence while we sip our shakes.

"Hey, don't mention what I told you to Damon or Miles. They like to tease me about bringing up any of that stuff, and I would hate to have to beat the shit out of them for no reason." He smiles, so I think he's joking. "But seriously, thanks for going out with me. I know I have a...reputation of sorts. But you can't believe everything you hear." He looks at me with his honey eyes, and I can't help but think what it would be like to wake up to those eyes. Then I remember the party.

"So, then, is it true? You've never woken up in someone else's bed before?" I stick the straw in my mouth for something to do, while I pretend not to care what his answer is.

"It's true, I've never felt close enough to anyone to want to wake up in their bed."

I don't say anything for a moment.

"Does that...surprise you?" He lifts his eyebrows at me, and I shrug. I make sure he's looking right at me.

"It excites me." I can't believe I said that, I mean, I was thinking it, but I totally said it!

Leto plucks the milkshake right out of my hand and tosses it, and his own, in the trash can right outside his window. He puts the truck in reverse and heads towards Edgewood. Instead of continuing up to the top, he takes a side street off the narrow road, and we come to a lookout. We can see the lights of the valley below us and the dark wooded hills beyond it.

When the truck is in park, Leto looks at me.

"Why is it do you think we met? I mean, why did you go to a party where you didn't know anyone? And then talk to me?"

"Umm...as I recall it, you talked to me first. You got my number, you texted me, you got my address, and you picked me up." I gesture to the scene around us.

He smiles, and I realize he wants me to ask him the same question.

"So, what's your answer then? Why pursue *me*?" My heart is racing, and I can't read his facial expression.

"Because I have spent most of my life with the people at that party, in that room. And not one of them interests me. Not one of them is someone I would want to get to know. Not one of them, but you. Ray, do you even know how beautiful you are? I can tell you don't, and it makes me crazy to think about."

Extremely flattered would be an understatement. I am floored. Like my jaw and soon-to-be panties are on the floor. I'm kidding, but I mean, come on. I, on occasion, think those things of myself, but always keeping everyone at arm's length, I have never had it confessed to me like that. And you know what? Why shouldn't he? I am fun and desirable. And I have been really, really careful. What would it feel like to be really, really reckless?

Just as the thought leaves my head, Leto's hand is in my hair. The other is holding onto my hip, pulling me towards him. He tips his head down and looks at me, holding me loosely, giving me a chance to pull away. But instead, I fully sit on his lap and wet my lips with my tongue. Before I can take another breath, his lips are on mine. In unison, we move. Our bodies do all the talking. Just as I feel like I might not want to stop whatever happens next, I hear a sound. A sound so out of place from the kissing and breathing noises, we both freeze.

Crunch, crunch, crunch. It sounds like something is right outside the truck. We both look all around us and see nothing, no other cars, no flashlights, nothing. Then I jump and let out a yelp.

A high-pitched scraping sound has us scrambling to start the truck.

"What the hell is that?!" Leto throws the truck in reverse.

"I don't know! Just go! Go!" I click my seat belt and peer out the window.

He is trying to back up and turn around, and not drive off the overlook, all at the same time. Once he has righted the truck, he steps on the gas. I look in the side mirror as we lurch forward and can't believe what I am seeing.

There, just behind the truck, is something or someone, crawling on all fours back into the tree line.

I reach under the seat where I stashed my phone and see that I have ten missed calls. Half from my mom, half from Winnie. Oh no, what time is it? I check the top of the little screen on my flip phone, 10:25 pm. Oh no.

"My mom is going to kill me! Drive faster!" I tap on Leto's arm eagerly, and he guns it. Then looks at the time on his own phone.

"Why do you have a 10 o'clock curfew? You're twenty years old?" He smiles out the side of his mouth.

"I don't know, it's usually midnight, which I know, I probably shouldn't have one, but it's not my house, so, not my rules."

"Your mom seems...interesting."

We pull up just a few seconds later, and I jump out with a wave over my shoulder.

"Thanks, see..." But before I get the rest of my sentence out, something hanging from the side of the door catches my eye. A note, torn out of a note-book, hangs there. An old rusty magnet holds it in place. I pull off the magnet and read the yellowing note.

April 1972

H. followed me home after work today. He told me I had the most beautiful eyes he'd ever seen. I guess he was trying to make up for me almost falling the other night. I wish I could tell Dot what's been going on. I just...Dot is different. She's innocent, whole. I'm...not.

Nothing else is written on the paper. I turn it over to make sure.

"What the hell is this?" I hand the note over to Leto, and he skims it and hands it back.

"I have no idea. Maybe someone was pulling a prank? Instead of shining a flashlight into parked cars, maybe they've moved on to creepy nonsense notes?" Then he turns to me, "Wait, Dot is your mom's name, right?"

"Right," I answer slowly.

"That's a weird coincidence." Leto shrugs, then points to the porch where my mom is now standing, holding the door open for me to come inside.

"Bye, thanks for tonight." I shut the truck door before he can respond and run up the porch stairs.

"I know, I know. I'm sorry, we were drinking milk-shakes and lost track of time." Half true.

"Well, you could have at least called me back, Rayel."

She pulls me into a hug and hears the paper crinkle against her.

"Oh, umm, someone put this on Leto's truck. I have no idea what it is. Do you?"

I show her the piece of paper and watch as her eyes go back and forth, reading it.

She goes white as a ghost and turns and goes inside the den. Okay? What is going on? I follow her and see that she goes over to the bookshelf along the wall under the window in the den. She pulls out a binder and opens it. There are two sheets of paper in the binder. She lays the one I brought home next to them and is studying them.

"Mom? What's going on?" She looks up from the binder like she's going to be sick.

"Ray, someone is..." her voice catches. "Someone is taunting me about my sister's disappearance."

"What do you mean? I thought the guy they suspected was long gone. Didn't he go to jail shortly after she went missing? Who else would even be thinking about it? I mean, besides us."

"I don't know Ray. There were a lot of people who didn't believe he was the one who did something to her. By the end of it, I was one of them."

"What? Well, why do you think it has anything to do with your sister?" I sit down on the couch and try to wrap my head around what is happening.

"I mean, he could still be alive, he could be back..." I start to say until my mom interrupts me. "Look, when I was a teenager, a couple of days after Rosie went missing, I found her journal. I only read the first page. This."

April 1972

I almost died tonight. I didn't. But I thought I might.

It was the same yellowing, notebook paper torn out, and dated at the top.

I gasp and look at my mom. "Who did you give her

journal to? Surely whoever has it now is the one trying to mess with us."

"No one, I read the first page, then I hid it. I came home from work, and it was gone; this note was in its place. She turns the page to show me another note.

I just can't anymore.

It feels like I'm living two lives.

I just need a break from it all...

My hand is over my mouth in shock.

"Then how did you get the other note?"

"Last night, while you were at the party, I heard the doorbell ring. It was sitting on our front porch under a rock. And either someone wants me to figure out what happened, or they want me to be scared that maybe I'm next. Or you, or someone else I love."

TWELVE
RAY 2007
NUTMEG

I stand there glued to the floor, realizing that's what I saw my mom put under her bathrobe last night. How long had she been staring at that thing before I sauntered in last night?

"As much as I want this to lead to some answers, my gut is telling me that it's going to be just more hurt." She takes my hand and guides me to the couch. "Sweetie, I really just want to put this all behind me. I don't know if I can handle reopening any of it. Not anymore."

I understand where she's coming from, but I don't know what to say. We sit there in silence, lost in thought. I'm sure my mom is thinking of the horrors she endured trying to get to the bottom of this so long ago. I had only heard bits and pieces of it. No one would come right out and tell me what exactly happened to my mom at that time. I never had the heart to ask her. To make her remember that pain. I'm wondering if, again, I should keep the strange figure sighting to myself. My mom has been through so much. I hate to think of her worrying about me. She is usually strong, but I can see how fragile this side of her is, with the people she's lost. Not tonight, maybe tomorrow, but not tonight. I lean over to embrace her, and we both jump at a knock on the door. We slowly look at each other, wondering who would be coming over this late.

"Hello?! Ray? Dot? It's me, Winnie!" The muffled voice makes me remember. I had totally forgotten I had invited her over to talk about my date. And I never even called her back. My mom looks relieved with the mood change. She shuts the binder, tucks it under her arm, and starts to make her way up the stairs.

"Don't stay up too late, girls!" She calls halfway up the stairs over her shoulder.

I run to unlock the door and pull Winnie inside the house. Locking up behind her, I drag her up the stairs at lightning speed.

"Damn, girl, what is the rush?" Winnie is dressed in a matching polka-dot pajama set with two braids down her back.

"Is that what you wore?! Ray! You look hot! Your hair, though... what happened?" I turn around after locking my door and slip into a giant t-shirt.

"Thank you, Leto thought so too. Oh, I had to dry my hair in the heater of his truck." I can't help the giant smile plastered on my face. But I really need to confide in Winnie about the serious stuff first.

"Okay, I am going to tell you all about my date with Leto, but first, there's some really weird shit going on, and I need you to hear it."

Winnie sits down slowly and nods her head for me to keep talking.

"Okay, we both saw that creepy person at the slaughterhouse, correct? Correct. And that is how I know I'm not going crazy. I saw them again last night in my front yard. They were staring at me through the trees, right into my window! And then tonight! We were bridge jumping at the lake, and when I looked up. They. Were. There. It gets worse. We were at the lookout, you know, the make-out spot by my house? We were parked, and I'm about ninety percent sure they were there! They literally stuck something to Leto's truck and crawled. CRAWLED. Away. And that's not even the worst of it."

Winnie's eyes are as big as saucers, and she looks positively terrified. But I barely stop to take a breath.

"My mom told me that her missing and presumed dead sister's journal went missing right after she did. And someone has been leaving pages from it for her to find. And now I guess for me to find."

"Wait, I thought the guy who did it served his time, then left the state?"

"He did, or so I thought. But then tonight, my mom told me she's not even sure he's the one who hurt Rosie! He never fully confessed to it. And ended up going to jail for something else."

"Whoa, that...is...insane." Winnie looks over at me, biting her lip.

"But Ray, there's one thing. I didn't see anything specific at the slaughterhouse. I just saw...something. And I'm not even sure what it was. It could have been a shadow or a tree branch. You're the one who said it was a *who*. Remember?"

As soon as she reminded me, I played back the whole encounter in my head. She was right.

"Oh...yeah. But you saw something. That's good enough for me."

I realize I have been pacing back and forth in front of Winnie. I start to catch my breath and sit down.

"Okay, so now what?" Winnie asks me, picking at her nail polish.

"Well, now I gotta be the one to solve her murder. Obviously."

"Yes, okay, I was afraid you were going to say that. Can't we ever just like, go to the mall, Ray?"

"Yes, after, I promise." We both start laughing, and she throws a pillow at my face. I put my hands up to block another from hitting me.

"Okay, okay, don't you want to know about Leto?"

"Yes, actually, I do." Winnie puts the other pillow down and resumes sitting peacefully on my bed.

"Well, we ate, and then we went bridge jumping, and then got dessert. And then we made out."

"What?! I don't believe it. You never kiss guys on the first hangout." Now it's my turn to throw a pillow.

"Yes, I do! Just not like a lot of them. I like to be picky."

"How did he convince you to kiss him?"

"He said some really nice things. Like how hot I was, and fun and outgoing. You know how I like compliments. And I don't know, it felt right." I shrug and can't help it; I just keep smiling.

"Okay, then, when are you going out next?"

"Well, I don't know, my mom was on the front porch, so we didn't really get to say goodbye."

"Well, I'm sure he sent you a follow-up text,

though, right? *I had the time of my life.* That sort of thing."

I check my phone, nothing.

"Umm...also no." I start to question myself. Maybe it wasn't exactly as good as I thought it was? Feeling a tad deflated, I switch our conversation to what is going to be on our summer bucket lists.

Later that night, I can hear Winnie snoring, and I decide I'm going to text him. Why not? Who says the girl can't say she had a really great time?

I open my phone and type out.

Thank you for tonight, I had an incredible time!

I push send and close my phone. There, now I will surely wake up to a text from him.

I fell asleep thinking about Leto's lips on my lips, my neck, my collarbone. But fell directly into a nightmare. I dreamt that I had woken up, and there standing over me was a woman, a girl? I don't know, she might have been my age. I started to scream when the first shovel of dirt hit me. She was burying me. My scream came out as a rasp of air because there was dirt filling up my lungs with each mound she piled on me. Why couldn't I move? Get Up! I was shouting in my head. Get Up!

I woke up and yelled. I startled Winnie, and she yelled too. Then I heard my mom run down the hall before she burst into my room. She was half-dressed for work and had her toothbrush hanging out of her mouth.

I put my hands up, "Sorry! Sorry! It was just a

nightmare. Sorry, Mom!" She glared at me from the door and walked back down the hallway.

Winnie and I were trying to stifle our laughter in our pillows, but from down the hall we heard my mom yell.

"It's not that funny, girls!" Which, of course, made us laugh harder.

A short while later, I dared to look at my phone; ten in the morning seemed like plenty of time to text me back. I open it and see that there are no messages. Not one. Great.

"Winnie, can I tag along with whatever you're doing today?" I lay on the floor as Winnie was flipping through a magazine that she brought.

"Leto still hasn't texted you back?" I roll over onto my stomach.

"Is it that obvious?"

"Yes, and I'm not sure if you'll want to." She gives me a sneaky smile. "I have that co-ed city soccer league I'm trying out for today."

I think for a second, mulling it over, that might actually be exactly what I need. "Okay, I'm in." I jump up to go find my shorts.

"Wait, are you serious?! Yes! This is going to be so fun! And I think Ashley and some of her friends might be trying out too!"

Oh, great, Ashley. But I put on a smile and opened my closet to find my shin guards.

"I haven't played in a while, but I don't really care if I make the team; I just really don't want to be alone today."

"Yeah, I get it. But let's be honest, you were always

better than me on your worst day than I was on my best."

"You're just trying to make me feel better," I smirk, jokingly.

"Yes, yes, I am."

I lightly punch her arm as we head out the door and down the stairs. I leave a note for my mom on the table about tryouts. She is still upstairs with the hair dryer going.

It only takes five or so minutes to get to the field. We can see from the parking lot that there are quite a few people here already.

Winnie locks her car, and we start making our way down. I have on white soccer shorts that match my cleats and socks, and a lime green sports bra. I tied my hair up in a high pony, but it still reaches down to the small of my back. Cursing myself for not bringing an extra hair tie, so I don't whip myself in the face with my own hair.

Winnie and I both jog over to where the most people are, half-circled around a man and a woman not much older than us.

"We want to start with a few warm-up drills, just to get everyone's blood flowing. Then we are going to split you up by positions, and end with a scrimmage." The woman yells over the crowd standing around her. I do a quick count and see that there are about fifteen guys and five girls, counting me, Winnie, and Ashley, who is standing next to a tall, tan, and broad Miles. He looks so out of place here in his gym shorts and t-shirt. This was a stark difference from the bedroom-eyed guy who was watching me from the wall of the party. Ashley bumps his shoulder playfully, and he returns it with a smile. I wonder if Ashley is the girlfriend Leto was talking about.

My thoughts are brought back to Leto. I left my phone in the car so I wouldn't be tempted to keep checking it. I'm still staring at Miles when he turns his head suddenly and catches me staring. Instead of looking down, I smile and wave. He gives me a nod and puts his arm around Ashley. Alright then, message received, I guess.

The coaches have us running sprints back and forth down the field. Winnie and I are chatting and laughing as we run. Ashley catches up with us, and I look to see that Miles is not with her. Ashley is pretty cute, I mean, she is average height, blonde, and blue-eyed. Lots of freckles dot her fair skin. And so far, she seems fairly athletic.

Looking up, I wonder if the clouds are going to burn off or if it's going to storm.

"Hey, ladies, beautiful day we are having." Now we all grimace at the darkening clouds above us.

"How can it be eighty degrees and be about to rain!" Winnie whines while we run to get a ball and start dribbling between cones, like everyone else.

"Nice of you to join us." Miles' deep voice comes out of nowhere and makes me jump. He notices and starts laughing. "Oh, if you're that easy to startle, this is going to be really fun." Miles jogs ahead and, with expert precision, weaves in and out of every cone at a sprinting pace.

And though I haven't played since high school, I start to remember just how much I enjoyed this sport. It wasn't a wonder that I was good; I was built for it. Short, petite, but very strong. Especially my legs. I could sprint for a very long time without becoming winded. And people have commented on my ball control before. It's easy for me to keep close to the ball and not let anyone near it.

When we've all been split up into our different positions, the coaches divide us into two teams accordingly. Our team gets red pinnies to wear.

Winnie and I are on the same team, Winnie as her usual second striker, and me as striker. Miles and Ashley are on the other team, Ashley as a defender and Miles as a striker as well.

He and I stare at each other across the centerline. Miles winks at me, but when the whistle blows, we both leap into action.

"Nutmeg!" Miles yells and wastes no time kicking the ball right between my legs and back to himself.

What the hell? Okay, that's the only one he gets, I tell myself as I throw myself in front of the ball, stopping it with my right inner thigh. I pass it to Winnie, and she and I start back up the field. We are weaving and dribbling just like we always have. We are getting close to taking a shot when I hear thunderous footsteps behind me. And a yell, "Nutmeg!" Oh, hell no, I speed up and just as I am in shooting distance, WHAM. I feel a crushing weight, and my face meets the grass. I am pinned to the ground under what feels like two hundred pounds of pure muscle. Spitting out dirt, I roll out from under Miles.

A whistle blows, and Miles hops to his feet. He reaches his hand out to me to help me up.

"Oops, sorry about that." But his dimpled, wide grin says otherwise.

Rolling my eyes, I take his hand and pull myself up.

Pretending to brush my shoulders off, I walk over to the ball. I can hear Miles's chuckling behind me.

"That's a penalty kick!" The male coach yells, and I pick up the ball.

Sticking my tongue out at Miles, I make quick work of scoring our team's first goal.

He looks up at me through dark lashes and jogs to the centerline. We are ready to continue when the first raindrop falls. Oh, this is going to be fun. The whistle blows, and this time our team wins the ball. Winnie is fast taking the ball down and me diagonally from her, ready for whenever she needs. The sprinkle turns into a drizzle, and wet, soggy shirts start to come off.

Miles's sweatshirt is the first to go. And when I say everyone stopped to watch, I mean everyone. Guys, girls, coaches. Everyone was mesmerized by the sheer size of his tanned muscles. Then he started sprinting right for me. I passed the ball, just as Miles yelled, "Nutmeg!" and tackled me again.

"What the hell is wrong with you?!" I yell while he is still pinning me to the ground. This time, my back is getting soaked, along with my white shorts. My boobs are squished under his slippery chest. I keep trying to push him off me, but he's just so damn slippery. He is hysterically laughing, and through tears, as he finally starts to get up, I can hear him telling the coach he slipped.

I get up and look down. I am soaked. It is pouring down rain, and I am almost certain my shorts are ruined. But the whistle blows again, and I make another penalty kick goal.

This goes on for the rest of the scrimmage. Winnie and I are in the scoring zone, and whether or not I have the ball, I hear *Nutmeg!*, and then I get tackled, and earn a penalty kick. I make every single shot.

When the tryouts end, I am pretty sure I look like I wore mud instead of clothes. Miles stalks over to his stuff and takes a drink of his water, looking about the same as me. I can't help but think about how Ashley must be feeling. I would be pissed if my boyfriend were 'nutmegging' the same girl over and over again.

Winnie and Ashley jog over to me, laughing.

"Okay, what is going on between you two?" Ashley lightly punches my shoulder, then looks down at the mud it left on her hand.

"What? Nothing, I mean, nothing from me. I don't even know that guy." I breathe out really fast, so she knows I do not want any trouble.

Ashley puts up her hands, "All I'm saying is, I have been playing pick up with Miles for years, and I have never seen him not take soccer seriously. Like ever." I look at her, confused.

"Wait, are you and Miles not dating?" I barely finish the sentence before she interrupts me with laughter.

"Me and Miles?! Yeah, I wish. Miles might have a girlfriend, he might have one hundred, but I sure as hell ain't one." The look in her eye makes me believe she actually does wish.

"Why? Ray? Are you interested?" It sounded like a challenge. But I am saved from answering. Winnie interjects before I can.

"No, she isn't. She and Leto went out last night. And by the sound of it, things went really, *really,* well." I smiled and appreciated her emphasis on *really*.

A strange look crossed Ashley's face for only a

moment, but it quickly turned into a practiced grin. Winnie looks over my shoulder to where Ashley is grinning. I hear what they both see.

"Hey, Nutmeg!"

Oh, my hell, why? I turn to see a still very shirtless, muddy-chested, way too jacked for his own good, Miles walking towards us. I crouch down and start untying my cleats. Pretending not to hear him.

"Hey Miles, you played... aggressively today," Ashley says in a much sweeter voice than she was using just moments ago.

"Oh? Was I? I didn't really notice." His shit-eating grin said it all.

He's holding something in his hand. A clipboard and a pencil. He holds it out to me.

Slowly standing, I take it. It is a list of names and phone numbers. I notice Winnie's, Ashley's, and a few other names already written with their numbers next to them. I see mine somewhere in the middle, but no number beside it.

"The coaches wanted me to get everyone's info for callbacks." He scratches his neck and waits for me to write my number down.

"Okay, thanks." I do not want to give him any satisfaction that my legs feel like jelly, and I am most certainly going to have a bruise on my chest from, well, his chest. So, I write my cell number as fast as I can and give it back to him. He looks down at my number, as if counting the digits to make sure it wasn't going to be fake. I let out a laugh, and he clears his throat, embarrassed.

All four of us are standing there awkwardly when Ashley decides to speak.

"So, Ray went out with Leto last night." Ashley stares into Miles' eyes, like what she's saying out loud isn't what she wanted to say. They share a look, and it's clear they are both on the same page mentally, something unbeknownst to Winnie and me.

"Yeah...I had a really good time." I feel very vulnerable suddenly. Then I remember I am in my sports bra and muddy soccer shorts. And the feeling increases.

"That's...interesting," Miles says, slowly. He looks like he wants to say more, but his face relaxes, and he gets a wicked grin. "You know, you really shouldn't wear white shorts when it's raining." He tilts his head and gives me a once-over.

Instinctively, I turn and look at my butt. Oh no.

"I could see your entire butt when the rain started, just so you know." We all start to laugh, but my laughter has a very thick edge of embarrassment.

"That was until it got covered in mud." He winks and walks away with the clipboard. Ashley follows him close behind. I pivot in the mud to Winnie.

"What the hell, Winnie! Why didn't you say anything?!?" I stare at her incredulously. She starts to laugh again.

"Well, to be honest, Ray, they were see-through before the rain started, too. But you have a nice ass, so I didn't think you really cared." She shrugs, and we both start laughing.

We make the trek back to the parking lot to Winnie's car. Winnie ducks into the driver's seat and starts her engine. I'm about to get in when I hear whisper shouts just two or three cars away.

"I just don't understand why he does this." It's a guy's voice.

"Okay, but it's not *my* fault. At least I know what I'm getting into."

The other voice is a girl. My brain tells me these two familiar voices can only be the only other people I know here today, and they are talking about the only other person we have in common. Leto. I bend over and see that I'm right. Ashley and Miles are standing between two cars, in an argument or heated discussion of sorts.

Miles looks down at his phone, "Great, speak of the Devil."

He puts his phone to his ear, "Hey man..."

I really don't want to be a part of this.

Throwing my dirty cleats onto the passenger side floor, I get in and shut the door. Hastily, I grab my phone from the glove box, my gut sinks, and I see that I have zero missed calls and zero texts.

"Still nothing?" Winnie looks over, eyebrows raised.

"Not. A. Damn. Thing." I decide then and there. Last night was not *really fun*. In fact, it wasn't fun at all.

THIRTEEN
DOT 1972
RIDE ALONG

" I 'm in." Rodger smiles with a wide grin that
meets his eyes.

"No, I mean, now *I* go find her." There is
no way Rodger is inserting himself in this. Not after
months of him chasing me. I am not falling for his
whole, *I care about your sister*, game.

"Well, hey now, that's not fair. I gave you a ride,
introduced you to my family, let you use my room, and
my yearbooks, bought and paid for by yours truly." He
points to his chest, which just gives me further
conviction.

"No, because you're right, life's not fair. And I
don't owe you anything." I don't know where such
crossness came from, but I was going with it.

I snatched the notebook paper, with Mia King's
name on it, from the bed and left his room with him
sitting stunned still on the floor.

As I weaved my way through dolls, dress-ups, and
art projects, I didn't look back till I got to the front

door. Standing at the top of the stairs with an amused grin was Rodger.

"Would you at least like a ride home?"

I thought about it and decided that it would probably be a good idea. I did have my skates after all. And they were heavy to carry after a shift.

"Yes, thank you."

As we make our way back to my little blue farmhouse on Elm Street, I can't help but look out the window at the rain-soaked trees and think of Rosie. My Rosie, out there all alone somewhere, probably wet, cold, scared. Waiting for someone to bring her home.

In no time at all, we are idling in my driveway. I look down at my uniform, skates, and crinkled piece of paper. Remembering my bike is still broken. I suppose it wouldn't hurt not to have to plan on walking everywhere.

"Fine. Pick me up at nine in the morning tomorrow." I don't wait for him to answer before I make a run for it through the drizzle to my front porch.

I guess I'll find out tomorrow how much he really wants to help me. Walking through the sitting room, I look up at the cuckoo clock on the wall. My mom loved that clock. We have had it ever since I can remember. Every morning, she pulls down the chain that makes the weighted pine cones rise back to the top, and the clock starts anew. I see that it's almost eleven at night and curse myself for being so late.

Tiptoeing up the stairs, I sneak a look into my parents' room. Both are fast asleep. That's odd. They always wait up for us and want to know about our evenings. Us. That's right, there isn't an *us* anymore. Just me. I wonder if they didn't wait up because they know she isn't coming home.

Well, they're wrong, I think as I climb into bed. I'm going to bring her home.

I lie there and go over the plan for tomorrow. So far, I have *use Rodger and his car to find Mia King*. Before I can add any other items to the list, I hear something. A low scratching, almost like an animal not wanting to make itself known. An animal that means to sneak up on its prey. It starts as a scratch every few minutes, and then I hear a creak or two. I feel paralyzed in place because I realize someone is trying to get into my room through my window. I get up as slowly as possible and move to the window. My lace curtains lie still, and I say a thankful prayer to God that I've kept my window locked since Rosie's notebook went missing. It's been a few minutes since I heard the last creek, but I pull back the curtains and peer outside. Nothing.

I don't see anyone under my window. I let out a breath of relief, but then my eyes go to the dark fields beyond my window. And there, standing in the wheat, is a figure. They are slight, and I don't know how I know, but their posture is manic. I put the curtain down and double-check the lock on my window. I'm creeped out enough that I sleep with the lamp on. It takes me hours to finally fall into a fitful sleep.

In the morning, I am dressed and ready long before nine. I don't give another thought to the strange visitor from last night. My mom must have washed my summer shorts while I was at work yesterday because I found them hanging out on our line in the yard. After I eat a quick oatmeal breakfast, I make my way out to the swing. The sun came up over the hills and trees this morning, but was quickly engulfed in today's overcast rain clouds.

There is a fog that has rolled in over the farmlands, making it almost impossible to see my parents and the other workers in the back corner of our land. As I sit there and swing, I now think back to the person I saw last night. How is it that they were able to get from my window to the field in such a short amount of time? This being a working farm, there are tools and ladders around just about every corner. It wouldn't be hard for someone to get access to my second-story window. I can't help but feel like whoever it was wanted to cause me harm. I had a fleeting thought that it may have been Rosie, but she would have just used the key hidden under the pot on our porch. Or thrown a rock at the window if she really needed to come in. Heaven knows she was not one to be ignored.

I had thought about it being Harvey, and actually, I haven't ruled him out. If he did end up seeing me up by the wall, he would have reason to make sure I don't repeat to anyone what I saw.

So, first things first, I need to talk to Mia King. Then I need to confront Harvey. Rodger might be an annoying, arrogant know-it-all, but I bet he could throw a punch if he needed to.

Rodger interrupts my thoughts when he comes into view. Walking around the back of the house in jeans and a t-shirt. No letterman's jacket today, despite the rain clouds. I stand up and grab my shoes from the laundry line. They are still quite soggy from my last excursion to the wall. I put them on anyway, not knowing if I am going to have to run, jump, or climb at some point today.

"Do you always hang your shoes out here?" Rodger eyes me skeptically, knowing they have to be damp from the rain, by the way I'm trying to jam my foot into them.

"Only when I fall down a mountain."

He chuckles, shaking his head. He doesn't even ask what I mean by that. He knows I probably won't answer.

We make our way back to his Mustang just as the rain starts. In the passenger seat, I have to pick up a notebook before I sit down. My stomach does a back flip. I immediately start thumbing through the pages. It looked just like Rosie's notebook, same light brown cover, with dark brown tape on the spine.

"Hey! Do you mind?!" Rodger rips the notebook away and tosses it into the back seat. "That has some personal stuff in there. I already have my sisters nosing through every single thing I own. I don't need any more girls in my life touching my things." He seems more embarrassed than mad, so I ask him the obvious.

"Then why did you bring it, when you knew you were picking me up?" I raise an eyebrow, folding my arms.

"Well, as I said, I have seven sisters butting into my life, every second of every day. My car is the one place I have that they can't take over. Though in a year or so, Jenny is going to be sixteen, and that's all going to change when we have to start sharing the car." His answer actually seems very reasonable. I mean, Rosie put her personal journal far out of my reach and eyesight, and it didn't stop me from snooping.

"Oh, I'm sorry." I don't know what it would be like to be the only boy in such a big, chaotic family, but I do know that I value my alone and quiet time. Rodger probably doesn't know the meaning of the words.

"Plus, I didn't know if we would need something to write on, so I just tossed it in." His words make me feel grateful that he's here with me, that I have one other person looking out for me, but not just for me, for Rosie, too.

"Thank you, that was really thoughtful." You would have thought I slapped him. His face turns from embarrassed to shocked.

"Are you feeling alright, Dotty?" He gently puts the back of his hand to my forehead, like he's checking to see if there is any sort of temperature.

"Umm...I think so? Why?" I pull my head out of his weirdly soft touch.

"Because Dotty, you are being nice to me."

I roll my eyes.

"Very funny." I smile, and we continue driving to the south side of town.

"Now, I do think it's time that you tell me why we are going to be seeking out Mia King. From what I can remember, she is somewhat shy. I don't think she looked me in the eye at all on our date."

"Or maybe she just had better taste than you thought." I quip.

"Oh, there she is! The Miss Dotty I know and love!" He fist pumps the air, trying to make me laugh. It almost works, but my focus is on Rosie. Well, first Mia, then Rosie.

As we get closer to the area that Rodger said he picked her up from, my leg starts to shake. The houses were looking more and more run-down. Some even looked abandoned altogether.

"Are you sure this is where...she came from?" My face slackens as we slow down in front of one of the most dilapidated houses I have ever seen.

The roof is sagging and looks to be on the verge of caving in. The front porch is full of rot, and the railing, which I'm sure once helped individuals up the narrow stairs, is lying on the grass, covered in moss, long forgotten. The small, square, pale green house was probably only about eight hundred square feet. Included in my observations were no signs of life. There was no smoke out of the small chimney. And it was clear that no one was keeping up the yard. I don't even see a mailbox.

"Trust me, this is the house she came out of," Rodger says quietly, reading the expression on my face.

I mean, my house was small and considered somewhat poor. But it was clean and well-maintained. You could feel the love pouring out as soon as your foot hit the edge of our property.

Rodger throws out his finger and points to the small window on the sunken-in porch.

"There!" He waits for me to see what he's pointing at.

There in the window is a small, dirty-faced child with red hair, not Mia, but her sister for sure. Looking at her, I couldn't help but see another version of her, an older version, clutching her dress, getting hit. The horror of it flashes across my mind.

Reaching in the back seat, Rodger pulls out three

big bags full of stuff from his back seat. He's
creaking up the porch, making sure not to step in
any holes before I can ask him what those are all
about. I snap back to the present and quickly follow
his lead.

With a loud creak, the front door pulls open slowly
before either of us can knock. It's the small redheaded little girl. Dirty faced and sad eyes.

"Well, hi, little miss, is your sister Mia home? Do
you remember me? I'm her friend, Rodger. And this is
my friend Dotty." I wave my hand, but I have to stop
my eyes from watering after gazing around the residence. Dirt, filth, and liquor bottles litter the floor.
The girl doesn't seem to be more than five or six, but I
don't see or hear another soul here.

"I'm not supposed to open the door when daddy's
gone. Mia's at work." She squeaks out in a small
mouselike voice.

"Where's your mom?" Fearing I already knew the
answer to that.

"Dead. Before I can remember." She gulps, and I
wonder with her tiny little frame, when was the last
time she ate?

Rodger steps over the threshold and, in a few
steps, is in the kitchen with his bags. I hear him
unloading things. Peering around the corner, I see it's
fresh milk he puts in the fridge, bread, cereal, fruits,
and vegetables. It takes me great effort to swallow
down the lump in my throat. His kindness. He
remembered what it was like when he was here last.

The little girl jumped up on the counter and
started helping put groceries away. Rodger slid something out of his pocket and put it in her hand. A

chocolate bar. That ball of emotion was stuck in my throat as I watched him.

"Now remind me, little miss. Where does Mia work these days?"

She already had a mouth of chocolate, but through bites, she said, "The mean meat factory." At his confused look, she adds, "You know, the place where they're mean to the animals. And then they kill them?"

He nods and pats her head.

"Well, little miss, is there anything else I can do for you?"

She hops down off the counter and looks up at him, thinking.

"Come back and bring more food."

I turn to leave and feel a tear escape and roll down my cheek. I had been holding it in since she first showed her face. I have seen poverty my whole life. But never such blatant abuse or disregard for a small child. Her sad, unjust life circumstances disturbed me, but Rodgers' thoughtfulness touched me. He looked at me with a furrowed brow, walking me slowly back to the passenger side door.

"From what I know, her Dad isn't real bright. He works down at the cannery, and they have a neighbor girl who is in charge of her sister most of the time. But I do know, no one here is a good housekeeper. And that little girl looked hungry the last time I was here, and I couldn't get it out of my head. Had to make it right."

If I were ever able to describe what it felt like to fall in love with a moment, that would have been it. To see the big brother to seven little girls' side of Rodger was jarring. In my mind, he was a skirt-chasing jock. One-dimensional. And now? I don't know. He was helping me, without question, and so far with no motives of his own.

We pull away from the weed-filled gravel out front of the King's home. Rodger doesn't ask me where we should go, but I realize exactly where he's taking me.

"To the slaughterhouse we go." As if I hadn't already guessed. Still, I couldn't help but appreciate his willingness to keep helping me. I looked over at him, his dark hair and blue eyes. His skin looked summer-tanned under his white t-shirt. His jeans look nice, but well-worn. And boy, he wore them well. I looked down at my own jean shorts and loose shirt, feeling suddenly self-conscious. I had left my hair down, long and blonde. As if sensing my sudden mood shift, Rodger turns and smiles.

"So, Miss Dotty, I think it's about time for you to tell me what it is we are doing out here." I keep eye contact and shake my head. Not even his selflessness is going to convince me to tell him what I think may be going on. If Harvey is the one who hurt my sister, this is about to be a giant accusation. And I was going to get Mia to help me make it.

Bumping down Elm Street, we passed my house. We rounded the corner, and just the flat roof was visible between the green canopy of trees.

Rodger parks a little way back on the narrow street.

"Okay then, what's your plan? How can I be of service?" He does a little bow towards me.

"Umm...stay here, maybe keep the car running?"

He nods, and I climb out of his Mustang. Checking to make sure my shoes were tied, I crossed the street and ran over to the front entrance.

There, through the window, I could see an older woman at the reception desk. Her yellow blouse and pinned-up hair made her look like a human beehive.

"Hi, I'm Dorothea."

"Well, nice to meet you, Dorothea. How can I help you?" I couldn't help but be distracted by the unmistakable smell of death. Through the hallway, I could see that two big pieces of plastic were the only separation from the front office and the actual butchering, saws, machines, and beeping. It was almost too loud to hear the bee lady.

"Umm, I'm looking for my friend Mia. She works here." The receptionist looks at me, confused.

"Well, from what I know, there are no ladies who work here except me."

"Are you sure? She's...umm...tall and has red hair."

"I'm sure." She looks me up and down and sighs. "But I will go ask, this is only my second day here."

I stand there while she stalks off between the plastic curtains, and the putrid smell wafts over in her wake.

I start to breathe through my mouth, but realize I can taste it.

Plastic crinkles, and I look over in horror to see a blood-covered Harvey. And he looked mad.

"What the hell are you doing here, Dot?!"

The receptionist's eyes widen at his outburst. She grabs her blouse but doesn't say anything to Harvey. Rushing past him, she busies herself at her desk, avoiding eye contact with either of us.

"I...where's Mia?" I find my voice, it's steadier than I feel. He slowly looks me up and down.

"So, it *was* you." A statement, not a question. I don't move or act like I know what he's talking about. Even though I do. He had been chasing me down the hill through the woods. He had seen someone. And he even suspected it was me.

"Where's Mia?" I ask again, even louder than before.

"How the hell should I know? She didn't show up for her last shift. They hired this lady yesterday to take her place." I hadn't realized I had scooted back all the way against the door. Harvey had been stepping closer with every word. He's so close now I can smell the blood on him, taste it.

"A little piece of advice, if you don't want to end up just like little Rosie, you'll shut your mouth and mind your damn business." I didn't even wait a second after his threat to open the door behind my back and sprint away. I only got two feet when I ran into a crushing brick wall.

The familiar brick wall's arms shot out to grab me before I could crash to the ground.

"Rodger!" I screamed, half terrified from the impact and half from Harvey's rotting threat.

"Dot, get in the car." I don't see where he goes. I assumed he was following me to the car, but when I turned around, he was gone.

FOURTEEN
RAY 2007
SILENCE

I stayed silent the whole way home from the tryouts. I felt so stupid. Why was I so quick to trust him? And even worse, why did I care so much? I have been jilted by guys before. Plenty, though in those moments, it did feel like I was relieved to not have their attention when the time came. I feel like I would become bored and just wait for them to end it, so I didn't have to. Unless there was something alarming that had to be taken care of up front.

When I was fifteen, my first *boyfriend* and I were on a walk. Not much you can do when you grow up in a small farming town. Especially when you're not old enough to drive, and there are no shops anywhere near your house.

We had been walking and talking about life. I liked to get really deep with people, pretty much off the bat. I don't know if it is for shock factor or to try to find out what people's secrets are. But it was easy for me when I was a teenager. Very sure of who I was, I knew that anything I shared or did, I didn't care if it was repeated.

Well, I couldn't say the same for Lance. The more I got to know him, the less I wanted to know.

We had come across a small farm down one of the winding roads. Lance had walked a little ahead of me. He turned around and put his finger to his lips. Motioning for me to be quiet. Beyond him was a huckleberry bush, just off the dirt road. It had started to rain, so silently I crouched down under the overhang of the bush. I shrugged my shoulders to Lance, waiting to see what he was going to show me.

Slowly, he bent down and picked something up. Next thing I knew, that very something was being flung at my face. I felt a wet, slimy rope slap me across my cheek. I remember thinking *What the hell was that?*

Well, I didn't have to wonder long; turns out it was a giant gardener snake. Once I wiped off the dirt and residue with the sleeve of my jacket, I saw it dangling in his hand. He was laughing like he had just pulled off the funniest prank of all time. I smiled and was quiet as we made our way back to my front yard. He had no idea that would be the very last time he ever had the privilege of being alone with me. Once he rode away from my house on his bike, I texted him, letting him know we were no longer dating. That was easy, though; I felt almost nothing about moving on. He had told me very little about himself. Our relationship was basically holding hands and making out at bonfires, nothing too crazy for this *careful nun*. But when it was clear I no longer wished to be around him. I simply stopped.

This was not that. And I know I'm being dramatic. I *know* that. But I can't stop myself from feeling.

I felt myself open my heart to Leto, just a crack, and it felt like he opened his just a crack too. I suppose sooner is better for disappointment, though. Imagine how bad I would feel if it were months or years down the road?

Winnie and I are sitting in her car, in my driveway. She can tell I'm upset, but since I am only spiraling in my head, she lets me go after I assure her twice that I'm fine.

She has no idea that I'm giving this stupid boy the power to wreck my entire day.

I decide a hot bath is what I need. I make a stop at the laundry room before I head upstairs. Taking off all my clothes, I throw them in and start the machine. My mom would die if she saw all that mud in her washer. It feels important to get that done before she comes home. I already feel like a mooch as it is. I didn't picture myself at twenty years old still living with my mom. I'm sure she didn't picture this for me either. Wrapping a towel around me from the pile of clean laundry, I feel a little less dreary.

From the laundry room, I gaze down the hall to our back door. My grandparents brought it from their farmhouse in Sumner. The top half was a wood diamond pattern over glass. And the bottom was a wooden X on the panel. It made one of the creakiest squeaks when you opened it, but my mom loves it. And so do I. My grandparents must have too, to bring it with them.

The rain had stayed a heavy drizzle, so I almost didn't see it. But then it moved, and it was unmistakable. A person peered at me through the rain, into the house from the diamond window. I let out a yelp, and as I did, the figure disappeared. I always lock the front door, and I see that the back door is still locked too. My breath has not eased by the time I make it down the back hallway. Standing a foot or so back from the door, I look out across our backyard and into the dripping tree line. No one. I see no shaking branches or bushes disturbed. Whoever it was must have slipped around the side of the house.

I squint, and out of the bottom of my vision, there is something stuck to the door below the glass... my heart starts to race when I see a piece of paper stuck to the door.

Slowly, I unlock the door so it doesn't make a sound. I know I'm going to have to make this fast.

I rip open the door, and it screeches. In one motion, I grab the paper and pull it inside the house. The moment the door is shut, I deadbolt the lock. My hands are shaking, and my heart feels like it might pound up my throat and out of my mouth.

"Rosie," I say her name, and it comes out as a breathless whisper.

April 1972

You know when you just know? Like when you know you've met someone who understands you. Who makes you feel...alive? He challenges me more than anyone ever has. Makes me think that together, he and I could leave this town. See the world. Sometimes it can be hard to stay in that place, though. Hard not to be a disappointment to them. Hard to always try to be exciting enough. Good enough.

Holy. Shit.

Just when I didn't think my heart could beat any faster, I feel like I am going to black out. I stumble to the stairs in my towel, clutching the paper, on legs that feel like lead. Wobbling up the stairs, I go into my mom's room. She always keeps it tidy. Long curtains frame her window, a white bedspread on her queen-sized bed against the north wall. To the left is a window overlooking the back yard, and a closed closet to my right.

I spot the binder on her nightstand. I wonder if she was looking at it this morning. I walk over and open the plastic cover. Lying the new note next to the other ones, my mouth goes dry.

Same exact paper and handwriting.

Who is doing this? And why?

I take the note back to my room and put it underneath my underwear in my drawer. It's clear my mom doesn't want to share with me everything that happened thirty-plus years ago. That's fine. But it's not going to stop me from finding out what happened.

Who the hell is Leto anyway? A distraction. Not anymore, I tell myself, as I quickly get dressed in some shorts and a sweatshirt. The bath will have to wait. I only have two more hours to do some research before my mom gets home.

I don't know why I never googled it. Seems so simple. And I'm nosy. And I love mysteries. But because it was my own family, it just felt so intimate.

Every time I brought it up, my mom couldn't even look me in the eye.

From what I understand, the little bits and pieces that I heard through the years, my aunt Rosie went on a date and never came home. The guy they suspected of having taken her ended up hurting someone else. He went to jail for about twenty years. When he got out, he moved away or something. They could never pin Rosie's disappearance on him, and he never confessed. And they still haven't found her. Around the same time he got out of prison, my mom and dad got pregnant with me. They had been married a while before they decided to have me. From what I'm told, I was a very wanted baby. But the day my mom told my dad she was pregnant, he left and never came back.

Leading up to my mom getting pregnant, he had been acting really strange. He would be gone for long hours at random times of the day. Even got in trouble at work for showing up late a few times. So, when he left, my mom thought he most likely ran off with someone else.

The police said they found credit card activity a few states away, so she didn't pursue him. She filed for divorce, and that was that. She gave me her last name, and we have been a team ever since. I know she's been in pain for a long time. I can see it in everything she does. But she has never let it stop her from living her life. I admire her in every way for it. She simply gets up, fixes up, and shows up. She doesn't just live through the pain; she has thrived through it.

I'm on my mom's laptop in the den, a few minutes later, and Google is confirming everything I already knew, and not much more. Other than the person that

Rosie's suspected murderer hurt was a minor. I knew it was a young girl, but I thought they would have a name for me to track down.

Back to square one.

I feel my phone vibrate in my pocket. I can sense it's Winnie checking up on me. I say a silent *thank you* prayer that I have a friend like her. Without taking my eyes off these accident police reports, I answer my phone on the fifth ring.

"Hi, bestie! I was just about to call you!" There is silence on the other end, and then someone clears their throat.

"Umm...hi?"

Oh my gosh, I pull the phone away when I hear a male's deep baritone answer me instead of Winnie.

Leto's name is at the top of the screen.

FIFTEEN

RAY 2007
PHONE CALL

"Ray? Hello?" I try to compose myself, closing all the tabs I have open.

"Oh, hey...Sorry, I thought you were Winnie." I force a laugh, but there's sweat collecting on my upper lip. I can't help the tiny flip my stomach does at his voice.

"Why do you have Winnie's name saved to my number?"

"I don't, I just...I wasn't...actually, it doesn't matter, what's up?" I get up from the couch and start to pace around the den.

"Well, I was going to ask if I could see you tonight." His voice sounds strange, almost out of breath.

"You were?"

"Yeah? Does that surprise you? I thought we had a nice time last night."

"I mean, yeah, we did bu-"

"Then I'll pick you up at seven. Do you have to be home by ten on a weeknight? Isn't that right, nun?" He says, cutting me off.

I don't think I like this. My gut is telling me, I don't like this. And yet, my skin heats thinking about sitting in his lap again. Feeling his arms around me. Smelling him, tasting him.

And I suppose if we hang out, I can ask him why he gave me the silent treatment. I don't know, though, this feels too vulnerable. Wasn't I ready to never speak to him again?

"I'll be ready at six, I'm busy later."

"Okay then, six it is. See you then." He hangs up before I can confirm, but the edge in his voice sounded, to me, like curiosity about my later plans.

I glance at the cuckoo clock. I only have an hour to get ready before he comes. I sit back down on the couch and text Winnie.

Hey, can you hang out with me and Leto tonight? He just called me and will be here at six. I'm trying to play it really casual, so I was thinking if you came, then he would think that I thought he and I were casual? Make sense?

I only have to wait a few seconds for her response.

Yes, duh. See you in a sec.

And that is how you wing woman. I shut my phone and the laptop, making sure nothing lingers on the screen that has anything to do with Rosie. That would give my mom a panic attack for sure.

My mom gets home as I'm rotating my laundry.

"Hey sweetie, how were soccer tryouts?" She's standing in the entry, taking off her raincoat and boots. I can't help but stare. Even in her older age, she is stunning. Her naturally blonde hair is swept back in a claw clip, and her petite, in-shape frame is what I can only hope for at her age.

"What?" She tilts her head and smiles.

"Nothing, I just missed you today." I hug her extra tight, and she kisses the top of my head.

"Soccer try-outs were really fun. Winnie and I are going to hang out with some of Ashley's friends in about an hour."

"Is it that Lee boy?" Her eyes look at me with serious focus.

"Leto Lee? Yeah, he's the one picking us up." I try to sound as casual as I can. Even throwing in a shrug.

"Just be really careful, I hear he has a bit of a reputation."

"From who?!" I suddenly feel very defensive of the boy whom I just met, who ignored me for a whole day.

"From Winnie's mom." She started laughing, and I couldn't help but feel relieved. So just two moms gossiping, got it.

"Winnie and her big mouth," I grumble on my way up the stairs to get ready.

I shower quickly and decide to let my hair dry wavy. I don't want him to think I spent an hour drying my hair for him. Plus, I don't have time since I spent too long picking out the right outfit for him. Short shorts and a hoodie. I hear Winnie come in the house a moment later and run down the stairs to greet her. Winnie looks great in her black sweats and tight white t-shirt. Her curly, fiery red hair is pulled up in a messy bun. We both look at each other and say "Casual" in unison just as the doorbell rings.

I open the door to find a very good-smelling Leto leaning against the door frame. He's in jeans and a long-sleeved blue shirt. His golden eyes give me a once-over, then another. I clear my throat.

"Hi, you look amazing." His eyebrows furrow for a split second when he sees my hoodie. I smile and pretend not to notice.

"Thanks." I open the door a little more to show Winnie beside me.

"Winnie is going to come if that's cool?" I raise one eyebrow at him.

He doesn't skip a beat.

"Yeah, for sure, might be a tight fit, but the more the merrier." He grabs my hand and leads me out to a black SUV. Opening the passenger door for Winnie, she looks at me over her shoulder and climbs in.

Leto opens the back door, and I can now see that Damon is driving and Miles sits squished in the back seat.

"Hey, Nutmeg." Miles smiles at me from inside the car. I notice Leto's eyebrows pull together.

The more the merrier indeed. Did Leto have the same idea as me? Or is this, in fact, *casual?* He squeezes my hand as if in answer to my unvoiced question. No, the way he put his hand on my lower back to help me into the car feels anything but regular.

Buckled in, Leto puts one arm around me and the other arm across my lap, holding my other hand. I feel Miles stiffen slightly on my left. I'm trying not to make eye contact or think about just hours ago when his bare chest was on my almost bare chest. My face flushes at the memory. But I bat away the thought.

"So, I heard you made quite a scene at the soccer field today." Leto jokes, but his eyes have an intense look about them.

"Oh, yeah, I don't know if I would put it that way. I mean, I didn't exactly play my best."

"Really? That's not what I heard." Leto smiles, and everyone in the car starts laughing. Winnie turns around.

"Well, if it hadn't been for Miles tackling her every time the rain washed the mud away from her shorts, she would have made even more of a scene." I couldn't help but laugh at that, too. Leto only chuckled slightly, and his grip tightened on me a small amount.

Is that really what Miles had intended? To make sure my butt stayed covered? Seems like he could have just given me his sweatshirt to tie around my waist instead of jumping on top of me over and over again.

Besides the laughing and the initial greeting, Miles has stayed extremely quiet.

"Where are we going?" I suddenly think of asking.

Leto stays quiet, and it's Damon that answers.

"Well, we heard you like getting scared, and we decided it was time to let you in on our little...secret." It's crazy how alike Damon and Leto look. If it weren't for the eight-inch height difference, it would be hard to tell them apart from a distance.

"What the hell does that mean?" Winnie says, as she looks back at me in agreement.

"It means we are letting you into our inner circle. Very few girls have been where you two will go tonight."

"Well, how long is this going to take? Winnie and I have plans later." I look out the window and see we are winding down the road from Edgewood to Sumner. All three of these guys have lived in Sumner their whole lives. We could be going almost anywhere in Sumner tonight.

"Then here is your chance to cancel those plans before we lose cell service," Leto says slowly but loud enough for everyone in the car to hear.

For some reason, his words make me wary. Shit, he's calling my bluff. After some quick thinking, I say out loud to Winnie.

"We might as well see what these three idiots are talking about. I'll text Mat and have him tell Taylor." Leto suddenly stills.

I pretend not to notice, pull out my phone, and go to my contacts. Finding Mat, I send him a text.

Hey Mat. Winnie and I can't make it by ten tonight. I'll call you when we get home, and we can meet up with you guys after. Text Taylor for me, would you?

I see Miles side-eyeing my phone. I make sure Leto can see that I actually sent the message. I quickly turn it on vibrate and shove it in my shorts pocket before Mat can text me back. Mat is going to be confused as hell. I haven't spoken to him or Taylor since high school.

"I told them we would call them when we got back to my house." Still playing the game, Winnie turns around and nods.

I can't help but feel like I have the leg up here. I might not even bring up Leto not texting me back last night, or all day today.

"So, Leto, Ray said she had a nice time last night. Why didn't you text her back?" Dammit, Winnie, I give her a look, and she just smiles.

"Oh...I didn't get a text. My phone died last night, and I didn't get a chance to charge it until just before I called you." I look out the window past Miles, and I see his eyes roll.

If Leto was who Miles was talking with in the parking lot today, then Leto is lying, and Miles isn't going to say anything about it. Or he's not lying and is totally in the clear for not responding. Either way, I must act like I don't care because, *casual*.

"Man, that's crazy," I say.

Winnie starts laughing at my thick sarcasm.

"Hey, in case you forgot, I work on my family's land for most of my day. Not a ton of time for much else."

Winnie doesn't respond, and I'm grateful because if she was going to say what I was thinking it was not going to be casual or nice.

The SUV bumps over some train tracks, and I see we are turning onto Elm Street.

"Is the secret just your creepy ass farmhouse?" Winnie says to Damon.

"No, much creepier."

I feel uncertain, but I tell myself that's only because this is the same street where I saw the creepy figure. That seems so long ago. Could it really have only been days ago?

"Wait, is it the slaughterhouse?" Damon smiles in the rear-view mirror.

"Getting warmer."

We pull over to the side of the narrow road, the car is halfway in the ditch and halfway on the road.

We all climb out with a bit of difficulty, and Winnie and I stand close together waiting.

Leto walks over and takes my hand.

"Ladies, I hope you aren't too tired from soccer for a bit of a hike." Winnie and I exchange glances.

We start following the three boys away from the slaughterhouse and into the tree line. Thankfully sun is still out. It makes it a lot less scary to be following these men into the woods that I just barely met.

"What do you mean?" I stop, crossing my arms. I feel entitled to a bit more explanation than that.

Miles finally speaks, "We are going on a hike up the hill, it's really cool. And a lot less scary when it isn't pitch black, so we should go." Miles gives a tight-lipped smile, but his dimples are still visible. He's wearing a black t-shirt and cargo shorts.

Leto drags me along with him deeper into the woods. Winnie is up ahead next to Damon, but Miles stays to my left. Silently walking beside me.

We come to a quick-moving stream and a very old bridge that looks to be made of rotting wood. Winnie and Damon make it across in a few very shaky jumps. Damon helps Winnie from crashing into a tree on the other side. He's a lot stronger than he looks. Miles jumps the width of the creek and holds out his arms, smiling. Leto wastes no time. He grabs me around the middle and literally throws me across the creek. I scream as I slam into Miles' arms and solid chest for the one hundredth time today.

"That seemed really well rehearsed for not ever bringing girls here," I say. Winnie laughs and nods in agreement.

"We didn't say no girls, just not very many girls." Leto smiles and puts his hand on my lower back, guiding me forward.

It's getting darker as we go; the incline is getting

steeper. And even though the sun is still out, all the rain today has the ground slipping away under our feet. Damon has already slipped and almost fallen twice. Winnie and I couldn't stifle our laughter. I felt a little bad when his cheeks burned red.

After a few minutes, Damon and Winnie were in front, Miles in the middle, and Leto and I in the back.

"So, you had fun at soccer today." It was a statement, not a question.

"Yeah, I haven't played in a long time. It felt so good to get out there again." I give him a sweet smile, but he doesn't return it.

"What part of it *felt good*?" He looks at me, waiting for me to answer, his fingers still laced in mine.

"The part where I forgot how good I was, and how much fun I have playing." He stays silent for a moment. "Leto, are you mad at me? What's your deal?" So much for *casual*.

"I just didn't like hearing about you and Miles wrestling in the mud all morning. He's my friend and all, but he and I have a complicated history."

"I'm not sure what concern that would be to you. It's a co-ed soccer team. Boys and girls will come in contact with one another. Plus, what are you to me anyway?" It came out harsher and a bit louder than I wanted, but I meant it. "What am I to you?" He drops my hand but keeps walking.

"Right now, your friend. But I thought we were both on the same page with this going somewhere further."

"Well, I don't sit on my friend's laps and let them put their tongues down my throat. And I sure as hell don't ignore them and then lie about it." Now it was

Leto's turn to blush. I see Miles slow his walk, obviously listening to our not-so-quiet conversation.

"Wait, you're mad at me?! You're the one who showed up in some other guy's football sweatshirt for our date. And invited your friend, whom you obviously talked badly about me to, beforehand."

Shit, I *was* wearing one of my ex's football sweatshirts. It seemed like so long ago that I didn't even think of this sweatshirt as his anymore. But I look down and sure enough see his last name and jersey number across my chest.

"At least I only brought one friend, you brought two!" A weak argument, but someone had to point out the hypocrisy.

At this point, I think the entire woods were listening.

"So, you wouldn't have minded if it had just been the two of us? Here? In the woods? All alone? That wouldn't have seemed strange to you?"

I had stopped walking and was trying not to see his point. But I did.

"I guess that would have been a bit...awkward."

"Yeah, no shit. You just expected me to pick up the nun and take her into the forest? Hike up a mountain with no cell service? When everyone knows you have the most protective mom? She would probably call the National Guard if she found out you were out here with me. Even with a group of people."

"Wait, why would my mom single you out specifically?" My anger has cooled off a bit. I reach out and touch one of his arms that's shoved into his jeans' pocket.

His temper seems to calm at my touch.

"It doesn't matter. I guess what I'm trying to say is I like you, Ray. I don't want to play games with you. I just want to be with you."

Miles and the others are still walking. I can see them in the near distance, but I'm not sure if they can hear us anymore.

I don't know what to do. What Leto is saying feels genuine. But something in me says to keep my guard up.

"I...really want to keep getting to know you. And I don't care what people are saying or not saying about you. You didn't care what my reputation was, and that means a lot. So, if we can just be honest with each other going forward, I don't see why we can't still keep hanging out."

"So, you'll stop wearing other guys' clothes around me?" Leto playfully bumps my shoulder with his.

"I'll do my best." There, I didn't commit to anything solid. And it feels right not to become what I think he is describing as his girlfriend after two dates.

"I can live with that." He smiles and turns me to face him. Grabbing my face in his hands, he plants a kiss on my lips. I kiss him back greedily. Forgetting where we're at until I hear Winnie whistle from up ahead.

"Hey, you guys! Get up here!"

We pull apart and jog the distance between us and them. We have reached the bottom of the steepest part of the climb. There's an old rope, but Winnie and I are still going to need help ascending. Leto goes first and waits to pull everyone up, one by one.

Damon goes after Leto to help. Then Winnie.

Damon and Leto are slipping and almost falling trying to help Winnie. Miles bends to my ear.

"Hey, I just wanted to let you know that I'm helping the coaches announce callbacks, and you're in." His breath is hot, and immediately goosebumps rise over my arms. Miles notices and gives me a wicked grin. Then gestures me forward before I can answer him.

Not wanting to give him the satisfaction, I hustle up the rope and into Leto's arms. Miles close behind me.

Leto grabs my hand and leads me a little way through the trees. Parting the branches so I can see.

"Welcome to the wall."

Winnie's scream cuts through the air. And I look in the direction her head is turned, and I almost fall backwards down the hill.

Because, there, in the setting sun's twilight glow, was a girl. Standing on the wall motionless.

We all jumped when we saw her. It wasn't until she started laughing and making her way over to us that we realized we knew her.

"Ashley, what the hell are you doing here?!" Damon scowls in her direction, but there's a smile on the corner of his lips.

"Yeah, you scared the shit out of us." Leto walked over to her and hugged her.

"I heard you guys were going to bring Ray up here and didn't want to miss the fun." Her eyes look Leto up and down before she turns to Winnie and me.

"How was the hike up?" She raised one eyebrow like she had heard the argument that had taken place very loudly just minutes before.

"It was great." Leto quickly says before I have a chance. He smiles, but is looking at Ashley strangely.

Leto takes my hand and starts leading me away from her up the side of a grassy incline up to the wall.

The wall is massive. About five stories high. It looks like it was built right in the middle of these two big grassy hills. I can't see what's on the other side, but it would seem to be water. It almost looks like a dam or some sort of reservoir retaining wall. It's covered in moss and looks ancient.

I hear Ashley and Winnie behind me talking to Damon and Miles. Saying something about camping out up here sometimes. I don't know why, but the thought of it gives me the creeps.

In front of the wall is sort of an opening, or clearing. But all around us are dense woods. It would be really easy for us not to see what is seeing us. And that uneasy feeling washes over me again.

Leto and I walk up the hill and stand on one side of the wall. It looks even higher from up here. I look down at the group and notice Damon hanging on every word Ashley says. Same with Miles. Just how close are these four? What is it they are all saying to each other without words?

"I'm really glad you're here." Leto motions for me to sit down. We do, and hang our legs off the wall.

I give him a smile and scoot a little closer to him.

"Ashley has been my friend forever. She has known us all since we were kids. I think you and her could be really good friends." I consider for a moment. "I don't know. How does she feel about us hanging out?"

In years past, I've never had it go very well for the guy I was seeing to have a girl best friend. The girl is either in love with the guy, or the guy is dating me because he can't have the girl. Either way, there wasn't ever a lot of *getting along*.

"Well, you guys have a lot in common. Soccer, for one thing. And I don't know, she's just a good person. She's been there for me through...a lot."

He tosses a pebble he'd been handling into the trees.

I nod, but I feel like there's more. But I don't want to push it. I'm a guest here. In these woods, with this group. The last thing I wanted to do was make assumptions.

"Yeah, Winnie seems to like her. So I probably will too." It wasn't a lie. And right now, this large man was holding onto me, asking if I would be a little more involved in his world. And I wanted that very much.

I look down to see Damon slip off his backpack and pull out some supplies. It was hard not to notice the cousin's differences now that I really looked at him. Not as tall, not as athletic, and not as easy to converse with. I can tell he relied on Miles and Leto to be the faces and clowns of the group. Firewood, blankets, and some bottles full of something. It all feels very routine.

Young adults getting together to drink and sit around a fire. It seemed so normal. But there was a pit in my stomach. And I couldn't explain why. I wanted to be cool about Leto. I didn't want to overthink it, but that's exactly what I was doing.

As it's getting darker, my awesome brain reminds me of the figure I saw staring at me through the back door just today. Oh yeah. Plus, the letters. Plus, my aunt. I couldn't seem to get her off my mind. It all started to crash down on me at once. Elm Street, my mom's old street, the slaughterhouse, the woods.

That's why I feel this way. I tell myself there's no other reason. Leto is fine, we are fine. I'm just dealing with a lot right now.

Leto squeezes me, and I'm brought out of my spiral. He starts to stand up.

"Come on, I hope you're ready for some ghost stories." I give him my hand, and we make our way down to the others. They have a fire going, and Damon is passing around drinks from his apparently bottomless backpack. I notice everyone but Leto and I take one. I think it's just beer, but the thought of not being at the top of my game in the woods is too unsettling. Leto has already made it known to me that he doesn't drink.

We all settle in, Damon to my left, Leto to my right, Ashley, then Winnie, and Miles across from me.

Miles' eyes stay on the fire for most of Damon's fake-sounding story about Bigfoot. It causes all of us to burst out into laughter when he says something about the only living comparison to Bigfoot's man parts known to the experts, are his own. He stuck out his foot and claimed they wore the same shoe size.

When silence settles over us, and it's just the crackling of the fire and Leto's arms around me, his chest starts to rumble as he begins his story.

"Now I'm certain you ladies didn't come all the way up here to hear about Bigfoot, or in Damon's case, and I am speaking from eyewitness account, Smallfoot." Leto smiles, and everyone laughs. Damon laughs, but I can tell Leto's jesting stings.

"These woods have a history. You can feel it when your feet touch the grass, or when the rain drips from the leaves onto your skin. You hear it when the wind whistles through the pines. There have been others before, others who will come after, and others who are here now."

A chill runs down my spine, and I give a slight shiver. Leto answers my shiver with a quick brush of his lips on my neck and continues.

"It's not the ones we can see that we should be wary of, but the ones we cannot. Once you leave, they can stick to you like the sheet moss that grows overnight. The mold of them creeps into you and plants ideas you would have otherwise never thought of."

"Who?" I can't help but ask.

"Ahh, I'm glad you asked, the impressions of the people who were hurt here," Leto says slowly. "As you know, the slaughterhouse is just down the hill from here. When my grandparents were young, they used to hike these hills, young lovers looking for adventure on a summer's day."

Miles' eyes met mine across the fire briefly. The fire danced in his coal colored irises.

Leto goes on, "They used to come across many of the deposits of what they thought were decaying animals from the slaughterhouse. Big holes were dug in the ground, filled with blood and innards. The creek used to run red at times with the runoff of the slaughters. Even leeches lurked under the surface of the water. It was common knowledge that you did not want to fall in. It wasn't until a girl a little younger than we are now went missing that people grew suspicious of the deposits. When it all of a sudden stopped, folks were beside themselves. A conspiracy that someone had used the location of the slaughterhouse to hide massive crimes was born. The slaughterhouse, of course, denied all accusations and was never linked to any of the missing girls or the blood found. Even though there was a former employee who did go to jail at one point for crimes against some girls. He was still never linked to these hills. Not in that way anyway. When the cops searched the woods, they found no evidence of these deposits anywhere. But the girl who was last seen here alive with that very suspect has never been found. And it's curious because this very wall that we sit under tonight was the last place she was ever seen. By the very man who was found to be hurting women. So, where is she?"

Realization hit me in the gut.

"Wait, are you talking about Rosie?" I throw my hand out and grip onto Leto's broad chest.

Another silence falls over the six of us. Did they bring me here to tell me about my own missing, presumed dead relative? The way Leto had told the story was almost rehearsed, like it was one he told often, and with pleasure. My cheeks heated to think I was here just for him to embarrass.

"Well, if by Rosie you mean your aunt who went missing when she was in high school, yeah, the very same," Damon answers for Leto with a menacing grin.

"And what? You thought it would scare me?" I think pretending not to be creeped the hell out is my best bet here. Even though I was on the edge of standing up and running right back in the direction we came. They had information I didn't even have. Was it true? Did my mom know? Has my mom ever even been to this place? Is the feeling of impending doom that I've had since I got here because what they say is true?

"It's just a story, based on some *maybe* true events," Leto says, as he and Damon exchange glances. Ashley is just staring wide-eyed into the fire.

"Well, in any case, I don't think Ray came here to relive any of her family's trauma with us or give us any information we didn't already have." Ashley smiles at me sympathetically.

Bless you, Ashley. But I do think I could add to their *lore* without looking like what they told me has freaked me out as much as it actually did.

So, against all my better judgment, I tell them about the notes. And the figure that's been following me around.

"Wait, where did you change into Leto's clothes when you went swimming?" Miles says, after I just spent five minutes going over every gory detail of the past few days.

"Really? That's it? That's what you gleaned from everything I have told you?" Everyone starts laughing, and Leto answers for me.

"It's not really anyone's business where and when Ray chooses to put on or take off my clothes, or hers." I think he meant it as a joke, but it definitely came out more as a threat.

Miles puts his hands up in surrender and takes a drink.

My willingness to share seemed to have thawed the tension between us all. Winnie had stayed unnaturally quiet through it all. I look over and see she has actually fallen asleep. The rest of us spend hours talking about different theories and where Rosie's body could be, or if she did really just run away as her first note had led most people to believe.

After an hour or so, I had nodded off, not being able to keep my eyes open.

I don't know how long. But when I woke up, I looked around, confused about where I was. The fire had died down, and I saw Winnie still asleep, Damon snoring on my left, and Miles awake and watching me from across the fire. The two people I didn't see were Leto and Ashley.

"Where did they go?" I look at Miles, and he looks at me with what I think is grief. Or maybe guilt?

"Umm...I'm not sure." Miles says and looks down.

Damon stirs. I am surprised when Damon interrupts and speaks clearly. "They went to find more wood for the fire," I swear Damon had just been asleep, snoring.

Miles rolls his eyes, and then panic hits me. "What time is it!?" Suddenly, I remember I am a twenty-year-old girl with a new ten pm curfew, and the way I feel rested can only mean that I have slept through my curfew. Sure enough, I pull out my phone, no service, but it says one o'clock in the morning. Shit."I have to go." I get up and start to stumble back from the direction I think we came in, and Miles grabs my arm.

"Hey, slow down, Nutmeg." I turn to him, eyes watering in frustration. "Even if you make it down, how are you going to get home?" He stares down at me.

"I just need to get down so I can call my mom and tell her I'm okay, just extremely stupid." The last thing I ever wanted to do was make my mom worried. My whole life, I had tried to be her friend, her ally, not her problem.

"Okay, I'll take you." Miles grabbed my hand with rough, hot hands, pulling me along at a run. He knew I could keep up and did not slow down for me even slightly.

Miraculously, neither of us fell, and we made it back to Damon's SUV in record time. I pull out my phone, and sure enough, I have about twenty missed calls between my mom and Winnie's mom. I called them and accepted my verbal punishment from both.

Miles winced when he heard the yelling from the other end of the line. He stood there with his hand in his pockets and just watched me handle it with a small smile on his lips.

"What the hell is so amusing?" I quip, shoving my phone back in my jeans' shorts pocket and leaning against the car, arms crossed, staring at him. It's hard to see details of him, but it wasn't hard to see his massive frame and white teeth gleaming.

"I just think it's funny that you have a curfew for one, and two, that it isn't even midnight."

I think for a moment, it didn't seem like he was taunting me, just curious. So, I disarmed my defense a small amount.

"It usually is midnight. My mom is just a worrier. Her sister, as you know, played a huge part in the way she views life now. I understand her worries. Do I agree with them? Not always. But the least I can do for her is not go missing and never be found, you know?" I smile so he knows I'm not offended.

"Yeah, I get it, I guess. There's just..." He trails off as we hear voices coming down the trail. They sound far enough away that we know they haven't crossed the creek yet.

"Just what?" I step a little closer, so he doesn't have to talk very loudly. For some reason I can't explain, I think I could feel his anxiety. Sure enough, he comes in so close I can feel his breath. Smell him. Only it smells of mint and something sweet. Not alcohol, I could have sworn he had been drinking beer too.

"It's just, you don't seem like the type of girl that would want...Leto...around." I could tell by his pinched dark brows that it pained him to say that about his friend. He must have felt it was important to say it to me anyway. I don't take a step back; instead, I lean in.

"Oh...that. Well, to be fair, Ashley did warn me about him. But he and I...I don't know, we are just getting to know each other right now." I shrug and look to see if I can spot anyone coming through the tree line. No one yet.

"Ashley told you? Or warned you? Or whatever?" His face looks surprised and amused.

"Yeah, so it's not like I don't know his reputation. And in any case, Leto said you were probably going to marry your girlfriend soon anyway. So, I'm really not sure what your concern would be with Leto and me." He looks confused. And it makes me stop.

"But come to think of it, where is she?"

Wouldn't she want to be in on tonight? I know I would if I were her. I mean, there's no getting around it. Miles is one of the most attractive guys I've seen. Like ever.

"I guess you guys really are keeping it casual, I

mean, he was with Ashley last night. And maybe even tonight. And as for my girlfriend—"

Just then, the four others come crashing through the trees. But at his words about Leto and Ashley, my stomach crashed through my butt.

"Jeez, you guys took off fast!" Winnie says as she stumbles toward me, almost tripping into the ditch.

"One of us had to call off the search party, Winnie!" I say out loud, but inside, I am telling my brain to shut up and not think about what Miles just told me. I see a look of panic on her face as she pulls out her phone and sees all the missed calls and texts.

"Shit!" She quickly dials her mom back, and the yelling on the other end of the phone starts back up again.

Damon steps forward, "We'd better hurry, brothers. Leto and I only have a few hours before we have to be up doing all sorts of things back at home. And I know Miles shows up early every day at the site." He must be talking about the apple farm and Miles' construction job.

I don't have time to wonder, though, because when Damon unlocks his car, the lights illuminate Leto and Miles staring at each other. The light seems to have interrupted a nonverbal argument between the two. Leto breaks it up when he scoops me into his arms and puts me on his lap in the back seat instead of having me sit beside him. His hair is a little mussed, and his t-shirt looks a tad ruffled. He must have fallen asleep for a little bit, too, I tell myself. Instead of what my brain tells me to suspect.

Sitting on Leto's lap worked out because Ashley

lives close enough to walk, but didn't want to in the dark. So, she took my seat next to Miles.

Leto spent the entire ride home giving my neck small kisses and having his hands on my upper thighs. Nothing wild, but everything felt so exposed sitting so close to his friends. Is this how he acted with other girls? Had they all done this exact outing before? Just with a different girl on his lap? Something told me yes, but the heat that had risen in me told me not to care.

Looking around, I couldn't see Rodger. Then I heard what sounded like someone hitting a watermelon with their fist. I hurry back around the corner and see Rodger holding Harvey up by the front of his shirt against the side of the building. His nose is bleeding, and it is still pouring down his chin and mixing with the other animal blood already on his chest.

"You think it's funny to threaten Dorothea? You like feeling like a big man to little girls? Well, how about me? Huh? If you want to feel like a big man, go on, threaten me! See how well you can talk to women after I punch your teeth down your throat."

"Rodger!" He doesn't hear me at first, but Harvey's hands are up, and he's pointing over to me. It looks like he's trying to get Rodger to look over towards me.

Rodger shoves him into the building one more time, then drops him. Turning to me, Rodger wipes his hands on Harvey's pants.

"You ready?" He looks at me like he just asked if I

wanted to go for ice cream. I am frozen to the spot. Looking from Rodger to Harvey, who is still bloody, and trying to pick himself up off the ground. That was an insane gesture.

I can't speak, so I just nod. Rodger steps over Harvey and walks beside me to his car.

When we are driving back down the road, his grip tightens on the steering wheel, and I can see that his knuckles are cracked and bloody.

"Rodger, you are a maniac." The words are out before I can stop them.

He starts to laugh, and I can't help but smile.

"Look, when you have as many sisters as I do, you learn to have a little loyalty to the opposite sex. I told you, your sister helped me when I had no one else. Something I imagine one of my sisters would have done for me if they could have. So, no, I am not going to ever stand by and let anyone talk poorly about her or you. And if that makes me a maniac, then I accept the title gladly."

He nods in resolve, and we bump down the road. I don't even know what to say to that. Other than to feel relief. Finally, someone as crazy as me, willing to do what it takes to find Rosie.

A sinking realization I made recently was that my parents were not going to be the ones to find the answers. They were too shocked, too hurt, too traumatized, I don't know, too sad, maybe? It was all they could both do to take care of the farm. I could see it in their eyes, in their heavy walks. They said they would never give up, but I know what defeat looks like when I see it. Cruel acceptance was the words that came to my head.

But Rodger. Sweet, seven sisters, Rodger. He was going to help me. He and I were going to pick up the slack.

Not too long after, Rodger's mustang pulled down a long dirt road and up to the front gate of the Berry Farm.

"Why are we here?" I turned to Rodger when he turned off the engine.

"It's time for us to tell each other what we know, you first. Then me, then I'll tell you why we are here."

I looked at Rodger for a moment. It wasn't that I didn't want to trust him. It wasn't even that I felt I couldn't, I just...I didn't know if there would be any point in the future when he would disappoint me. I know it sounds harsh, insane even. But it was easy to rely on only your family. For me, it was at least. Mine were steady, reliable, and loving. People outside of it, on the other hand, were unpredictable. But I think Rosie going missing, finding out about her secret journal, and having my parents shut down, all in the same month, made me realize some things.

No one is without unpredictability, no one is without secrets, and no one is exempt from all-consuming grief. So I looked at Rodger, I mean, really looked at him. His thick black hair, olive skin, and blue eyes. All the reasons I should run. But I don't, I choose to let him in. Just a little.

"I saw Harvey Green attack Mia in the woods. The same woods where Rosie was last seen, and involving the same guy. Or at least I think it was Mia. She was tall and skinny with reddish-brown hair. And seeing as

Mia quit her job at the slaughterhouse recently and wasn't home, and I don't know anyone else who has red hair, really. I would say it is probably her."

Rodger's mouth drops open.

"What do you mean by *attack*? Did Harvey see you? Is that why he threatened you?! Did Mia get away?" His intensity calms me slightly. I put my hand on his arm in a subtle way of saying *stop*. He gulps a dry, hard swallow but stops asking me questions for the moment.

"I saw him hit her. Hard, across the face. I threw a rock at his back from up the hill, and she bolted. I ran too, and I didn't know he saw me. But I had suspected it. I haven't told anyone but you because my parents have the harvest coming up. Plus, they are already sick with worry about Rosie, of course. But I wanted to see if Mia and I could go to Sheriff Jones together and make a statement...But I can't find her. And now I'm worried Harvey got to her, like he may have gotten to Rosie."

Rodger is still staring at me with his mouth open, but his eyes look alive with excitement.

He lets me go on, "And there is one other thing I have been wanting to either confront Harvey with, or ask the police about still. Harvey made it sound like he and Rosie used to only stay out till ten or eleven at night, but I used to wait up for her sometimes, and she wouldn't get home till midnight or sometimes much later." I don't know why initially it bothered me, but if you had nothing to hide, why would you change that small detail? Unless you did have something to hide.

I think of something else before he can interject, "And there's more, Rosie had a secret journal that she left in our room. I found it, hid it under my pillow, and then someone broke in and stole it. Oh, and has been tearing pages out of it and leaving them for my family to find to make it look like she ran away."

"Holy shit! Sorry, excuse me. I mean, jeez Louise, Dot!" It's hard to hide my smile, but I try my best. Rodger is beaming like he just unwrapped a present.

"What is so funny?" My hand is still on his arm, and he makes no motion to move it.

"You. Are. Far out. This. Is. Far out." Now it's my turn to look at him open-mouthed.

"No, I don't mean Mia getting clocked by Harvey is good, or Rosie being gone, or the whole break-in scenario. I mean, yes, I do...but not like you think. Listen, something is going on here. Like, honestly, something wild. And I think we are going to be the ones to bring this town some justice, and hopefully Mia and Rosie, too." He looks at me with one eyebrow raised and his hands up as if to say *Are you still in? Did I pass the test?*

And I was, and he did.

"I don't think you're wrong, Rodger, but you need to work on your delivery. Okay, your turn. Why are we at the Berry Farm?"

"Well, one obvious reason is that Rosie worked here." I shoot a glance at him, and he puts his palms up.

"*Works* here, sorry. Rosie works here, and I want to know what it was like the last time she worked. What was she like? Who did she usually talk to and all that? The other reason is that I don't think Mia could afford to lose her job even for a day. My guess is she showed up to work at the only place we all know that is always hiring. Even if the money is garbage."

I nod and consider. I do like the idea of asking around her place of work. After all, now that I know she kept things from even me, who knows what or who she could have been into here at work all day? And Mia did seem like the kind of girl who would be in dire straits even after one day without work.

"Okay then, let's go." I turn to open the door, but Rodger stops me dead when he brushes a strand of hair from my cheek. My face flushes and he pulls his hand away.

"Sorry, you had a hair." Clearing his throat, he leans across me and pushes the passenger side door open. I remind myself that this boy has seven sisters. Looking out for girls is basically an involuntary impulse for him at this point.

But something reminded me that he hadn't tried to ask me out ever since I asked him for help. Hadn't tried to put any moves on me either. My heart felt a flutter for that. But I pushed that thought aside. I'm here for Rosie, for Mia.

Getting out of the car, we made our way up to the fruit stand where they sell some of their berries. I know their main income came from the berries that were shipped all over the state. This is where local folks came to purchase their berries, though. Sometimes Rosie would bring home a crate, and my mom would be able to make pie. Those were the times when I was thankful Rosie stayed at a low-paying, backbreaking work job. My mom's pies were that good.

There was a small main office where a lot of the trades between farms took place.

As we approached, my shoes made a crunching noise on the hay that lay strewn around us. There was a thin-lipped girl there. Overalls and a button-down dirty shirt. I could tell she tried to look as put-together as she could. Living on and working on a berry farm. She was sitting on a wooden crate in the shade next to a display of strawberries, blackberries, raspberries, and huckleberries. The colors were deep and rich, but I knew it took a toll to harvest these. Rosie used to come home with stained hands and blisters on her fingertips. And a fierce backache.

Rodger starts in, "Hi, I was wondering if you had any new hires here. I'm looking for my friend Mia. Tall, red hair, around our age?" Jeez, just cut right to the chase, why don't you? I narrow my eyes at Rodger, but he ignores me and strolls right up to the girl.

She looks to be about our age, but I don't recognize her from school. She stands up and brushes off the pants that have collected dust from the ground around her.

"She's just your friend?" The girl asks innocently, but her eyelashes blink way too many times to be a coincidence.

"Yeah, a family friend. I stopped by her house today and couldn't find her." He throws in an easy smile that exposes his straight white teeth.

"Is she in some kind of trouble?" The girl tilts her head, and I know then that Mia did come here to work. The girl must have seen just how hard Harvey had hit her. And I think Rodger realized it, too.

"Yes, but not from me. We are trying to make sure she is safe. If we could just talk to h..."

The girl cuts him off, "Yeah, last I saw her, she was fine, besides her eye and cheek. Black...and split pretty good. We hired her on the spot, but we only had half a day's work for her today. She took off about fifteen minutes ago. In that direction."

She lifted her chin not to the dirt road behind us, but to the tree line east of us. That explains why we didn't encounter her down the long dirt road. Her house is back in that general direction. It would make sense if she were on foot to take that as a shortcut.

Rodger nods to the girl, then points his thumb out to me.

"This here is my other friend. Dot. Her sister worked here, but we haven't seen her for some time. Is there any way we could get a little information?"

"You're Rosie's sister." Not a question. She doesn't wait for my answer; she turns around and disappears into the small make-shift front office for the farm. The one open window tells me it's better to stay out here in the shade than inside that sure-to-be-sweltering hot box.

The girl comes back out quickly, and sure enough, there are beads of sweat running down the sides of her face.

"Here. My dad told me to give this to any family of Rosie's that came by." She hands me an envelope, and I open it to see it's her last paycheck. And a pink ribbon she used to tie her hair back on the hotter days. The sight of it creates a knot in my throat I can't explain.

"Well, what if she comes back? She is coming back." I almost snap at the girl. But she just shrugs.

"Then I'm sure my dad would rehire her. But she

hasn't shown up for four shifts in a row. So, for now, she doesn't work her anymore." The finality of it makes me sick. I ball my fists up in my pockets to keep from saying or doing anything that will scare her or Rodger. But I feel like shouting.

"Okay, so when she *was* here, Rosie, I mean, what was she like? Who did she interact with?" Bless Rodger for talking calmly when I wanted to scream.

"She was nice, polite, and wore those wild boots more than once. Her job was to make sure the trades with the other farms went well. My dad said she had a knack for talking to people. Making them laugh and feel at ease around her. So, he made sure she dealt directly with them all." This girl can tell that I'm not at ease. I see the sympathy in her stare.

From somewhere behind us, a big truck pulls up, and I hear dogs barking.

Coming towards us is the young, skinny apple farmer and his two dogs. He was wheeling ten apple crates on a dolly toward the girl and her stand of berries. He seemed to be in his own world. Didn't pay any mind to Rodger or me.

"Hey!" He turned his head after replacing a few crates of his apples with berries. He looked over at us, and his eyes widened.

"Oh, I didn't see you there, Miss Dotty." He dipped his head toward me and then to Rodger.

"I was just asking about Rosie. Did you trade with her much?" I pointed to the crates on his dolly.

"Did he ever. I think he and Rosie did more trades than any of the other farmers around here." The girl answered for him. His cheeks burned red.

"I can't say no to my wife, she loves the berries to make pies, butters, jams, and tiny, sweet things. She says too much apples leave a bitter taste in her mouth."

"She sounds lovely." Rodgers' sarcasm is only caught by me. I stifle an odd snicker.

And then I remember the last time I saw this man. The last time he called me Miss Dotty. Did he hear it from Rosie? And there are those two dogs he had offered me. To help in the search. I look to see a couple of foxhounds. And I think I do have use for them after all.

Rodger looked at me and nodded. Like he knew what I wanted to ask.

"Are you busy right now? Apple farmer?" I tilted my head and waited for him to finish loading up his crates and dolly.

"I do mean to get back before dusk to do a few things, but I could spare an hour or two. Why?"

"And what about your hounds?" Rodger chimed in, already knowing where this was going.

"Well, they stay with me, so I suppose if I go, they could go."

"I would like to take you up on your offer from the other day. Can you follow us to the last known place my sister was? It would be really helpful if we could try and get a scent off this?" I hold up the pink silk ribbon in my hand; it catches the breeze and blows out beside me. I swear I can smell Rosie, and I put my hand down to hide it from shaking.

He stares at the ribbon now at my side for a second too long.

"Please, Mr. Lee." It seemed like a lifetime ago, but I remembered he told me his name was something Lee. And I think saying it brought him back in the moment.

"Dale, you can call me Dale. Sure, you go on ahead, and I'll follow you."

Rodger clapped his hands and rubbed them together. "Great! Thanks, Mr. Lee, it's not too far from here. Is it Dot?" Rodger looks to me.

"No, just down the road and east a bit."

A short while later, we pull up just down the road from the slaughterhouse. I see the flat roof just up ahead. I really hope Harvey doesn't come outside for any reason and find us. I turn around the other way and head to the creek crossing. Close behind me are Rodger, Dale, and the foxhounds.

Dale takes the ribbon and lets his pups smell it. Then, when he is satisfied that they have the scent, he unhooks their leashes, and they dart off into the woods. All three of us are following them at a sort of jog. Faster than a stroll, but slowed down by all the trees and bushes, and fallen logs on the ground. They are taking us exactly where I thought they might. In the direction of the wall. Both the dogs are out of my sight, but they are barking as they go. Finally, their barking seems to get louder. This must mean they have stopped.

There's no way they could have made it to the wall yet. As we get closer, I see they are barking up a tree. I hear a girl scream, and my stomach leaps at the possibility.

I look up to see two big green eyes staring down at me in terror. No, it is not my sister. But it *is* Mia King. A fresh cut on her cheek and a dark bruise on her eye.

Dale looks the most confused of us all. He looks at me, at the ribbon, his dogs, then back at Mia.

"What is going on here?" He seems more jarred than we are. But Mia slides down the tree and starts to laugh.

"Rodger, what are you doing here?" She claps her hand on his shoulder.

"Well, I went to see you today and wanted to ask how you've been. And you weren't home, or at work, or at your new job..." He trails off. Mia looks at him, confused.

"Why on earth would you be trying to track me down all over town?" Her eyes scan over to Dale and me again.

I start, "Because... I'm the one who threw the rock." Her head snaps to mine, and she involuntarily puts her hand to her wounded face.

"I think Harvey hurt my sister, and I need you to help me prove it." She hangs her head but doesn't answer me right away.

"That doesn't explain why my hounds found her." Dale seems angry about the confusion of his pups.

I hold out the ribbon and shrug. "I've watched Rosie put this in her hair a hundred times."

Mia eyes the pink silk. "I found that in the fields today, brought it to the Berry Farmer's daughter."

Dale breathes a sigh of relief. Happy to know there's nothing wrong with his dogs after all. We all stand there awkwardly for a moment until Dale breaks the silence.

"I'd better be going, I still have a few things I need to attend to before it gets dark." With a nod, he takes his hounds and tramples back towards the road.

Mia walks over to me and startles me with an embrace.

"Thank you, I don't know why you were there, and how you were able to hit him. But thank you for throwing that rock."

"I'm Rosie's sister." She gives me a knowing look.

"I know I shouldn't be with a guy like Harvey. I know it. But I don't know, sometimes he can make me feel so good. He even takes my sister with us sometimes when we go places. Like the movies, or out to eat. There's a good side to him. And I swear I didn't know he was seeing Rosie. Not until the other day, when I heard the rumors at work. That he was the last one to see her the night she disappeared. I confronted him and... he hit me. He brought me up to the wall to spend...time with me... but when I wanted to fight instead, he got enraged. I have never seen him that mad before. If it hadn't been for you...I don't know what would have happened."

"And why are you out here?" Rodger puts a comforting hand on her shoulder.

"I walked from the Berry Farm and was just wandering around in here having a smoke." She gestured to a butt of a cigarette on the ground between us.

"Then those two dogs showed up, so I hopped in that tree." She points above her head and tries to smile, but it comes out as a wince.

"Do you think Harvey could have hurt my sister?"

I already know what she thinks, but I want her to say it. To help us.

"Yes, I think he most likely did."

"Are you willing to press charges? To tell the police exactly what happened?" I can tell she's brave and strong. But I don't know what level of abuse she has endured in her life. And what level she feels is okay and what is not. I've only ever known kindness, so I can say for sure my threshold is zero. I would have no problem telling on anyone who crossed me to my dad.

"Yes, I think so." I'm so glad I wasn't wrong about her being brave.

All three of us are bumping down the road to Mia's house. Sheriff Jones is not my favorite person by any means, but I do think he cares, in his own way, about this town.

I'm in the back seat listening to Rodger and Mia chat.

"She really shouldn't be alone at home, Mia," Rodger says to her, but not in a cross way.

"I know, but with my mom gone and school out for the summer, I don't know what else to do." I hear the pain and love in her voice for her sister.

Rodger seems to think for a moment.

"Well, my sisters would love to have her. They are always doing all kinds of annoying things. Do you think your sister would want to hang out during the day with them?"

I could see tears sliding down Mia's cheeks as she nodded to Rodger. I even had to swallow a lump in my throat looking in on this moment. Who was this guy?

"Great, then it's settled. Have her ready first thing, and my mom will come get her in the mornings. Make sure she's hungry, or it will hurt my mom's feelings if she doesn't eat with us." He winks and keeps driving like he didn't just do the one thing these two sisters needed most in the world at that time.

EIGHTEEN
DOT 1972
CONFESS

I had moved up to the front seat of Rodger's Mustang and hadn't taken my eyes off the road since we dropped off Mia.

Our plan was to go to the police station first thing in the morning all together. As a team. We told Mia we would be with her every step of the way, and we meant it. I couldn't stop thinking about how I was going to tell my parents all that I had learned in these few short days. The thought of it was what kept me from hearing Rodger say my name three times.

"Dot!" He waved a hand in front of my glazed straight ahead stare.

"Sorry, what?" My trance broke, and I looked to see we were in front of my farmhouse on Elm Street.

"I was just saying, good luck with what you need to take care of tonight." His eyes looked me over, then went back to his steering wheel, then looked me over once more. It was obvious he wanted to ask me something.

"What, Rodger?"

"It's just... I'm not sure what is going on. But I wanted to ask..." He shifts in his seat so he's facing me. I shift in mine so we are almost nose to nose. Feeling like just about nothing else could surprise me more than anything I have already seen, heard, or felt in the past couple of weeks, I nod for him to keep talking.

"Do you...could you...ever give me a chance?" And I stand corrected.

I can't help but stop the smile that spreads across my face. This is why he was nervous? Because he is still trying to go on a date with me? A part of me feels wary; had his acts been just a show? To get me to like him? I guess I won't know until I give him a shot.

"I'll make you a deal. Get me through this. Help me bring Harvey to justice. Make sure Rosie's story doesn't get forgotten. Promise me...we won't ever stop looking for her. And I'll let you take me on a date."

I try to stop it, but my voice catches. I've said all the things I desire in this moment. All my hopes, and I know there isn't anyone who can make good on them all.

But instead of telling me no, Rodger leans into the small space between us. Cups my cheek with one of his hands and plants a perfectly soft kiss on my forehead.

"It would be my pleasure, Dorothea."

A warm sensation washed over me, and everything in me wanted to believe his sincerity. It felt hard to speak, so I nodded and got out of the car. Without looking back, I jogged up the steps and into my house.

Rodger wasn't going to tell his mom about our plan to take Mia to the police tomorrow. He felt like she would have too much to say about it. I agreed with him. I think the fewer people who knew, the better. Rodger was going to inform his mom of her new summer duty. Taking Mia's sister during the day. He was adamant that his mom and sisters would love it.

We agreed that telling my parents might bring them a little hope at this horrific time. Mia's only job was to stay safe and get her sister ready to be picked up in the morning.

Feeling good about our plan, I go into the kitchen to see if my parents are back from their farm obligations for the day. No one is there. I searched the rest of the small home to make sure. Not a soul but me. The heat felt suffocating inside, so I grabbed a glass of milk and went outside the back door.

The sun was at its hottest point. I look over and see the tree swing moving in the breeze. There is enough shade to keep me cool while I drink my milk. I was only swinging for a few minutes when something moved out of the corner of my eye. Goosebumps moved up my arm at the memory of the figure I had seen out in the field just a day or so ago.

I whip my head around and sure enough, just like last time, there it was. Tall and thin. Standing above the wheat. I could not see if it was a man or not, but it seemed to me to be facing me. No face was easily detected because of how far away it was, but my gut said there were eyes fixed in my direction.

The breeze was strong enough that it could have explained the movement. But I was certain whatever was out there was living and breathing. The probability of someone scratching at my window and then retreating back to the fields, and having this random scare*crow* here being two different situations, was not high. The chances of them being related are just about guaranteed if you ask me. And having both of them being related to Rosie going missing is almost too much for me to handle right now, but I know denying it will only delay me from the truth. So, I stare at the thing just beyond my property. Because if that's Harvey, he thinks he is clever. He thinks he can scare me into forgetting what I've seen, what I know. But he is in for a very nasty surprise.

I sit on the swing for what seems like seconds. But the sun is low in the sky when I hear my mom and dad coming up from the east side of our property. They are talking in low tones, and my dad is holding my mom's hand. They don't see me at first, so I just watch them.

My dad turns and takes my mom's hand in both of his. He brings it to his lips, and I can see it in both their eyes. They don't think Rosie is coming back alive. The resolution in them both leaves my stomach a black pit of snakes. Something I had told myself was a possibility when I saw what Harvey did to Mia. But not something I wanted to really think about. Because there was still a chance Harvey was just keeping her hidden, hurt, but alive. Until she could heal and come back. Even thinking it sounds crazy.

The promise my dad made to my mom and me stumbles through my thoughts. If she were dead, he could still keep his promise to us. To never stop looking, thinking, and praying to know what happened. But I wouldn't be able to keep mine. To have her walk back through the door.

They spotted me and motioned for me to follow

them inside to start helping with dinner. I got up from my swing and walked to the back door, which my dad was holding open for me. Before I walked through it, I turned to look at the scar*ecrow* one more time before I went inside. But it was gone.

Before I had the chance to really process it, my mom was handing me a paring knife.

I stayed quiet, and my mom and I worked in silence together. I peeled the potatoes while my mom made the pie crust. I cut up the meat while she sautéed it. I stirred the filling while she filled the pie crust and set the oven. Her hands worked quickly to make the lattice pie top and popped it in the oven. She cranked the timer while my eyes watched her closely. I chose to stay in the kitchen after she went upstairs to shower. I didn't say anything to my mom about not having a green salad. It was very unusual for my mom not to have prepared one, or not to have asked me to. But there was nothing usual about these past couple of weeks, nothing at all.

Both my parents came down the stairs as the timer was buzzing. I pulled out the meat and potato pie while my dad helped set the table. I watched him grab a fourth plate and then freeze. He looked down and, gently like the plate was an infant, set the plate back in the cupboard. He turned and sat down, not making eye contact with my mom or me as he did so.

"So, how was work today Dotty?" Startled at the sound of my mom's voice, I looked at the piece of her untouched pie.

"I didn't work today. I did something else, and...I actually want to speak to both of you about it." They both set their forks down and wait for me to go on.

"Okay, so this isn't very easy to say...But I think Harvey is the one who knows what happened to Rosie. Besides the obvious reason, he was the last to see her." I'm careful not to say I think he hurt her. Not yet, anyway.

"Well, spit it out then!" My dad stares at me with a deep intensity.

"I saw Harvey hit a girl named Mia King when I went up to the wall. When I went to Mia's work to ask her about it, I learned that she had quit. But I ran into Harvey there instead, and he...made me think he knew what happened to her."

Their mouths hung open in silent disbelief.

"What. Did. He. Say." My dad spat the words out slowly.

"He said if I didn't leave it be, I might... end up like Rosie." My voice had gotten quieter and quieter, while my dad's got louder and more out of control. He stood up and grabbed his coat that was hanging on a hook by the back door.

"Dad, no. I have a plan. Mia agreed to come with us to the Sheriff tomorrow to tell her story about what he did to her. And there is a witness that will corroborate what he told me. All three of us are going in the morning."

My dad isn't used to hearing the word no, but his shoulders drop a little, and he turns to face me.

"Who's the third person?"

"It's Rodger, Rodger Young."

Surprise crosses his face, and he thinks for a moment.

"The Youngs, that's a good family. Lots of girls.

Lots of girls. Okay, I will drive. And we will leave first thing in the morning."

I remember my mom and take a chance to glance at her. She doesn't hide her tears. She lets them fall freely down her sun-kissed cheeks onto her completely intact piece of pie. She doesn't say a word, just reaches her hand out to cover mine. She gives it a squeeze and gets up out of her chair. Together, they walk upstairs. My dad is practically carrying my mom. And I am left alone to clean up dinner.

NINETEEN
DOT 1972
ASSAULT

I lay in bed staring into the closet. Counting our four dresses. Looking at Rosie's boots. Then back to the ceiling. I do this most of the night until a little brightness starts to peek through my lace curtains.

I wonder if Rosie is also witnessing this sliver of morning dawn, or if the moonlight of the Friday night she went missing was the last she had ever seen.

The more I see and hear about Harvey, the more convinced I am she never made it out of his sight alive. My parents' withdrawal and somberness suggest that they, too, suspect the very worst.

Instead of dwelling on the worst, I decide to get up and get ready to go to the Sheriff's office. Grabbing my summer shorts and t-shirt, I tiptoed to our family's shared bathroom. My mom's favorite colors were pink and blue. This is reflected on just about every surface in our home.

The bathroom has no shower, but a tub against the back wall. To the left is a small sink with one cupboard underneath. Across from that is the toilet, with extra toilet paper stacked on the tank. My mom wasted no time painting the sink cabinet white and the walls a light blush pink. She laid the laminate flooring herself, too. I remember her coming home so excited, she had found a pattern that had both pink and blue throughout the embossed squares. It was small, yes. But it was always clean.

Her smile, when she put her hands to her hips and said *ta-da,* as she swung the door open to show off the finished product, was from ear to ear.

I dip my chin, thinking of how I may never see that smile again. Not the one that reaches her eyes, at least.

I soak in the tub until the sun rises all the way over the dark green hills. The water has gone lukewarm, and my flesh is a wrinkled, prune mess.

"Dot? Are you almost done in there?" I hear my dad's hushed voice. My mom must still be asleep. His deep baritone still rings out despite his efforts to be quiet.

"Yes! Just a sec!" I make quick work of getting dressed and drying off. I open the door to see my dad, red-eyed, with sunken skin, and a forced smile. He moves so I can go past him, and I swear I hear a sniffle as the door closes behind him.

I walk over to my parents' room, not bothering to hide my footsteps. I can see my mom is awake and sitting up in her bed. She is staring straight ahead, out the window.

I gasp when I see her. I can't help it. Her eyes are unfocused and hazy. Her hair is wild and unkempt. A far cry from the curlers and headscarf she usually wore. I covered my mouth and hurried down the stairs. She didn't even look my way when I all but screamed. She must have been lost in thought. My heart was breaking for my parents a little more every day. I prayed today was the day we would get some answers.

I only had to wait twenty more minutes until my dad was coming down the stairs, ready to go. We planned on picking up Roger first, then Mia.

"I understand Rodger is an okay fellow. But why are we dragging him along? As far as I have been informed, he neither adds nor takes away from anything we're about to tell the Sheriff."

"Well, Dad, Mia knows Rodger really well and trusts him. He's been taking care of her family a bit. I think she would feel more comfortable with him than alone. Plus, he overheard Harvey's threats. Remember?"

He must have because he doesn't say another word about it. Just stares at the road and drives.

Rodger is sitting on his porch when our old red truck crunches along the driveway. He has his Letterman's jacket and jeans on. I tell myself that there are only two reasons why I'm glad he is here. Roise and Mia. And not the heat I still feel from the kiss on my forehead his lips left behind. What kind of man gives his all and asks almost nothing in return? Only asks if I would consider letting him be around me.

"Hey." He says breathlessly as I climb to the back seat. It's hardly considered a seat at all, but there is no way Mia or Rodger could fit back here.

"Would you mind if I had a word with your parents before we pick up this Mia girl?" My dad doesn't try to, but his voice is sharp and threatening.

"Well, Sir, I wouldn't mind at all, only my dad is at work already, and my mom is on her way to pick up Mia's little sister. She's been home alone while her sister and dad are at work. She's only six, I think, so..."

My dad waves him off before he can finish his sentence. I can't tell what my dad's impression of him is, but I have a feeling it's not great. I, on the other hand, feel like putty when he mentions his plan to keep Mia's little sister fed and cared for.

We arrive at the King's residence to a familiar scene. Almost caved-in roof, sagging porch, and chipped paint.

I swear I can hear my dad's eyes popping out of his head when he observes this abandoned-looking shack. Before Mia comes out, my dad turns to Rodger.

"If your mom needs help with the child, let me know. We would be happy to take a turn."

Rodger's head tips up in acknowledgment, just as we hear a door shut.

Mia walks slowly to the truck and slides in next to Rodger.

"Mia, this is my dad. He is going to take us to the station. He knows the Sheriff." Mia shrugs and curls her shoulders in to look as small as possible.

What I should have said was my dad knows how to threaten the sheriff and throw him on his hind end right out of our house.

.   .   .

The station smells like musk and window cleaner. Kind of like when you try to clean something really old, but the dusty smell never goes away, and now you just have both smells fermenting together. It forms a completely new, unpleasant smell altogether.

By chance, the Sheriff is standing at the secretary's desk, laughing and drinking a cup of coffee with the woman sitting there. He is standing just to the side of her, leaning casually on the back counter.

As soon as he spots our unlikely crew, he coughs, and it turns into him choking on his drink.

"What are you doing here?" He sputters out while the secretary stands and pounds on his back. He waves her off, and her head swivels from him to us and back again.

I involuntarily smile when it looks like panic in the Sheriff's eyes at my dad standing just feet in front of him.

"It's about Rosie." Rodger steps forward, and I am taken aback when he is the first one to speak.

"Well, about Harvey Green rather." Rodger continues to step forward until he is almost covering me completely. I crane my neck around him to see Sheriff Jones blinking and wiping coffee off his mustache with the back of his hand.

"Who are you?" The Sheriff stands there awkwardly, eyeing all four of us.

"Rodger Young and I witnessed him making threats to Dotty yesterday, telling her that she was going to end up just like her sister if she didn't mind her own business."

I can see my dad's fists clenched tight at Rodgers' statement.

"And the rest of you?" He made no indication that he believed Rodger.

"I witnessed Rodger hitting Mia King in the same place where Rosie was last seen alive, and with the same person to whom she was last supposed to have been with." I must have practiced saying that a million times last night, lying in my bed staring at my ceiling.

"And with the shiner, I'm guessing you're the girl he hit?" The Sheriff tilts his head to Mia. She nods and twists her hands deeper and deeper into the pockets of her sundress.

Sheriff Jones rolls his eyes and gestures for us to follow him into a cramped room with a table, a trash can, and two chairs. The walls are blank except for a window on the back wall. My dad pulls the chair out for Mia. It was most important to get her statement on record first. And we were all in agreement about that. Mia sits and scoots as close to the table as possible. The rest of us stand behind and to the left of her, closest to the door. She puts both her hands on the table, and instead of looking down, she tips her chin up and speaks.

"Harvey Green and I usually meet at the wall in the woods, behind Salmon Creek. We've been meeting there for a better part of a year. It became less once he and Rosie started up."

The Sheriff puts his hand up, and Mia pauses. He is taking notes in his notebook.

"What did you do at these meetups?"

"We used to have sex." She said it as a matter of fact, as if she were reciting a grocery list. My cheeks heat at her forwardness. Rodger and my dad, standing beside me, look equally as uncomfortable. To Sheriff Jones' credit, he just keeps writing.

"Okay, so we used to meet up at the wall. He told me about Rosie and gave me the choice to stop seeing him or not. Probably the only decent thing he ever did. Rosie didn't know about me; he made it clear that if I told her, then it was over between us. So, I never did. Harvey was the only thing I really had going for me. Until yesterday. Yesterday we were up at the wall, and I asked him about Rosie. I asked him if he knew what happened. And he lost it. He hit me. And if Dot hadn't been there, I think he would have killed me."

The Sheriff looks up slowly and turns his gaze to me. I take a step closer to Mia and tell him about seeing Harvey and her at the wall.

After I'm done, Rodger steps closer and recounts what he overheard at the slaughterhouse. He conveniently left the part out about breaking Harvey's nose, though.

When all our stories are told, the Sheriff only asks one question.

"And since you all know this isn't enough to bring murder charges with, I'm guessing you mean for Mia to press charges for the assault?"

"Yes," Mia says while starting to stand.

"Well, considering all of what I already know, and what you all have come here today and told me, I'd like to offer one piece of advice. Stay out of sight until we pick him up."

The next hour is Mia getting her face photographed and our statements retold on a tape recording device.

By the time the folks at the station let us go, we are emotionally and physically spent. They said they wouldn't pick Harvey up until they could get a warrant from a judge. None of us had experience with how long that could take. Our prayer was that he wouldn't catch wind of it until it was too late to run.

H ours later, we sat around the dinner table. Just the three of us. It's wrong, but starting to feel like the new normal.

My dad gave my mom an overview of all that has happend, and she openly wept. It cut a strip out of my soul to see her that raw with emotion. It didn't stop her from somehow making a roast and potatoes through her tears. I watched them fall onto her apron as she peeled the carrots, and I set the table.

My dad looks at me with a dead serious expression, "Tonight, I need you to lock up as soon as you get home." My dad was supposed to help out on a neighbor's farm close by today, but was late, so he could be with us at the station. So, he and my mom are going after dinner. "It shouldn't take more than an hour or two. Are you sure you can't get the night off? I wish you would just ride along with us."

"Dad, I'm not afraid of Harvey. He is a big, dumb coward. And yes, I'm sure. I need the money. Plus, it might be safer for me to be out in public instead of home alone."

What I really wanted was just time to think. Something about Harvey felt off to me. Sure, he was a jerk. Any man who would lay hands on a girl ought to be punished, but I couldn't shake the feeling that I was missing something. And I planned on figuring out what it was that bothered me about him. I mean, besides the obvious.

"Mom and I will drop you off, and Rodger's mom said he could drive you home."

Both my eyebrows raised in unison at his surprise arrangement.

"You would trust me here? Alone? With a boy?" I make my voice an octave higher, in an attempt at a damsel in distress impression. A part of me can't help but feel excited about Rodger. The thought of him. The kind of boy he was, the kind of man he would turn out to be.

"I think we will be home before your shift ends, but just in case we're not, yeah, I think I will take the chance of Rodger here versus Harvey."

The Drive-in was dead tonight. Barely a customer every thirty minutes. Rodger sat in his Mustang in stall five. Every now and then, I would skate over to him to chat.

"What was Mia's plan tonight? Surely, she's the one Harvey would come after first?"

Rodger nods and takes another bite of a cheeseburger I had just brought him. With a full mouth, he manages to mumble,

"She told me that her dad is home tonight, so she isn't too worried about it. And honestly, I think Harvey is more scared of her dad than Mia is of Harvey."

When I get back into the restaurant, Daryl points to the clock.

"I don't think it's gonna pick up anymore tonight, Miss Dotty. You can go ahead and take off early."

I look at the clock and feel somewhat relieved. It's been two hours, and my parents should be home soon.

"Okay! Thanks, Daryl!" I call over my shoulder as I make my way to Rodgers' car.

"I'm off! Let's go!" Rodger starts up his engine and smiles at me in the front seat of his car.

He rolled down his window and let a yell out to the passing trees. It reminded me of Rosie. Her carefree spirit, her love for all things fun. I missed her, a deep ache that I knew would not, could not be filled until she was here again. Then I remembered one of the reasons Rodger had said he decided to help me was something Rosie did for him last year.

"Rodger, what did Rosie do for you last year? You said it was why you decided to help me."

"Oh...it was...nothing really." Passing under a streetlamp, I could see his cheeks darken.

"No, I don't think it was nothing."

Rodger scratched the back of his neck and let out a long breath.

"We had study hall together last year. Every day. And every day she would watch me struggle to read and write even the simplest of sentences. Don't ask me how I got this far; it's a mystery to everyone. But she watched me struggle until one day, the teacher gave up. He said he had never seen a kid dumber than me. So Rosie pulled up her chair and asked if she could help me. At first, I didn't let her. But she sat by me every day until I finally told her yes. She brought me a notebook. That one you saw in my car. She had one just like it, and she would write in it all the time. But she brought me that notebook, and we practiced until I memorized probably every word in the English language. She also talked. A lot. About the wheat farm, her friends, sometimes boys, though she would never name them. But she didn't talk about anything as much as she talked about her little sister Dotty. She loved you. *More than she'll ever know*, she used to say. Rosie told me that she had been seeing a couple of guys, but that she hadn't told you about them yet. She wanted to be perfect for you, to be the sister you deserved because you were her everything. She told me several times how much she relied on you and your unconditional love. And it touched me. It made me want to make sure that's how my sisters saw each other, saw me."

I didn't realize I had started crying until a tear rolled off my cheek and hit my hands folded in my lap.

"And Rosie told me if there were ever a boy to fall in love with you, that he would be the luckiest guy in the world. And so, I tried and failed to get to know you." He chuckles, and I'm sure he's thinking about all the times I was cross with him in the past. I wipe another tear and stay quiet, hoping he will say more.

"And then Rosie went missing. And I saw you at the Drive-in. And I remembered all that Rosie had done for me. And I... wanted one last chance to have the privilege to know the person she loved most in the whole world."

It was the things I had hoped Rosie felt about me. The very things I had seen in her, knew about her, but hadn't had a chance to tell her. A sister's love is really indescribable. But listening to someone else succeed at capturing a glimpse of what it was to have a sister was exactly what I needed.

We had been in front of my house for a while. Rodger reached across the car and brushed a tear off my cheek with the back of his hand. Then he let his hand drop to mine that were still folded on my lap.

"And Rosie was right. About everything. You especially."

Even though we were mere inches from each other, it didn't feel close enough. I turned to face him, and his eyes went to my mouth. I leaned in and could smell his sweet breath mixing with my own.

I closed my eyes and gasped when I heard a crashing sound like breaking glass, and felt something sharp hit me in the forehead. I open my eyes to Rodger's Mustang door being wrenched open and Rodger getting yanked out by the back of his shirt by a familiar frame.

"Hey! What the hell is going on?!" Rodger yelled as Harvey Green punched him square in the jaw. That's all it took, and Rodger was out cold on the ground.

Harvey leaned in and took the keys out of the ignition. He chucked them over his shoulder with a bloody hand covered in shards of glass. He must have punched the window out.

I put my hand up to my forehead and feel a deep cut across my left eyebrow. I pull my shaky hand away as my door gets ripped open. Harvey grabs me under both my arms and is dragging me towards his car. I started yelling and kicking and screaming. "Dad!! Help!! Dad!"

"They aren't home." He says in my ear with a voice that makes my skin crawl. I don't stop fighting, though. I rear my head back and hear a crack.

"Dammit!" Harvey yells, but he just holds me tighter. But the back of my head is warm with his blood or my own. By the sound of it, it's his. I hope I hit him in the same spot Rodger did.

Despite my resistance, he gets me in the trunk of his car. I am kicking and punching and screaming until he finally pulls over. We had only been driving a few minutes, so it must be somewhere close.

He opens the trunk and yanks me out. I see that his face is covered in blood and his nose looks crooked. Good.

He is pulling me to the side of a building I have seen before. The slaughterhouse. No, no, no. If he gets me in there, no one is going to find me. I fear that no one is going to know where to look until it's too late.

But I exhale as I notice he's taking me behind the building, not in it.

"Thanks to you and that whore Mia, I lost my job today. Apparently, Mia is pressing charges, and I don't have to guess to know who pushed her to do so. They must not have enough evidence, though, because I haven't seen the Sheriff yet."

It sounds like he's talking more to himself than to me. I am still laser-focused on trying to get away. He doesn't even have to use much effort to hold me. With one arm around my middle and the other wrapped about my long hair. No chance of me getting away without leaving a lot of me behind.

He continues up the hill, still talking frantically.

"And Mia, she'll get what's coming to her. As soon as her drunk dad isn't around. Which won't take long at all. I mean, can you blame me?"

With every pull, I feel my scalp protest. Harvey's body odor sits in my nostrils. Burning them and making my eyes water. He looks filthy, like he got fired mid shift. Still covered in animal blood and now his own blood. The smell of death mixed with his sweat was horrific.

After about ten minutes of him ranting and trying to carry me up the steep side of the hill, he stops.

"Well, I guess this is as good a place as any." He lets out a manic laugh that makes the hairs on the back of my neck stand on end.

I keep quiet and watch him pull out a skinny rope from his pocket. Grabbing my wrists, he winds the rope around them until I can't move my wrists at all. Then he lifts them above my head and winds the rest of the rope around a branch. My toes are barely scratching the soggy ground beneath me. My arms feel like they are going to pop out of their sockets. "Stop! Please Harvey! I'll take it back, I'll get Mia to drop the charges. Please!!"

Harvey stops tightening the rope to the branch once he's satisfied. He stands with his twisted nose almost to my own. It looks like he is almost considering what I said. Then his eyes change.

"You're a liar, just like Mia, and just like your bitch of a sister."

I scream, and he punches me in the stomach. It

takes the air from me. And I am left there gasping. "Better not yell again. Or I have better ways to silence you." He unsheathes an eight-inch blade from his pocket. It looks like a smooth, skinny butcher's knife. My gut tells me that's exactly what it's intended for.

"Then please." I start to say in something close to a whisper."Please just tell me where Rosie is. I just need to know."

"You know that's the reason for all this, right? If your sister hadn't been such a liar, she would still be here."

"What do you mean?" I hang there and wait for him to respond.

"She was seeing another guy. Tried to use it to get me to go steady with her. But instead, I broke up with her. I'm not desperate, and I don't go steady. But since there's no proof of this other guy, it's me who'll pay for Rosie. So I might as well be guilty of what I'm surely gunna go down for."

"If you didn't kill Rosie, then you have no reason to kill me. Don't you get it?" I still didn't believe him. How convenient another guy would be. Someone else got hold of Rosie that night? I don't know if I should buy it. Rodger did mention Rosie saying *guys,* but who knows what she meant by that. I feel the blood running down before the pain sets in. He had taken the knife and cut a line straight down from the front of my ear, all the way to the top of my breast. I could tell it was deep from the amount of blood that was seeping down the front of me.

"You know I'm not such a bad guy; in fact, I'm going to make sure you see your sister very, very soon."

I spat on his face.

He back-handed me so hard stars danced across my vision. The edges of the woods started to dim, and then it all went black.

I woke up to rain hitting my face. I tried blinking my eyes open, but it stayed dark. Then I remembered what was going on. I tugged on my arms that had fallen asleep and looked down at the blood that hadn't stopped flowing. Then I spotted Harvey. He was between two trees just a few feet away, yelling into the woods.

"Who's there?!" followed by his sickly laughter.

I put my head down and to the side to try to close the wound on my neck and make him think I was still passed out, so I could listen to what Harvey thought he had heard.

Sure enough, I could make out faint voices. It sounded like whispers in the wind. It took me back to the times when Rosie and I would tell ghost stories about the woods, about the slaughterhouse, about the dark. I never imagined she and I would live one.

"Come out, come out, wherever you are." Harvey mocked in a sing-song voice that would make a grown man shudder.

Then something came crashing through the trees to Harvey's right. A silhouette of a man tackled Harvey around the middle. I saw him go down, but through a break in the clouds, the moon gave off the smallest bit of ambient light. To my horror, I saw the glint of his knife going up and down. I started to scream in frustration when I heard Rodger's voice.

"Run! Dotty! Run! Get out of here!!" But I couldn't

run, not to him, not out of this hellscape. Nowhere. I was strung up like a dead pig just waiting to be gutted.

But then another voice came from the darkness.

"Dammit, Rodger! I told you to wait!" Relief shot through every pore in my body. Dad.

My dad was on top of both Rodger and Harvey for about two seconds before he jumped up and had the bloody knife in his hand.

I screamed again when a cold hand touched my wrists.

"Shh, sweetheart, it's me, Mom. I've got you, I've got you." Somehow, in the dark and without a knife, my mom got me untied and into her arms. She tossed the rope over to Rodger, who was helping my dad restrain Harvey.

"How...did you... know?"

"Well, it wasn't hard to guess. We got home and found the boy passed out cold in front of our house. He came to and told us who took you. And said you might be at the wall or the slaughterhouse. And he was right, right in the middle of the two." Even in the dark, I could see a light in her eyes that I had missed. It was the part of her that sparkled whenever she was with her family. I hugged her, and she pulled me arms' length from her.

"Oh, bless your heart." She bent over and tore the bottom of her hem off and started to dab my gash. Behind us, I could hear my dad and Rodger struggling to carry Harvey, who was now hog-tied, down the slick hill.

"Come on now! The sheriff should be waiting at the bottom for us."

It should have been harder for them to carry him,

but once they fell into a rhythm, they all but ran down the trail. My mom and I struggled to keep up in the rain. Very in character for my dad not to wait for the police to show up.

Sure enough, we saw flashing lights and more than one police car across the creek.

There was an ambulance, and my mom walked me straight over to it and insisted I get stitched up immediately.

"We don't really do that here, ma'am; that doesn't happen until she gets to the hospital."

"Then what exactly are you here for?" My mom eyes the poor EMT.

"Just hospital transport and life or death intervention."

My mom puts her hands on her hips, "Got it. Dot, let's get in the car and go to the hospital." I tilt my chin and start to follow her.

"Wait, just a second, did he confess?" It was the Sheriff; he had his notepad out, with his pen poised.

I managed to say, "No, he didn't; in fact, he said he broke up with her because she had met another guy."

"Then why would he hurt Mia and try to kill you?" He asked.

Exactly, I thought, but was too tired and too hurt to respond.

My mom was on the porch again when Damon dropped me off. I climbed out of the back seat. Leto grabs my arms.

"Have fun with those other plans you had." Gives me a wink, and I roll my eyes and shut the car door. Winnie was going to spend the night, but her mom said absolutely not after she couldn't get a hold of Winnie. For her mom, it wasn't the curfew aspect. She didn't have a certain time she had to be home. Her mom's only requirement was that she be able to get in touch with her. So, when she couldn't, she insisted she come home and talk to her in person. So, now my curfew is not only getting me in trouble, but also other people in trouble, too. Thanks, Mom.

I didn't bother kissing Leto goodbye or waving to the others; I just ran up the steps, past my mom, and into the house. If there was going to be a scene, the last place I wanted to have it was in front of witnesses.

I heard the door shut and lock behind me as I walked into the den. On the couch was a binder with the notes in it, including the one that was on the back door, and I thought it was safely under my undies. Dammit. "I had some time today, you know, between the three hours where you were supposed to be home and when you called me." She had followed me into the den and sat in the oversized armchair across from the couch. "It was so strange because the Ray I know would have never done that on purpose. The Ray that I know knows that she only gets the privilege of living here rent-free, because she affords her mom the decency to not go missing." Her eyes look wildly at my muddy shoes and legs. I open my mouth to speak, but the look she gives me has me closing my stupid mouth right back up.

"My daughter, Ray, doesn't lie to me, and doesn't keep things from me either. So, either you honestly *fell asleep* somewhere with no cell service, and the boy you were with had no respect to wake you. Or you are lying and turned your phone off, and still the boy you were with didn't care."

"Mom." I calmly find my voice again. "It was the first one, I swear, only Leto wasn't there when I fell asleep. He had gone to get more firewood. And Winnie and I, I swear, were asleep. As soon as I woke up and checked the time, and freaked, I ran all the way down a dark trail to call you."

Her expression changed from wild to puzzled.

"What do you mean? Where were you?" I could tell by her look that she already knew and, for some reason, did not approve.

"I was at this place they call... the wall." Her lips made a thin line, and I knew I was right.

"And that Lee boy? He's the one who took you there? Why?"

Her response gave me the courage to challenge her. Why should I feel like a scolded kid when we are both adults? And evidently, I wasn't the only one keeping things around here.

"Yeah, he and his cousin. And you know what? The mom I know wouldn't have kept me in the dark about my aunt for my whole life. The mom I know wouldn't have kept from me the place she went missing or about the night when her killer got arrested. My whole life, I have been trying to be perfect. All the years spent trying to be the daughter you wanted and needed. The effort I put into trying to replace a ghost. And you can't even be honest with me about what happened to her?! I have to get all my information second-hand?"

In that moment, my mom didn't look like my mom; in her pajamas and slippers with tears now rolling down her face, she looked like Dotty. A sixteen-year-old girl who had lost her person.

I continue, "It's hard, you know, not being allowed or feeling like I can't ask about my own dad. Or about the person you were closest to in the whole world. It's hard trying to fill both the holes in your heart. I have holes of my own, you know. A big, giant dad-sized one."

I stand there waiting for her to yell, or scream, or maybe just hit me. I was ready for anything. Except what happened.

She crosses the gap between us and grabs my shoulders.

"Rayel, I'm so sorry. You are everything to me. You

have been since the moment I knew you were coming to us. You don't have to try to replace anyone. My demons are my own. And as for your dad... It's just really painful. Rosie didn't leave by choice. And your dad... He was there through it all. The whole thing. He knew Rosie and helped me... helped me recover after my accident. I just... I never understood how he could leave us, leave you. How could he choose to do that, knowing what Rosie's disappearance did to both of us? Even all these years later, I don't know what is worse, someone leaving involuntarily, or someone choosing to leave. They both have caused me so much anguish."

She pulled me into her, and her embrace was everything I had been needing.

"Rodger Young was my whole world after Rosie." She said his name so quietly I almost didn't hear her. I had only heard my grandparents say his name once or twice when I was very little, and my mom wasn't in the room. They told me not to ask her about it, so I never dared. But here she was, letting me in.

"Please, Mom, you can talk to me about him. If you need to." She nods and wipes her tears.

"I think it's time you heard about the parts of my life I tried to forget. And we will start with the reason I have been so worried and off since the notes started coming again."

"Well, obviously because it could be the guy they arrested for it, right?" I offer, immediately, more than curious.

"No, that's not why. In fact, I wish we were getting harassed by Harvey Green. But we aren't, because he's not the one who killed Rosie."

I wasn't sure if I had ever heard her say those

words, that someone killed Rosie, it was always she was missing, or someone hurt her, never killed, though.

"Harvey Green was the last person my sister was known to be with the night she went missing. And he was the person who hurt another girl in our town... and...the person who tried to kill me...in the woods by the wall."

The flames from the fireplace danced on the top of the scar peeking through her shirt. She followed my gaze and touched it.

"Rodger and my parents stopped him just in time, but that's why he went to jail. There was never any evidence against him for Rosie."

She crossed the den and opened the binder. In a sleeve hidden behind one of the journal pages was a handwritten letter on much newer notebook paper.

"Then I got this. It's a letter from Harvey Green's daughter. He died from cancer a year ago, and she just had the mind to reach out this week. She said even on his deathbed, he swore to have had nothing to do with Rosie. He insisted she had a different guy she was seeing. She said he made her promise to reach out to me and tell me one last time. And you know what? I believe him."

But this would mean the person is still out there and still looking to harm us. But why? Why after all these years?

"I don't know." My mom answers what I didn't even speak out loud.

"And I'm sorry for lecturing you about your curfew. I know I can trust you. It's the Lee boy I don't trust. I just don't know him well enough, and so far, he hasn't brought you home on time either of the times you have been together."

He also could be sleeping with his *best friend,* Ashley, but I'm already bent out of shape about that one. I don't need another reason for my mom not to like him. Because, despite my mom's hesitations, Ashley's, and Miles' warnings, I wanted to see where this goes. Needed to see.

"I can handle Leto. Trust me, it's not that serious. But what do we do about Rosie?"

"I don't know, I've been thinking about contacting the Sumner police department. They have a lot of new technology now to be able to find people, or bodies, or... bones. DNA even."

"Well, for whatever you need, I am here." I wipe the last of the tears on her face with my dirty sleeve, and she wrinkles her nose.

"Thanks. I mean it. Thank you."

I start to stand and decide to end on some good news.

"I made the soccer team," I say with a big smile and a little bounce in my step that might have everything to do with Miles and his nutmeg moves.

"Good for you!" She claps, and I take a bow before I run up the stairs two at a time to jump into a hot shower.

After I've scrubbed off the night, I climb into sweats and a hoodie. I threw my clothes into the hamper in the closet and heard a thud. I fish my phone out of my pocket and look to see that I have a text from Leto.

Sneak out.

Not a question, or a suggestion. A command.

Crap. I knew I shouldn't, but knew I would. I can handle it, handle him. Just hanging out, seeing if we work well together. My stomach does a flip as I creep out of my room and listen to my mom's door. I hear her slow breathing.

I slowly unlock the front door and check the cuckoo clock. It's two thirty in the morning. I'll give him thirty minutes. That's all.

On the porch, I see him a little way down the driveway. Wow, he is presumptuous. How did he know I would come?

He smiles and leans against his truck in a fresh t-shirt and shorts.

"Couldn't resist, I see." He flashes me a wicked grin.

"You've got thirty minutes. What is it that you need from me?"

His eyes look me up and down, and a hungry look crosses his gaze. "Everything."

"Umm, no." I look down at my sweats and baggy sweatshirt. He must be joking.

"Why not? You like me, and I like you?" He doesn't sound mad, but he does carry an impatient tone.

"That's not enough for me. I don't even know you." I tilt my head to the side.

"Well, I know you, you're beautiful and pure, and everything that's good. I must have you." He jokes, but makes no move to get closer, so I don't feel scared even as his words startle me.

"You *must have me*?" I can't help but start to laugh, and luckily, so does he.

"I had to at least try." He shrugs and pulls my hips to his. "Is it at least okay to kiss you?" His breath is so close I can already taste him. I answer by kissing him. Letting go and welcoming his hands in my hair. They slowly make their way down the back of my sweatshirt, and my skin heats at his touch.

I pull away, and he doesn't pull me back. Just watches me.

"Times up." I plant one more kiss on his mouth and leave him standing there in the dark.

I snuck back inside, locking up behind me, and listened at my mom's door to hear her breathing. Still sleeping. Good.

Lying in my bed, I look over at my closed closet door. And I wonder if I had closed it when I got my phone out of the hamper. I didn't remember doing that, but I must have. I didn't think about it too much as I drifted off to sleep, dreaming of Leto, his hands, his smell.

Then I found myself in a nightmare. I was in my bed and awake, but still must be dreaming because I couldn't move a muscle. And in the corner of my room was an old woman. Face like a crinkled paper bag. It looked like she spent years staring at the sun. Her eyes were glassy and sunken; she just stood there staring at me. Who was she? Was this who was haunting us? But who? And why am I dreaming of her? I try to scream, but can't. I try to swallow the lump in my throat. Closing my eyes, I try to fall into another dream. It takes minutes until I can move again, but it must have been hours. Because I opened my eyes, and there is light from outside filling the room. And my closet door is open.

TWENTY-TWO

RAY 2007
SWEAT

I'm still feeling uneasy about my dream, my phone vibrates, and I jump.

"What is going on today, Ray?" My mom's brows pull together as she surveys me over her eggs.

"Nothing, I just...I had such a vivid dream last night. It feels like I didn't sleep at all." I shovel another mouthful of peppered eggs into my mouth.

"Well, that just won't do; you need all the strength you can muster for your practice today."

I look up at her in surprise. "And just who have you been talking to?"

"Winnie's mom, duh." She rolls her eyes and takes her plate over to the sink. My chair scrapes against the wooden floor as I make my way to wash my dishes.

"Well then, she must be psychic because I have heard nothing about it." I bump my mom out of the way so I can clean up breakfast.

My mom and I had never had to break certain routines. She would cook breakfast in our kitchen. Washing produce in our white farm sink that overlooks the southern side of the property. And I would sit on our marble countertop, swinging my legs against the oak cabinets below.

She would pick a CD to listen to, and we would sing and dance until the meal was made. I used to set the small white painted oval table, and we would try to have every meal we could together. I got to choose the cleanup music. After we ate, it was my job to do the dishes.

Today, though, neither of us put on music. The air was still from all that was laid out last night. My head felt foggy from my dream. And I am pretty sure I still had no idea what was actually going on.

I stared out the window at the dark gray clouds threatening to spill. My mind was trying to put together this soggy jigsaw puzzle that I was missing half the pieces for.

So Rosie went missing, and the boy she was last seen with went to jail. Harvey. But the same boy has maintained his innocence from day one, even on his deathbed. Except that my mom was attacked and almost killed when she was a teenager for snitching on this boy for hurting another girl. And ultimately he went to jail for hurting her and my mom. But my mom has always been suspicious that Harvey wasn't the one who took Rosie, and now she is almost sure it wasn't him. Because of the notes showing up. And on top of all the Rosie stuff, my father, Rodger, split the day he found out my mom was pregnant with me. But had been just as obsessed with finding Rosie as my mom and grandparents. So that doesn't add up at all. And to put the cherry on top, I am being followed by strange figures and have been having nightmares.

Oh, wait, I forgot about Leto. What are we? I know he's a distraction, and a very enticing one. What I don't know is how hurt I'm going to be when I find out he really is the guy everyone has warned me he is.

I look down and realize the water has run cold, and I've only rinsed one fork. My phone vibrates again, and I turn to grab it off the table. My mom must have left the kitchen, but I was so in my own head that I hadn't heard her go.

Two text banners blink on my phone. I open it and see one from an unknown number and one from Winnie.

Nutmeg,
Soccer practice at 2 pm today, same field
Wear less see-through shorts.
-Miles

For reasons I'm not ready to think about, my stomach does a tiny flip. I can't stop smiling, remembering stupid Miles and his stupid tackling.

Then I read Winnie's text.

So what time are you picking me up?????

I decided to reply to Winnie first.

1:30, better not make me wait.

Then I think about what I should say to Miles.

But then you'll have to think of another excuse to get on top of me?

As soon as I press send, I regret it. That was way too much. My anxiety over my flirtatious text increased after Miles didn't text me back.

I was putting on my black soccer shorts, red sports bra, and grabbing a hoodie, and my phone went off again. I dropped it trying to open it as fast as I could.

But it wasn't Miles, it was Leto.

Come to a party with me tonight. I'll pick you up at 8.

I didn't even bother texting him back. After all, it wasn't a question, and he knew I wouldn't say no. The thought half pisses me off, but it's true.

I throw my water bottle into the backseat of my little blue car and pray it starts. It's been a while since I've driven it, and since my mom is at work, I would have to call someone to jump it.

Luckily, it starts right up, and I'm on my way to Winnie's in seconds.

I'm waiting for her to come out of her canary yellow house on Thirty-Fourth Street, and my phone goes off. a message from Leto.

Oh, so you're pissed if I ignore you, but it's okay if you ignore me? That's fine, I found someone else to take to the party anyway.

Excuse me, what? I check the time between texts. Just a couple of hours. What the hell? I quickly text him back,

Hey, sorry I was hanging out with my mom, getting ready for soccer, and then driving to pick up Winnie.

When Winnie comes out a few minutes later, he still hasn't responded. Embarrassed and feeling guilty, I don't share what's going on with Winnie.

"Hey, you seem quiet. The music isn't even making my ears bleed." She says to me jokingly.

"Sorry, just tired from our late night last night. And I had the strangest dream." I could hide the pit in my stomach well enough, but Winnie knew me too well for me not to be talking a million miles an hour.

"Oh my gosh, how scary was your creepy ass boyfriend last night? It took me an hour to fall asleep. I couldn't stop picturing those pits of guts or whatever." She shudders, and I'm thankful for the distraction.

"And my mom was so pissed when I got home. Your mom really knows how to get her riled up. It was lucky you woke up, and Miles ran you down the hill. Are you excited to see your much less creepy boyfriend? Ready for him to nutmeg you?"

We were both laughing so hard, I could barely get the words out.

"Shut the hell up!"

"Yeah, I guess you aren't ready. Why on earth did you wear black shorts?"

I really wanted to tell her about the risky text I sent and the text I didn't send in time and all the other shit that was happening, but instead I just kept laughing with her. All the way across the parking lot and down to the field. I left my phone in the car again. That way, I wouldn't be worried about Leto.

After the coaches gave a little speech about us making the team and going over fees and what to expect from the season, it had almost taken up fifteen minutes of our practice. I looked around and didn't see Miles or Ashley.

"Yeah, that's strange. Ashley told me she was going to be here." Winnie offered when she noticed me looking around.

"Yeah, Miles too." Winnie punched me in the arm.

"What?! You talked to Miles? When? Where?" I rub the spot on my arm that she punched.

"Okay, ouch. And relax, he just texted me about practice."

We break off into positions and start running drills. Every time a car drives by, I look to see if it's them. The clouds and fog have burned off, and the searing eighty-degree sun is out. Not even bothering to wear a t-shirt, I have no layers to take off. I'm in just my sports bra and short shorts, and I'm still sweating into my own eyeballs by the time we start our scrimmage.

I fall into a familiar rhythm with Winnie and another girl on our team whose name I can't remember. Dribble, dribble, pass, dribble, pass, dribble, score. Between the three of us girls, the other team has only scored one, while our team has scored five. I start to gain even more momentum when I hear someone catching up to me. Heavy footsteps that I immediately recognized. Instead of scoring, I quickly pass the ball off and bend over to examine my shoe laces.

Just as I suspected, I hear "NUTM—" and then something slams into me and careens over the top of me, face-first into the ground.

The entire field erupts in laughter, and even the coaches are clapping from the sidelines. I stand back up and pretend like I hadn't been planning that since last night.

"Oh my gosh, Miles, are you okay?" I hold my hand out to help him up, but gasp when he rolls over, and I see one side of his face caked in mud from the wet ground of yesterday's rain. And a bloody split lip. His lip has no mud on it at all. So, he came here like that.

"How did you get that? Who did that?" I demand, as he grabs my hand and pulls himself up.

"You did." He says through a sideways grin, then runs to the side to peel off his already drenched in sweat sweatshirt.

I was certain I did not, but I shook it off, and we

kept the game going. Surprisingly, Miles didn't try to tackle me again. I don't know if I was disappointed or not. I shouldn't be, it was Leto and I that were hanging out, right? I should leave Miles alone. Although it sounds like Leto won't be hanging out with me tonight and will most likely be hanging out with another girl. Probably Ashley. I had seen her across the field after Miles had flipped over my back. I heard the whistle blow, and this time it was the other team who was driving the ball towards their goal. Winnie, the other girl, and I chased them to put a little more pressure on their players. I caught up to Miles, who had just been passed the ball from Ashley, and decided on a whim to get a little more payback.

I yelled, "NUTMEG!" and made my very best attempt at tackling Miles so he couldn't score.

However, not only did he score, but I slammed into a sweaty brick wall of flesh and bounced off so hard I fell onto my butt and hit my tailbone so hard I was seeing stars.

Instead of laughing, I heard gasps at the sound of my impact.

"Holy shit, dude, what are you made out of?" I moaned, rolling on the ground, before Miles scooped me to my feet like I was a small bird that just hit a window.

"Are you okay? You have like...a lump on your fore-head." I reached up, and sure enough, there was a small goose egg above my eyebrow.

I didn't say anything, I just regrouped with my team and finished the scrimmage without causing any more scenes.

After practice was over, I ran to my water bottle

and chugged the entire thing. The sun seemed to just keep getting hotter. Through the trees, you could see Mt. Rainier. It felt like such a beautiful day of summer despite the sweat that had pooled in between my boobs and all down my back.

Winnie walked over to me with wide eyes and an expression that told me she had something to tell me. I glance over to where she just was, and Ashley and Miles were lying in the grass under a tree, talking.

"What?" I turned to her excitedly.

"You sent Miles that text." I nodded.

"How did you...?" She put her hand up, so I stopped.

"Ashley was there hanging out at Leto's, and Miles texted you about soccer practice. Then you sent him a semi-flirtatious text back. Leto was standing behind him, reading the whole thing! Leto punched Miles and snapped his phone in half!" My jaw just about hit the floor.

"That's why they were late. He and Ashley went to the mall and had to get him a new phone!" Winnie was so excited that she was giggling. But I felt so bad. I had gotten Miles in trouble and myself. No wonder Leto was pissed. Weirdly, I was also kind of flattered that Leto would care that much.

"What did Miles do? Did he punch him back?"

Winnie's smile got even bigger.

"Ashley said Miles picked him up and literally threw him across the room, but that Miles couldn't stop laughing, and that's when Leto broke his phone."

"Wait, and Ashley told you all this just now?"

"Yeah, and Miles walked up halfway through and confirmed it."

So, he was telling the truth when I asked him what happened to his lip. Inadvertently, I had done that to him. I smiled and turned to see Miles watching me, propped up on his elbows through dark lashes and dripping wet hair. Ashley is still talking to him, but he's giving me a wicked split-lipped grin.

"What the hell is wrong with those people?"

Winnie laughs at my conclusion, as we make our way back to my car together.

Winnie and I were lounging in my room a couple of hours later. I had turned on the radio, and my mom ordered us pizza. We had both agreed to a girls' night in. I finally filled her in on what happened with Leto and about the dumb so-called *party*. I still felt like I had done something wrong. But Winnie pointed out that Leto and I were not exclusive, and that what I had said was a joke.

"If he had even bothered to ask about it, then he would have known, and wouldn't have had to be thrown across a room." She shrugs. Winnie makes another great point.

"You know what, you're right, I should just forget about it. I mean, I'm the one who said casual. Right? Right."

Winnie starts nodding her head, but then tilts it to the side. Something like a mischievous glint twinkles in her eye.

"Or..." She says with a feline-like smile.

"Or...what?" I say, a smile widening across my face.

"Or you could text Miles, and he could take us to the party."

I mull it over for only a few seconds before I grab my phone and text Miles.

Hey, what are you doing tonight? Winnie and I are craving tacos.

Winnie looks over my shoulder,

"Tacos? Nice touch. He won't suspect a thing." She rolls her eyes, and I press send.

We start planning what we will wear if he texts back. I lay out my red sleeveless dress and patchwork boots on the bed. The v-neck and buttons down the front give it almost a western look. It goes well above my knees but hugs me like a glove. It's similar to the dress I wore on my first date with Leto. Just a little tighter and a little shorter.

Winnie finds one of my black cocktail-like dresses that poofs out like a cupcake. She pulls out a long strand of costume pearls and drapes them over the dress.

"I hope you have some backless sandals that match; otherwise, I'm going to have to wear my cleats." Winnie's feet were about two sizes bigger than mine. And my dress will be extra short on her because she is about 5 inches taller than me too. But it's going to look so good with her bouncing red curls. My phone vibrates, and we both turn to each other, smiling.

Tacos? That's so crazy, I was just thinking the same thing! I'll pick you guys up at your house. And then, do you guys want to hang out after?

"Oh, this is too easy." Winnie squealed.

Uhh, sure. What did you have in mind?

I text him back eagerly.

"Okay, this is perfect because my mom is going out with her coworkers tonight, which means I bet I can get a later curfew," I tell Winnie, feeling my eagerness start to bubble in my stomach.

"Or... you could say that you're spending the night at my house?" Winnie chimes in helpfully.

"Done," I say as I run out of the room to tell my mom about Miles taking us to tacos and then spending the night at Winnie's. She seemed jazzed about my not mentioning Leto.

I run back to my room and check my phone.

How about a party in a barn?

Winnie's already getting dressed when I send our reply.

Sounds great, we will be ready in thirty.

I take the time to straighten every strand of my hair. It goes just past my waist, and I part it to the side and put on some mascara.

The doorbell rings, and I put on my boots and throw some black flat sandals to Winnie that lace up her ankles and calves.

I can hear my mom talking to a guy with a deep voice in the hallway. From the top of the stairs, I can see him smiling with those damn dimples. A real smile that reaches his eyes, telling my mom about him flipping over my back at soccer. She starts laughing way harder than necessary.

"Well, I can't say that I'm surprised at all. In fact, you should consider yourself lucky that was the only thing she did." She cackles proudly.

Miles is wearing baggy cargo shorts and a white t-shirt that glows against his tan skin and dark hair; it's wet like he just showered. His lip looks bruised but isn't bleeding anymore.

My mom turns to me and mouths, "He's hot." And then her eyes go to my boots, and she smiles.

"Yes, thank you, Mom. Hey, so like I said, tacos, and then I'm going to spend the night at Winnies. Bye."

I grab Winnie and Miles' arms and pull them towards the door. But I get jolted back when Miles doesn't budge.

"Actually, I'm also going to take them to a get-together in my friend's barn. There will probably be drinking, but I won't drink since I will be the driver." Miles gives another big smile.

I slowly turn to him and mouth, "What the hell is wrong with you?"

He starts to laugh, and my mom puts up her hands.

"Listen, as long as you get them to Winnie's by curfew and safely, you have my blessing." Winnie and I stand there in shock. And then I take a good look at my mom. She looks...hot. Like dressed up, heels, a lot of makeup.

"Wait, Mom, do you have a date?" I don't think I remember her going on a date ever, like in my entire life. Why now? Why at the most uncertain time in our lives? Then I remind myself that no, this is not the scariest, most unsure time in my mom's life. Not by a long shot.

My mom's cheeks turn bright red, and Miles saves her from my question.

"Well, you look lovely, Miss Luis."

"Yeah, Mom, you really do." And I meant it.

Without too many other words, we head out to Miles'…bike? He senses my hesitation.

"Don't worry, I swear we can all fit, and I brought you guys helmets!"

He unzips a side pouch and, sure enough, produces two helmets, one for each of us.

"So, one of you will sit behind me, and one of you will sit in front. Whoever is shorter sits in front, so you don't burn your leg on anything."

Even in my boots, I'm the shortest one there by a long shot.

We both look at each other and shrug, climbing onto his black motorcycle. I have no idea what kind it is, but it looks fast.

He starts it up, and Winnie puts her arms around Miles and me, forcing my back to be completely flush with his chest and lap. I'm extra glad it's getting dark and that no one is facing me in my way-too-short, for a motorcycle, dress.

Miles pulls my hands up to the handlebars and puts his hands over mine.

We start winding our way down Edgewood to Sumner.

It isn't long until we find ourselves in front of the taco bus that's usually parked in the Fred Meyer parking lot.

All three of us climb off the bike carefully. I make sure to go first so I can fix my dress. Miles hangs our two helmets from the handlebars and puts his own on the seat.

"You guys go find a table; I'll order."

We choose the table closest to the bus, and I wait

to hear exactly what Winnie thinks about all this so far.

"He just keeps getting hotter. Tell me why you still want Leto?"

"I can't explain it, but I just do. But yeah, he does keep getting hotter." We laugh as Miles walks over with a platter of probably every taco on the menu.

"Wow, that was quick."

"Yeah, I know the owner. He's worked on some of my dad's sites with me."

He sets down the food, and we all dig in.

"Ashley told me that you told Ray about how I really got my bloody lip. And I half wondered if you guys texted me just to see if you could get me a black eye to match." There is so much taco in his mouth, it's a miracle we both understand him.

"Now, why would I want to go and do something like that?" I try to cover my laughter with a bite of taco.

"I don't know, but then Leto told me you weren't coming to his party, and I put it all together." Miles winked, and I swear my heart skipped a beat. So, he knew we were using him and still showed up and took us out? Yup, just keeps getting hotter and hotter.

"And I decided I would play along, but only because I really like to watch Leto squirm. And not get what he wants. It happens so very rarely these days."

"I didn't realize it was his party that I was uninvited to." The words are out and a lot more bitter than I meant them to be.

If Miles and Winnie notice, they don't act like it.

"Yeah, pretty lame. But luckily, I'm invited, and so you guys are too!"

The three of us stayed there eating tacos and laughing about soccer well past dark.

We helped him clean up the table, and all three of us hopped back on the bike.

I couldn't help but feel nervous as we turned onto Elm Street. Would Leto throw me out? Make a scene? Or would he act like this was his plan to get me there all along? And what would I do?

We pull up to his familiar driveway, but the massive white farmhouse is dark. It doesn't make sense with all the cars parked along the driveway. But a little way ahead, there is a tiki torch-lit path that circles the right front of the house and leads to a white barn around back.

The barn door is open, and there are twinkle lights hung all over.

It looks like they went to the Salvation Army and bought every piece of furniture you could sit on and put it around the walls of the barn.

There is a table full of drinks and a keg to the left of it. The music is blasting, and it looks like the party is in full swing.

I don't see Leto and relax a bit. Winnie and I look at each other and go right into the middle of a group of people dancing.

We both understand that the best way to play *nonchalant* is to blend. Like, we were totally invited, and we totally know everyone here. Some of the faces did look familiar from the party in the farmhouse.

We are both laughing at each other's dance moves, and I sense hot breath in my ear. I let my body fall back and feel hands wrap around each of my hips. I start dancing, having a really good idea of who is behind me. We move in sync, and after a few seconds, I get a whiff of beer. Looking up at Winnie, I see her eyes go wide. Panicking, I turn around, and Damon grabs me. He puts one hand on my lower back and the other on my spine. I push his chest, but he only pulls me closer. His lips are on mine before I can get away.

Everything happens all at once. I hear Winnie yell. Damon finally releases me after what seemed like forever, but was probably only a second or two. Winnie takes me into her arms. Out of the corner of my eye, I see Damon get slung back like he's on a bungee cord. Winnie and I both whip around, and Damon is on the floor. He looks pissed and gets up as fast as he can. Miles is standing there, laughing. "Oh, sorry, dude, I didn't see you there."

Damon's face changes, and he gives Miles an awkward half-grin. He holds out his fist to Damon, and he bumps it. Guys are so weird.

Miles looks at me, and I know he can see it on my face. The embarrassment of Damon's kiss. But before Miles can say anything, someone grips my arm above the elbow. And these hands I know. Rough, hot, and desperate. Winnie releases me when she sees who it is. Before she lets me go with him, she raises her eyebrows as if to say, *Are you good?*

"I'm okay." I barely have time to say, Leto is pulling me through the crowd, leaving a stunned Winnie, a pissed off Damon, and...a...Miles. I don't know what he is right now; all I know is he was there. And he threw Damon on his ass for kissing me.

Leto leads me up rickety stairs to a loft that is

stacked high with hay. There's a little path to the back, and through the maze, the music gets quieter and quieter. It opens up a little, and there is a blanket and a lantern. Leto walks over and turns it on, illuminating the small space.

"Why did you come here?" Leto's voice doesn't sound angry, just curious.

"Because Winnie, Miles, and I were hanging out after soccer, and he invited us. Why were you such a prick to me today?" I was surprised by my boldness, and so was he.

"Oh, I'm the prick? I was the one who joked about your best friend? I was the one who ignored you after inviting you out?" It felt like he was twisting what happened, but I didn't want to fight. I mean, what a dumb fight to have.

"I'm sorry, I just wasn't by my phone. And you know that was a joke. I've made it pretty clear I'm into you. Right?"

He seemed to relax a bit, but his jaw was still clenched.

"Yeah, I guess you have. Maybe I haven't been as clear." He takes a step toward me, and I can smell his soap. Mint, and something lemon.

"I want this." He says it into my mouth as he kisses me. Our lips are moving together. Each of us is hungrier than the other. We move to the floor, never breaking contact. His weight is on top of me, and I pull away from his mouth.

"What do you mean you want this?" I can see him clearly, even in the lantern light. He has on a tight black shirt and jeans. I can see his thick arms through the sleeves of his shirt.

"You, this, all of it. I want to be with you. Holding your hand in public, going on dates. I want everyone to know that you belong to me." I have never had someone say all the things that I earned for. Never had anyone lay it out so plainly. I hadn't dated a lot, but I knew I wanted to be wanted. Not ignored or pushed to the side. I wanted to feel pursued. I wanted to belong to someone.

He took my kiss as a response and immediately started to unbutton my dress. I kept kissing him, but put a hand over his hand.

"You can't have me like that, not yet." He threw both his hands up in surrender.

"Okay, Okay." He kept kissing my mouth, my neck, then lower. I crawled backward out from under him. Then thought of something.

"Where's your date?" Didn't he say he had found someone else to bring?

"Who cares, Ray? I'm up here with you, aren't I?" He sits back on his knees.

"Well, yeah, but who did you bring? Won't she be... upset?" I re-button the top of my dress and start to stand.

"No, she won't care. It's not like that with her. We're just friends. It's just Ashley." I can't help but remember when he and Ashley were missing from around the fire after I fell asleep. Or the look Miles gives me whenever I bring them up.

"So... nothing has ever happened between you two?" I try to make it sound as casual as possible.

"Shit, Ray." He looks angry. I shouldn't have asked him. But if I'm going to belong to him, doesn't that mean he'll belong to me?

"Never mind, it doesn't matter as long as you're with me now, right?" I walk up to him, kneeling in front of him, running my hands through his hair. His honey eyes soften, and he hugs me.

"Exactly."

He stands to his full height, leads me through the hay, and back down the rickety staircase.

As we descend, the beat of the music washes over me. Everyone below is dancing and drinking. Scanning the room, I find Winnie talking to a guy who looks like someone from one of our classes at the community college. She has a drink in her hand and is laughing at something he said. Wow, she's either drunk or into him. It's not usual for her to laugh at anyone's jokes but mine and her own.

Looking past Winnie, I see Damon. A dark look on his face as he sees me hand in hand with Leto. I had almost forgotten about his forced kiss earlier. I scowl at him. What a bastard.

I turn because I feel another set of eyes on me. Miles leans against the wall and has his arms crossed. A sad half smile on his lips, he dips his head as our eyes meet. For some reason, it makes me nervous, like Leto is going to see our exchange and freak out. I look away, and when we reach the bottom of the stairs, he drops my hand. Leto's face changes into that *life of the party* mask he wears so well when he's entertaining. How easily he can go from my honey-eyed Leto to the curious-eyed Leto unnerves me. He looks towards the back of the room.

"Hey, I need to go take care of something," and without a glance back, he disappeared into the crowd.

I stand there for a minute, trying to decide if I

should wait for Leto or go find Winnie. Before I can choose, there's someone standing next to me.

"Hey, we need to talk." Ashley looks at me with a pleading expression.

"Okay?" I fold my arms and wait for her to start talking.

"So, you need to know something. I swear I'm not saying this because I'm jealous. I'm saying this because it's true. Leto and I are involved." My stomach drops.

"What do you mean?"

"I saw you guys come down from the loft. I know that damn hay maze and blanket all too well, Ray. Listen, I like you. But he won't ever be yours. Or anyone's really. He doesn't know how. I don't think he ever will."

I can't tell if she is lying or not. If he really was like that, why would she be involved with him? And what is her real motivation to tell me?

"What do you mean by involved exactly?" I don't need my imagination running wild with this.

"We hook up, like all the time. In fact, if you didn't have sex with him just now, he's probably looking for me as we speak." What a horrible thing to say. Who would subject themselves to the scraps of a relationship like that?

"Listen. Ashley, that's pretty pathetic. I'm sorry he doesn't want to date you. But if that's true, that's really sad that you would settle for that kind of treatment. And if it's not true, you are a maniac and should probably get some help." I pat her on the shoulder, and her face is frozen in embarrassment. I feel a little guilty at the blush in her cheeks. But it doesn't stop me from turning around, leaving her, and making my way to Winnie across the room.

"Hey, Ray! You remember Kyle!" Yup, she is definitely drunk.

"Yeah, you had Econ with us, I think?" Instead of answering, he lets out a loud belch that sends Winnie and me into hysterics. Glad for the distraction, I laugh a little louder than I need to.

Winnie starts to pull me away, "Hey, come with me to get another drink, Ray. We will be right back!" I follow her over to where the plastic cups and keg are, just to the right of where Kyle is waiting.

"Ray, what the hell is going on? Why did Damon kiss you? And then Miles coming out of nowhere and sending him sprawling on his ass?! And what happened upstairs with Leto? Do NOT leave anything out." She stares at me with much more sober eyes than she had for Kyle just a second ago.

"Oh yeah, I keep forgetting about Damon. I don't know, that was super weird. Gave me the creeps. And Miles was just kidding around, you know, he's super close with Damon. It seemed like a joke to me. And okay...Leto wants to be like official. Wants us to be a thing. He said he wanted people to know I was his or something?" Saying it all out loud made it sound a little dramatic. I don't know Leto that well... is it all too fast?

"We need to be careful around Damon, starting now. And damn, Miles really does just keep getting hotter. And don't hate me, but Leto feels... fake. Like he's trying too hard to make you interested, acting jealous, bringing you upstairs, then leaving you in the dust, only to make you fall for him again the next day... I'm sensing a pattern." She looks down at her feet for a second before snapping her attention back to me. "Oh, and what was Ashley saying to you? Please tell me you were nice. She really does want to be our friend, I think." My gut twisted thinking about our conversation.

"Umm, I tried to be... but she told me that she and Leto sleep together. But they aren't exclusive. And that if I'm not having sex with him, then he's most definitely going to have it with her. And I told her if that's true, it's really sad she puts up with that, and even sadder if she's making it up." I feel some of those tacos rumbling around in my stomach. Winnie's expression looks horrified.

"She said that? What a bitch. I mean, if it's true, though, good thing she told you. What are you going to do?"

"Well, I'm afraid to ask Leto. Something tells me he isn't going to be receptive to a conversation like that. He's...sensitive. Especially if it's not true. He'll be hurt if I even ask."

"Yeah, I guess the most logical thing is to just start having sex with him so he doesn't go have sex with Ashley." She cracks a big smile, so I know she's teasing me.

"Well, that's one way to take care of it." I jump when Miles' deep voice interrupts our girl powwow. He looks annoyed and like he's about to say something to me. But shakes his head and turns to Winnie.

"Hey, so I'm guessing Leto will be taking Ray

home. I'm about to head out, wanted to let you know in case you needed a ride." He stands there with his hands in his pockets, looking down at us with dark eyes, no dimples in sight.

"Umm, no thanks. I'll play third wheel. With you gone, someone is going to have to keep Damon away from Ray."

"All you would have to do is tell Leto, and he'd have a way worse night than me." He points to his lip as he takes a step back to leave.

"Probably good for you to leave," I say. "Not sure your girlfriend would be too happy with you driving us around on your bike all night." I don't know where the venom came from, but his comment made me feel insecure. Like I wasn't capable of handling myself or something. And he wants to act all high and mighty when he himself has a girlfriend.

"Leto told you I had a serious girlfriend, right?" Miles says slowly, patiently.

I nod.

"Well, I don't. I haven't had one in three years. So no, I'm not the jerk you were hoping I was. I am exactly who I appear to be, no matter who is around." The next moment, Winnie and I were staring at the broad back of him as he disappeared through the crowd and out the door.

"Oooookay, what the hell was *that* all about!" Winnie squealed.

My face was hot with emotion. There was no reason for me to be mad, but my cheeks burned, and the corners of my eyes did too. I was embarrassed. Ashamed that I didn't correct Miles when Winnie had made her joke about sex with Leto. And that I had so readily believed what Leto told me about Miles. How did Miles know what to say to make me question everything?

"I don't know. And I don't know why I let that stupid guy get under my skin. Let's just dance."

We make our way back into the group of dancing people, and before long, Kyle finds us. He's taller than Winnie by a few inches and has a very golden retriever air about him. His blonde, straight hair is a nice contrast to Winnie's red and bouncing curls. He dances with us, and we start having fun again. I forget momentarily about Ashley, Damon. Leto and Miles. It all feels far away. I look down at my patchwork boots and smile. I wonder if Rosie had a chance to have nights like these, dancing with her sister or friends. The excitement of a brand new crush. I wonder if she had the chance to feel wanted. And I know it's fast with Leto, but why shouldn't he want to be with me? Why should I put up a wall? I want him to know me. If I get hurt, maybe it will be worth it.

Winnie's curfew was never. Except when she was with me. When she was with me, it was 1:00 a.m. Somehow, her mom could convince my mom. They had been friends since they were kids, and though she had been around when my aunt went missing, but was somehow able to give Winnie a little more freedom. And I did not want to push my luck with her mom. She's been there for my mom since way before I was born. So, I kept an eye on my phone, checking the time here and there. It had been about thirty minutes since Leto disappeared, and not that I was trying, but I hadn't seen Ashley since she cornered me at the bottom of the stairs.

I see some people gathered around a ping pong table and pull Winnie over to play. Even though drinking has never interested me, playing beer pong seemed harmless. We get in line, and Winnie knows her job is to take my drinks if need be. We start to play, and so far, everyone has to drink but us. So, we don't stop. Soon, everyone is gathered around waiting for us to miss, only we never do. And for some reason, we can't stop laughing about it. Every time we win, it makes it funnier and funnier.

But I stop laughing when something catches my eye. A door to the left of us that leads outside opens and makes a groaning sound. Over the threshold walks Leto, closely followed by Ashley. Winnie follows my gaze and takes me by the arm.

"Let's go." Before I can say anything, Winnie has her cell phone out and is texting her mom. We walk away quickly and right out the big doors in the front of the barn. Passing by the tiki torches, the fires looked like smudges of light. My eyes were burning, but I kept my breath steady and filled my lungs with the wet night air. Rain had started to fall. Through my suspicion and hurt, a thought popped into my head. I hope Miles wasn't on the road in the rain with his bike.

"Sorry, I just saw the look on your face and figured it was time to ditch. Do you want to go back?" She looks at me and then back at the barn, still alive with music and people.

"No, I'm ready. Even if that wasn't what it looked like, he left me there for over thirty minutes after pretty much telling me we were exclusive. I think it's okay to be done for tonight. I'll sort out the rest with him tomorrow."

"Well, that's good cause my mom will be here in about two minutes."

We stay huddled up together as the rain starts to fall faster and steadier. After exactly five minutes, Winnie's mom pulls up, and we jump into her minivan. Winnie only had an older brother, but for some reason, the Kings have had this minivan ever since I can remember. Winnie's mom was in the driver's seat, listening to an audiobook on CD.

"Hi girls, how was the party?" She looks around and senses it wasn't great. Winnie's mom was stunning, even in her older age; her hair remained brownish red and wild, her skin a creamy white.

"It could have been worse. Thanks for picking us up, Mia." I plastered on a smile and smoothed down some of my frizzy, wet hair.

"True, could have been better, and could have been worse. The tacos were good, though." Winnie winked at me.

Ever since that conversation with my mom about my dad, I had wanted to ask Mia something. Before my mom had talked to me, I was worried she would be as closed off about it. Like my mom, and not be willing to tell me anything, so I never bothered to ask. It hadn't occurred to me that she might be open to talking to me. My grandparents were dead, and my dad's family moved to Chicago when my parents were first married. My mom never mentioned them, and I never asked. The number of people I could get information out of was very limited.

"Umm Mia? I was talking to my mom the other

day. About...Rodger." Her eyes shot to mine in an instant. So she did know him.

"She told me he was like a great guy, that he was there for her through all the Rosie stuff, and then just split. I was wondering... Did you know him?" Mia's hands tightened on the stirring wheel, and a few moments passed before she answered.

"Yeah, I knew him before your mom did, actually. I owe him a lot." She swallows hard.

"My mom died when I was a girl. I had a little sister, a lot younger than me, to take care of. But my dad was a drunk, and I had to work. He would take off and leave her all alone. Until Rodger. He had his sisters look after her while I was at work and even brought groceries to us every week. He did this until I had enough money to move out and take her with me. Your mom and I have been best friends ever since. I think seeing your dad do those things for me made her fall in love with him. So yeah, I knew him. And he was a really great guy." I see her put her hand up to her eye and wipe a tear. That's all I can get myself to ask for tonight, feeling much more confused than before.

I know I should have asked way before now. I regret not being mature enough to demand answers from my mom from the very beginning. But it's easy to rationalize why I didn't.

Imagine the one person you can turn to, the one person who has always been there for you. Silently sacrificing day after day, all for you. I saw the pain she was in, even though she did her best to hide it. Especially the times when we should have been our happiest. When I graduated high school, when she got her freaking doctorate in Nursing. We celebrated, of course, but in her eyes, the agony, the loss, the fear. I saw it. Felt it in every hug and tight-lipped smile. My mom should have been whole. Deserved to be whole. It kept me from bringing it up. It kept me from resurrecting the past. And it kept me in pursuit of Leto. A distraction from both our pain.

I lay awake in Winnie's bed long after her snores filled her tiny bedroom. I was alone with my thoughts and glad for it. My phone vibrated and reminded me about tonight. What if Leto isn't lying? What if Ashley is? Shouldn't I give him the benefit of the doubt, at least for now?

I open my phone and see a text from him.

Can you meet me? I want to show you something.

I don't even think; I just respond.

Sure. Yellow house, first on your left after you turn onto 34th.

The benefit of the doubt, it is. It takes me a few minutes to pull on some of Winnie's sweats and a t-shirt from her closet. My dress was cute, but still sweaty from the party. And I wasn't about to show up in my underwear. Not yet, anyway.

I end up leaving the front door unlocked so I can let myself back in. It is a little past 2:00 a.m. I tell myself he's got an hour tops to show me whatever it is that can't wait till daylight.

I see his truck idling across the street, and I look down to see that I forgot to put on shoes. Running on tiptoes, I open his passenger door and hop in. He's wearing a gray hoodie and gym shorts. His honey eyes seem to glow in the dark. His real honey eyes, I think, he saves for me. There are no street lamps to speak of, so the fact that I can see the glimmer gives me a chill.

His hair looks slept on. I wonder if he was tossing and turning like me.

"So what is it?" I look at him, surprised by his question. He texted me to meet *him*.

"What do you mean? What is what?" I cross my arms, feeling defensive at his tone. I don't really care how big he is or how good he smells; if he's looking for a fight, he's about to find one.

"I tell you, I want you. Tell you I'd like to spend

more time with you. Be seen with you. And you leave. And you don't even say goodbye. You just leave. And super interesting because guess who also left? Miles, my supposed *friend*." I can tell he's trying to stay calm, but his breathing is pretty heavy. I stay quiet, thinking about how best to approach this. Remembering Miles' split lip.

"If you're trying to play hard to get, it's working. I mean, shit, Ray, I wanted to beat my best friend unconscious at the thought of him and you. Can't you imagine how this would make me feel? What did you think would happen? What did you think I would think?"

I don't think I like where this is going. I'm ready for a fight, but his mention of beating someone up has me rethinking my answer a bit.

"Ohhhhh, yeah, *super interesting*, huh? Well, I find it *super interesting* that you tell me those things, and then disappear. So, I guess maybe this is something you should learn about me sooner rather than later. I'm not going to wait around. If you're not interested in me, then fine, but I'm not going to stand by until you decide you are. And you losing your temper isn't something to be proud of." Though if I'm being truthful, it's kinda hot. It shouldn't be. But it is.

"And what about how *I* feel?" I start in. "Everyone is constantly warning me to stay away from you. How do you think that makes *me* feel? And not to mention you lying about Miles having a girlfriend. Who cares if he has one or not? What the hell was that about? I think until your actions start matching your words, consider yourself to be on probation. Unless you just want to call it. Because I actually have a lot going on at the moment and would be fine either way."

My words are steady, but I'm dying inside. Please don't call my bluff. Please don't leave.

"That's what I'm telling you, Ray. You make me crazy. I even had to make up Miles having a damn girl-friend, so you wouldn't even think about him." He was jealous. If I asked him about Ashley now, then he would know I was, too. No, thank you.

"Okay, but I don't know why you care. I'm here with you. I went to your party to see you. I told you I wanted to be with you. But I'm not going to put myself out there anymore if you're not going to meet me halfway." Please want me. Please don't leave.

A long silence stretches between the two of us.

"Fine. If you want me, you got me. What time is your practice tomorrow? I'll come watch. And we will go out after." I start to sweat; I can't believe it worked.

"2:00 p.m. You can pick me up, unless you'd rather I catch a ride with someone else."

"No. I'll pick you up. I'll be cutting it close, though. I'll be doing stuff in the orchards for most of the day." He leans in and brushes my hair behind my ear.

His hand lingers on the side of my face, and he tips my head up to kiss me. I meet him eagerly with my lips. I move my hands to the waistband of his shorts and start to pull his shirt up by the hem. And then I remember the line. If I let myself, he will no doubt cross it. I sigh and pull away.

"Okay, what did you really wanna show me? I have to be back in an hour." He looks at me with his glowing eyes. And gives me a feline-like grin.

"I heard you like ghost hunting." As soon as he said it, I got a feeling I needed to make him turn around. For some reason, I wasn't feeling brave just now. Thoughts of the hooded figure and the dreams of the old lady enter my mind. Why was it so unsettling suddenly?

"Where are we going?" I try to sound indifferent, but my voice comes out as just above a whisper.

"To the graveyard! I know it's not very original, but it's kinda scary and a great place to stargaze."

Okay, I can handle that. It's not the woods or the slaughterhouse. I can do this.

Leto's truck winds down the hill, back to Sumner. It feels like seconds, and we are already parked across the street from the cemetery. And as promised, the dense trees surrounding most everything on this side of the state open up to reveal a dark, tombstone-spotted final resting place. Perfect for gazing. Amazingly, the rain had stopped, and there wasn't a cloud in the sky.

I climbed out of the truck and walked over to the driver's side. Leto was grabbing blankets from the bed of the truck. He turned around and reached for my hand. He stopped and looked down.

"Where are your shoes?"

"Well, I forgot. Plus, I wasn't exactly sure what we were going to be doing, and all I had were my boots, and I was trying not to make any noise so..."

"Right." Leto crouched down in front of me.

"Get on my back." I took a little bit of a running jump onto his back, even though he was crouching; it was a little high for me. But he stood up like I had set a pillow on his back and not my entire body.

"Thanks," I mumble, and he runs across the street right into the edge of the cemetery.

There was one streetlight down the way, and across the street, so Leto was stepping carefully not to trip over any headstones. Once we got to the middle of the plots, he put me down and laid out a big blue blanket.

We both lay down on it and looked up. Every single star was out. Or at least that's what it looked like. Once my eyes adjusted, it felt like the stars were enough to illuminate all the stones around us. I turned and looked at Leto. His stare was a million miles away.

"So, you already know about my stuff." He looks at me while I speak, his eyes go to my mouth.

"What stuff?"

"You know, the single mom, missing aunt, dad split, only child stuff. I want to know about you. Tell me about your...stuff." He shrugs, but keeps talking.

"There isn't much to say. My parents were burnouts. They didn't want me. So, they left, and I stayed. My grandparents barely wanted me, but I knew how to be useful, so they kept me. They are tough, really rough around the edges. But for the most part, they let me do what I want as long as I put in the hours on the land. It taught me how to work hard. I guess it also taught me not take people for granted. People who want me." I take his hand and squeeze it.

I'm not sure what to say to that. As far as I know, I only have one parent who didn't want me. I can't imagine feeling that way about my mom or my grandparents.

"Is that Damon's story, too?" I wonder if this is the time to bring up Damon kissing me or not. I'm thinking...not.

"More or less. He had it a little worse. He used to spend some weekends with his dad. Always came back with more bruises than when he left. It went on until one day his dad just didn't show to pick him up. We were almost teenagers at that point. He's always been a little...off. I don't know, it's hard to explain. But he's really close with our grandma. She always gave him the easier jobs to do. Always lets him quit early. I guess I can get a little jealous of it. It took my grandparents so long to have kids, and when they finally did, they both turned out to be losers. Damon is a little more... persuadable than me. I think they knew Damon would be a good little sheep. Things can get pretty...dark out on the farm."

"That had to have been really hard for both of you. Probably still is. I know dealing with my dad drama feels heavy sometimes, dark even, too." I don't usually tell people about my dad; I don't want anyone feeling sorry for me. And they would usually ask questions I didn't have the answer to.

"Yeah, parents can suck. Your mom seems alright, though. Really overprotective but otherwise fine."

"Well, she's been through a lot. Her sister and all that." I let my voice trail off when I hear something that sounds close by.

"You know you bring up your dead aunt a lot..." I sit up and put my hand over his mouth to quiet him.

"Did you hear that?" I whisper, looking from side to side.

"No? Hear what?" We sit there in silence, and then I hear it again. A low humming noise. Like someone is singing.

"Oh. That." He starts to move my hand and smile. "I told you."

I look at him, confused.

"You told me what?" I'm still looking around to find the source of the noise.

"I told you up at the wall, sometimes things follow you home." Chills pricked the back of my neck, and I pulled the hood of my sweatshirt over my head.

"Can we go, please? This is freaking me out," I plead.

"I thought you loved ghost hunting and scary stories?" He raises his eyebrows at me.

"Yeah, when I'm with Winnie, and I know I can jump into my car and drive away. Not sitting here with no shoes smack dab in the middle of a graveyard!" I was trying to be quiet, but my voice was getting higher the more scared I became.

"I will protect you. I just thought of a scary story. Will you stay till after I tell it? And then we will go." He pulled me onto his lap, so we were both facing the woods. It felt a little safer to have him holding me.

"When I was a little boy, Damon and I used to play hide and seek in the apple trees. We could play all year round, but summer was our favorite because of how thick the leaves were. Summer had ended, though, and fall was almost over, too. Not all the leaves had fallen, but a good chunk of them. I must have been three or four, so about twenty years ago. But I had climbed up a tree that had most of its leaves still. I stayed as quiet as I could and made sure I didn't shake the tree at all. Then I heard singing." Leto's voice got so quiet that he was pretty much whispering in my ear over my hood.

"A lot like what we just heard. That's what made me think of it. I looked all around below me and didn't see a thing. Then suddenly, out of nowhere, a man came crashing through the trees. I had never seen him before, and it scared me so bad I stayed frozen as a statue. The man stopped under my tree and was catching his breath. When he looked up, we locked eyes, and that's when I knew I must be dreaming, because sticking out of his chest was a small hatchet. Blood was running down his shirt, and still I didn't move. The man saw me but didn't say anything; he just steadied himself and ran back into the trees. The singing stopped, and I stayed in that tree until it was almost dark. I was up there so long that Damon had given up finding me and went back into the house. I fell asleep up in the branches and only woke up after I heard my grandpa calling for me. When I climbed down, I ran as fast as I could and told my grandpa and Damon what had happened. No one believed me. When I told my grandma, she said it must have been a dream." After Leto finished, he let out a loud laugh, and I jumped.

"Oh man, I got you good!" My eyes started to water; something told me that wasn't a dream at all.

"And what do you think? Do you think it was a dream? Or how do you explain it?" I demanded. Fighting the tears, I did not want them to spill over.

"I mean, it must have been a dream, either that or some sort of ghost on the farm. I mean, our farm has been in our family for generations. Not as big as it once was, but still really old. A lot of history. Last year, my grandparents had to sell off a few acres on the north side. They didn't seem to be torn up about it, though. It was the side of their property that goes into Edgewood city limits, and they got a lot of money for it. Apparently, they are planning to build a parking lot on it or something. But yes, I think it was most definitely my imagination. I think the weirdest part was looking back, I think I was more excited than scared. Like it was just so bizarre."

I let out a sigh of relief, but still felt unsettled. Who would be excited about that? As promised, Leto scoops up the blanket and me, and we head back to the truck.

"It is weird, though." Leto looks at me when we are headed back up the hill to Winnie's house.

"Tonight. Whoever was singing or humming, that's the same song I heard when I was a kid, or like the same tune, I think."

"Ha ha, very funny." I roll my eyes, and Leto traces the back of my hand with his finger, his other hand on the wheel.

"How is it that you can go to bed so late and still get up so early to work?" He shrugs and laughs.

"Honestly, I wonder the same thing sometimes. I guess I just have never required much sleep. It seems like such a waste of life to me." We had arrived at Winnies, and I leaned over to give him a quick kiss. He pulls me in, and it's clear he has no intention of letting me get out of the truck. I put my hand on his chest, and he pulls his lips off my neck.

"I'll see you at 1:45 p.m. Don't be late, and if you are, you'd better call."

I hop out of the truck and through the King's front door. Locking it behind me and sprinting up the stairs. I look at my phone and see that I made it back in just over an hour. Winnie is still snoring, and in seconds, I am too.

The next morning, I fill Winnie in on everything. Even the creepy story about the guy with an axe in his chest.

"Are you joking? Ray, I'm all for being spontaneous. You know that. But you snuck out of my house with a guy you barely know. And hooked up in a graveyard? Are you okay? What is happening?"

"We did not *hook up* Winnie. In fact, it was all very PG." I was putting my dress back on from last night and my boots. She and I had slept so late that I was barely going to have time to shower and eat before practice.

"Did you want it to be PG?" Winnie pry's with a smirk.

"No. No, I did not. Because something tells me he is someone who is used to getting what he wants and when he doesn't. I'm afraid he will go find it somewhere else." Saying it out loud made me feel pathetic.

"Then let him. You know? I don't think he would, but if he does, then just end it. Sure, he's tall, and mysterious, and poetic. But if he would really consider cheating on you, then walk away."

"But that's the thing, I have no proof of anything, and if I bring it up, I will sound crazy. So I just have to... wait. And see how it plays out. He said he's picking me up for soccer practice today. Do you think you could drop me off at home?" I'm brushing the tangles from my hair, but I can feel her confusion. "But he doesn't play soccer."

"I know, he said he is going to come and watch the practice."

"Huh. Okay. Yeah, I can give you a ride."

A couple of hours later, I'm dressed in lime green soccer shorts and a black sports bra. The sun is particularly brutal today, so I grab two water bottles and set them by the door.

My mom has been in her room since I got home. The door was locked, and when I knocked, she said she wasn't feeling good.

"Don't you have work today?" I ask through the crack of the door.

"No, I took a sick day."

That is very unlike her. She didn't ask me about tacos, or the party, or what I'm doing today. Something is wrong.

I hurried and changed out of my dress, skipped the shower, and got dressed. Running back upstairs, I found the key at the top of her door frame and let myself in.

"Mom, are you okay? I..." Sitting up in bed in her dress from last night, my mom looks up. She is reading a notebook. It's brown, and old, and I know immediately what it is. Rosie's journal.

"Mom... how..."

"Someone left it on the porch. I can't believe it. It was just lying there when I got home. I've been reading it over and over again all night long. She was in trouble, and I didn't even know." She dissolved into sobs, and I closed the distance between us and climbed into bed with her.

"She talks about this guy she was seeing. Not Harvey. It couldn't have been Harvey because she

makes it sound like this guy was in a committed relationship and older than her. Harvey was neither of
those things. I've already decided to turn everything
we have over to the police. I think they could get
DNA off of it. Or I hope they can. This is the closest I
have felt to finding out what happened to her since
she left."

I sit there and rub circles on her back.

"Do you want me to drive you? To turn it in?"

"No, you have soccer, you should go. I am going to
call them to come here instead to get it. And the other
pages too." She reaches for the house phone on her
nightstand and is soon talking to a detective.

When I'm convinced she's settled, I hug her.

"Please call me if you need me." I hear a honk and
give her a quick kiss.

My mind is reeling, but I grab my waters, cleats,
and head out the door right into Leto's truck.

TWENTY-SIX

RAY 2007
RIVALS

Miles' dark eyes gave me a once-over when Leto and I walked towards him and Winnie on the sideline of the field. We were a few minutes early, and it looks like they were too.

"Hey, man, what are you doing here?" Miles' tone had an edge to it, and it was clear Leto noticed.

"I'm just here to watch Ray in action." Leto grabbed me and planted a kiss on my mouth. A little rougher than usual. But his point was made clear.

"And you said you wanted to use the track." I remind Leto, taking a fraction of a step away from him.

"Yeah, that too." Leto had one arm around my waist. He pulled me back against his side.

"Well, it looks like they're ready for us. I wonder where Ashley is. Have you seen her, Leto?" Winnie raises an eyebrow, not so subtly asking Leto.

"Um...No. I don't think I've seen her since the

party." He shrugs, gives me one last, way too enthusi-astic kiss, and jogs off.

"Alright, everyone, our first game is this Saturday morning. 9:00 a.m., rain or shine. But it looks like rain. Today and Saturday, unfortunately. Nonetheless, I think we have a pretty good chance. So today will be a shortened practice, and we will be scrimmaging and shooting." We all look up to the sky to see dark clouds rolling in. I can't say that I'm very sad about the temperature change.

We all line up, and the coaches split us up into teams. For the first time, Miles and I are on the same team. Winnie is on the other team, and Ashley is still nowhere to be seen. I take a nervous look around and see Leto jogging around the track, headphones in, and not looking our way. I remind myself I'm not doing anything wrong. I'm just playing soccer, on my soccer team, with my teammate. My hot, tan, tall, smells like fresh cut grass, teammate. Nothing to see here.

When the whistle blows, Miles and I take off up the field. Miles gets the ball, and we start passing to each other without saying a word. Winnie is close behind, and I only have a second before Winnie is going to catch up to me. So, I shoot the ball and score. Our team cheers, and Miles rushes toward me. I brace myself for impact, but instead of tackling me, he picks me up and spins me around.

"Let's go, Nutmeg!" I start laughing, mainly because I'm so caught off guard. I look past Winnie, who is laughing, to see that Leto has stopped running. He's just standing there staring. Shit.

I'm suddenly aware that I'm in a sports bra and tiny shorts.

"Put me down," I say, and start to climb down his massive chest. He looks at me, confused, and starts to slowly put me down. As soon as he does, I sprint back to resume the game. I look over my shoulder, and Miles is waving to Leto, who looks pissed. And maybe he has a right to be. The rest of the game, Miles uses every single opportunity to hug, high-five, or pick me up. By the end of it, everyone is laughing. The coaches, I'm sure, would have put a stop to it if he and I weren't playing so well together.

"That's exactly the kind of teamwork I want to see on Saturday, everyone. Come with this kind of energy and camaraderie." The coach gestures in my and Miles' direction. Miles pulls me to his side by putting his arm around my bare waist. Heats flushes my cheeks, and I sidestep away.

Instinctively, I look around but don't see Leto anywhere. Miles startles me by bending low to my ear.

"Just so you know, it would take a lot more than a co-ed soccer team to make me jealous." Miles doesn't wait for me to answer before he turns and jogs towards the parking lot. I grab my waters and drink them both. I guess I'd better find Winnie so she can take me home.

I walk towards her car in the parking lot, and she waves me over.

"Did he seriously leave you here?" There's a pit in my stomach. I look down, feeling extremely embarrassed. I turn at the sound of a horn honking. There in front of us is Leto in his truck. His facial expression is hard to read.

"I guess not. See you later, Winnie." I quickly

climb into his truck, just as the rain finally starts to fall.

"So, how was your run?" I say casually, pretending like I had no idea he was pissed.

"It sucked." Great, he's going to get right to the point. "I had to watch him touch you any chance he got. Soccer isn't supposed to be a contact sport." I sit still, not knowing what to do or say."I mean, I guess who can blame him, really. But I can't stop thinking about it. Why couldn't you have told him to stop? Did you even try? Or do you just love the attention too much?" My face must have seemed shocked or hurt because once he looked at me, his shoulders slumped. "I'm sorry, I just... Miles and I have a long history. And he's just... he's not the best guy when it comes to girls. Especially the girls I care about. I want you to be careful, that's all." I put my hand on Leto's arm.

"Look, I asked him to put me down. And soccer is somewhat of a contact sport. As far as the other stuff, we are teammates. And I don't know what to tell you. Our team plays really well together. If it makes you more comfortable, you are welcome to come and run when we practice." He nods and pulls me over so I'm sitting right next to him on the bench seat of his truck. For a moment, I feel like we are alright.

Later that night, Leto drops me off at home. It felt normal, easy to be with him when he's not mad. Or ignoring me. And he had kept his word, we hung out all evening after practice. When it's just him and I he doesn't have to put on an act. Or I guess not the same

act as when he's around his friends. I jog up the steps.
I'm eager to ask my mom about the police visit. She's
in the den on her computer. She's dressed and
showered.

"So? How did it go?" I lean down and hug her.

"It went well; they came and bagged it all up into
evidence. And had me give my statement. They actually seemed interested. Didn't give me the whole,
Harvey Green is dead, case is closed. They actually read her
file and are going to test the journal." My mom looks
lighter, like the burden of Rosie has been lifted slightly.
She hands me a pile of printed computer paper.

"In case you wanted to read it. I made copies
before I handed it over. It's hard to read…some of it."
I took the stack of paper upstairs and set it on my
nightstand. I know it must have been hard for my
mom to read this. I should have been here when she
first looked at it. I feel guilty about being out with
Leto for the past few hours.

But I'm here now. Not bothering to shower or
change out of my soccer practice clothes, I sit on my
bed and begin.

I skip past the entries that I've already read. I see
that in the back of the diary are sketches and drawings
from 71', but the really important stuff is towards the
front. There are a lot more entries, but I find one
that's dated May 1972.

*He makes me feel alive. When we are lying there naked and
exposed, it feels like there's no one else that exists but him and
me, and the moon. The third wheel on our trysts. I can see it*

staring at us through the perfect crescent cut out in the ceiling. And I think, how many miles did its light travel to be perfectly seen by me? How can it be possible to love someone this much? I am going to tell Harvey about us soon. Harvey was my...first love. When I thought I knew what it meant to be loved. He deserves to know I've moved on. And besides, I know there's no chance Harvey would ever go steady with me. I guess I'm just waiting to see if he really feels the same way about me as I do about him. Sometimes he promises me the world and then takes it all back in the next breath. He will tell me that we will run away together, and then I won't hear from him for days. But he's the only one who understands me. The only one I would risk it all for. And he's risking things too. He has a much different life than me, or anyone my age.

So, my mom's hunch was right. There was another man. And he must be older. The other entries are similar. Describing her internal struggle. Apparently, the man she was in love with was risking a lot to be with her, and she was asking him to risk more. And not yet ready to let go of Harvey. But Harvey was getting increasingly frustrated when all Rosie wanted to do was talk when they met up. But who was it? How hard could it have been back then to track down someone who was obviously local? And Rosie didn't have a car and didn't talk about getting picked up anywhere. She always says *I met him*. If the Police had her diary in the 70's, there's a good chance they would have found him. Or at least her body. I flip to another entry dated May 1972.

I never thought I would be the type of girl to string someone along. But until he can make a final decision, I'm not going to tell Harvey anything. He can suspect all he wants, but I want to keep my options open just in case. Wow, it feels so crazy to even be writing that. Last night I was ready to say goodbye to everyone and leave with him. And now I'm considering meeting up with Harvey tonight. How can someone make you feel so important and then discard you with a single sentence? It's painful for me to even write. But I'm going to. I want to remember it for the next time I feel I'm under his spell. When I told him I wouldn't wait any longer, he said, "That's okay, I was just about done loving you anyway." How am I supposed to come back from that?

I felt a tear hit my cheek as I read Rosie's words. I can't imagine giving myself completely over to someone and having to ask for the same in return. And then to have them basically tell me that they don't need to because they are *done loving you anyway.* I would have said and written much worse things. But how could she not see how he was manipulating her? How could she not want more for herself?

As I'm sitting there thinking, I realize something. She's not twenty. She's a kid, still in high school in the 1970's. Of course, he promised her the world, and she believed him. She was a child. Something else that bothers me is if she had told someone. Anyone. They might have been able to help her see. It hurts because if she had told her sister, my mom, then this journal would be an old childhood diary that you look back at and laugh. You read it to your kids and wonder how you could have been so dramatic. But she kept all her pain hidden. And now we just get to read about it and use it to help us solve her suspected murder instead. Nothing about this is right or fair.

My soul splinters when I reach the final entry. June 1972. The month she went missing. But after I read it, I realized it's the very day she goes missing.

Finally, he did it. He made a choice. He left me a note on my swing. How did he know I'd be the one to find it? I don't know. Maybe he watches me swing and has never told me so. He said to meet him at our spot, and we would make a plan to be together forever. Before I go, I am going to tell Harvey it's over. I'm not sure how he will take it, but I hope he can control his temper. And then I will hurry to meet him at our spot. When we make a plan, I'm going to finally be able to tell Dottie everything. For certain reasons, I've had to keep it hidden, even on these pages. In case anything were to go wrong. I wouldn't want to get him in trouble. But tonight. I will finally be able to breathe.

So, I guess the cops were half right in the beginning. She had been planning to run away. But this diary meant two things. One, that she had been planning to meet someone after Harvey, just like he said. And two, she hadn't run away because she planned to come home and tell Dottie everything before she went.

When I'm done studying all that Rosie had written, I walk down the hallway to my mom's room. I had heard her come upstairs a while ago. I hope she hasn't gone to bed yet.

I open the door and climb right into bed with her. Just like I used to when we shared a room.

She turned around and hugged me. Her emotions are plain to see on her face. Even in the dark.

"Mom, I..."

"It's okay. I mean, it's not okay. But for the first time in over thirty years, I feel like I'm going to see my sister again. Harvey was a terrible person. But he wasn't the worst person in Rosie's life. And now there is proof. Now there is a chance that I'll be able to bring her home."

The next few weeks went by in a haze. For my mom, it was a haze of waiting for answers. DNA isn't like the shows. There isn't a cut scene to a lab where things are tested the instant you find them. In real life, it's much, much slower than that. They did call my mom and gave her an update. There had been DNA and fingerprints that were recovered, and they were going to send them in for testing.

My haze was from being with Leto. He came to all the practices and games that he wanted to. Afterward, we would hang out, nothing too crazy. Just kissing, stargazing, and talking. We could talk for hours about the weirdest stuff. Lately, it was, what would we do if there was a disaster and we could only survive off what we could carry? He would say that he and I could make it. That we could survive and start a new civilization. The fact that he saw me that way made me feel special. Like of all the girls in the world, he would want to face the end of it with me. We didn't have a lot of things in common besides our views on certain things. He didn't want to hang out with his friends with me around very often. He said they were all immature. And then he would drop me off at my curfew. Sometimes he wouldn't show up to my games or practice and wouldn't say a word about it. When I would ask, he would make an excuse about helping out on the orchard and leaving his phone in the house all day. I didn't want to fight, so I didn't push it.

It was mid-August now, and last night he told me he would be there for my game. But he never came to get me, and he never picked up his phone when I called.

Besides practice and games, Miles hadn't tried to reach out to me at all. He still does his *nutmeg* stuff, I'm sure, just to piss off Leto, but otherwise will hardly look me in the eye. Winnie and I haven't hung out in a long time, either. Apparently, she and Kyle, that guy from the barn party, hit it off, and she had been seeing him a lot.

I called her when Leto didn't show.

"I'm so sorry! I'm already here with Kyle and Ashley."

"It's okay, I can always drive myself. I just thought if you hadn't left yet, I would see if you wanted to ride together. But it's all good! See you soon!"

I hung up and grabbed my keys, but heard a knock at the door. Well, maybe he wasn't a no-show after all. I could see a towering figure through the window.

"Well, I guess it's better to be late than ne-" my voice catches when I swing the door open and see Miles standing there. His eyes look sad for some reason.

"What are you doing here?" It comes out harsher than I mean it to.

"I just thought we could ride together." He scratches the back of his neck nervously and shifts onto one leg.

"Okay? But how did you know I needed one?" He just stands there and stares at me. "Have you talked to Leto? Is something wrong? What?" I demand and push his chest with my palm. He doesn't move an inch, but he grabs my hand and holds it there. My cheeks burn. And I pull my hand away.

"Come on, we will be late if we don't leave right now. I'll explain when we get there." He turns his back to me and walks off toward where his bike is parked. I follow him closely.

"No, you'll tell me now." I stand there with my arms folded, waiting.

"Look, I haven't talked to him today. But he was pretty messed up last night, and I had a feeling he would flake." He hands me his extra helmet, and I shove it over my long ponytail onto my head.

"What do you mean, *messed up*? He told me he had to be home early to be able to help his grandparents this morning." I get on the front of his bike, and he starts to laugh.

"What?" I spit out.

"You can ride on the back when it's just one person." I hop off and get on the back. Putting my arms around his middle, I scooch as close as I can to his back, so I don't fall off, I tell myself.

"Look, I don't know what to say. Leto has been one of my best friends since we were kids. But he has demons. He won't deal with them, and I'm worried he's going to leave you to do all the heavy lifting. His whole family dynamic is strange. The stuff he's learned along the way just isn't like what you or I have experienced."

His words spark curiosity in me. I knew very little about Miles' home life. Leto sure as hell has never talked about it.

"And just what would those experiences be, Miles?"

"Well, all of them really. I've got a mom and a dad who are crazy about each other. They met in college and have never spent a week apart since. They raised my sister and me to be extremely hard-working and God-fearing. There has never been a skill I couldn't learn or a girl I couldn't talk about with my parents. And I look at you, and I know you've been loved in that way too. You've been cherished by people in your life, and Leto never has. I don't care how this sounds, but I don't think Leto will ever love anyone more than he loves himself."

I just sit there, I am too dumbfounded to speak.

He takes my silence as his cue to leave. He revs his bike, and we take off towards the soccer fields.

Demons? What the hell does that mean? And what does being *messed up* even mean? Leto doesn't even drink.

And Miles, he was the kind of guy you prayed to be with. So what was so wrong with me that I didn't afford myself to be with someone like that?

Why did I think getting Leto to care about me would fix whatever was broken within me?

For no reason other than I felt like an empty shell, I squeezed Miles around the middle the entire ride there. I felt his breathing, and it steadied me. Helped me to calm down before the game.

When we get there, our team is already lined up and ready to start. Miles and I race over to our starting positions. I see Kyle on the sidelines, and Winnie waving to him from the field. Ashley doesn't look my way when the whistle blows, and the game starts. I steal a glance at Winnie, and she gives me a look that says *you have some explaining to do.*

We are playing terribly; Miles is distracted, and Ashley still won't look at me. What the hell is going on?

When it's halftime, the coaches want to know what the hell is going on, too.

"I don't care what needs to be said between you two, but you'd better say it quick." I look at the coach, confused; he is pointing at Miles. He must know what the coach means because he grabs my hand and pulls me to the side.

"Look, I wasn't going to say anything until after the game, but this is ridiculous. Leto was too drunk to come get you. He got so drunk that he was still passed out." I stare at Miles in disbelief.

"What are you talking about? You said you didn't talk to him. And Leto doesn't even drink."

"Yes. He does. And I didn't talk to him, because he was passed out. I don't know why he told you he didn't. But I assure you, he does drink. And often. He also has two black eyes, and I'm sure he was waiting till they looked a little better to show his face around you."

"What?!" I look down and realize I'm still holding Miles' hand. I rip it away.

"He got shitfaced drunk last night and told everyone you guys hooked up in a graveyard. And then started to describe it to people. Describe you... to people." No wonder he looked sad when he picked me up.

"Well...he lied. I mean, we did go to a graveyard. But we've actually never...actually, this isn't any of your business." Miles' face flashes a wicked grin.

"I knew it, and that's why I beat the shit out of him."

"You?! Miles! No wonder he didn't show up or call me. I've been doing my best to convince him that nothing is going on here." I wave my hand between us. "And you are doing your best to undo that! Stay out of it, Miles. I mean it. You have no idea how upset he must be." Miles stares at me for a few seconds.

"You know, if you don't care about who he is, then neither do I. I'm done trying to protect you from him. And trying to convince you that you deserve more than scraps that you call a relationship."

"Good, because you made it much worse. And I never asked you to." His words sting. I basically said the same thing to Ashley not too long ago.

"Good." He agrees and stalks off as the whistle signals that half-time is over.

I give Winnie a shrug, and we resume the game. We play even worse than before, and when we lose the game, our coaches promise us punishment in the form of torturous running at our next practice.

I'm so mad at everyone that by the end of it, I run to Winnie and ask if she and Kyle can take me home. Winnie is waiting patiently to drop Kyle off so she can ask me a million questions. I can tell from the looks she's been giving me in the rearview mirror. But then I remember, Kyle probably knows Leto.

"Does Leto drink?" I tap Kyle on the shoulder, and he turns in his seat to face me. He lifts an eyebrow.

"Haven't you guys been dating for like a few months?"

"Yes. I mean, I think so, yeah."

"I feel like you should know that by now."

"Know what by now?"

"That he drinks, he is the life of the party. At every party. Always has been."

I just nod and sit back down. Okay, so Miles wasn't lying about the drinking. But so what? Lots of people drink. Winnie drinks. Kyle drinks. Miles drinks, except I've never smelled it on him.

I jumped in the front seat the moment Kyle was gone.

"Winnie," I tell her everything: the diary entries from Rosie, Leto standing me up, and Miles showing up. I even told her about Miles beating him up. But I didn't say why. I wasn't ready for Winnie to hate Leto yet. If she did, she wouldn't want me to see him anymore. And there was something about him I just couldn't let go of yet. Something in me still felt like I needed to prove something.

"You aren't seriously letting him get away with lying to you, are you?" Now I'm really glad I didn't tell her about what Leto was saying to people about me.

"Well, of course I'm going to ask him about it. But I don't want to condemn him before I speak to him."

"You mean *if* you speak to him? He won't answer your calls or texts. Didn't even bother to pick you up when he said he would. Maybe that is your answer?"

"Or maybe, I should hear him out. Like I said." This was new territory in our friendship. We always agreed on things like this in the past.

Winnie put up her hands.

"Fine, but don't you dare leave a single detail out if he finally decides to talk to you." I roll my eyes and move to get out of her car. She grabs my wrist before I can.

"Hey, there's a dance. It's this weekend. Remember the end-of-summer formal the college puts on?"

"Yeah, I remember. I guess I didn't realize how fast that was coming up."

"Well, Kyle asked me to go with him. You should come with us. Even if it's not with Leto." I nod and shut her door behind me.

My mom is home when I walk in and take my cleats off.

"How was your game?" The look on my face must have told her.

"You lost?"

"We sure did, badly." She hugs me, then holds me out arms length from her.

"Well, the detective just called. They found DNA on the diary."

"Who's?!" But my mom shakes her head.

"They don't know yet, but they do know it's two different females and a male. One of the females could be mine, and the other Rosie. But the male..."

"Mom, that's really good news."

"I know, I know. I am trying not to get my hopes up. But I can't help it. I can feel Rosie. Like she's near. Waiting to come home."

TWENTY-EIGHT
RAY 2007
LUNCH

Seven days. Seven damn days until Leto decides to text me. He never called me back after he stood me up for my soccer game. The only sort of explanation I got from Miles wasn't enough. Too hungover to show up. But that didn't explain the past week. Not a word from him. Until now. Didn't even bother to call me, though. Just a pathetic one-sentence text.

Hey, do you want to hang out for lunch?

I was pissed, but my stomach still did a backflip, and that pissed me off even more.

Sure. What time?

I texted him back right away because he owes me an explanation or two. And because, despite how much it hurt to be ignored and disregarded, I missed him. He was mysterious, funny, and not bad-looking either. He had a way of getting everything to pull into his orbit, and right now, I was one of those things. Pushed out, only to be jerked back in just when I was thinking I could have survived without him. Everywhere he goes, people surround him. Waiting to hear what he has to say. If he would approve of them. Laughing at his jokes. It felt good to be the one he was there with. Until you weren't, and had no clear idea of what you even were to him.

I texted Winnie and filled her in. She had been playing the best friend and keeping me company when she could, for the past week. We went to the movies, ate way too much food, and played soccer. Miles wasn't talking to me, and weirdly, neither was Ashley. I don't care enough to find out what her problem is, but I can't help but feel annoyed about Miles. But I wasn't going to give Miles or Leto the satisfaction of asking why Leto was ignoring me. We figured out how to play together without speaking. We won our game this morning. I could tell our coaches had finally forgiven us for our last performance. Which we were all grateful for this because they had been punishing all of us at practice this entire week. Winnie surprised me by asking about the dance.

Are you still going to the dance tonight?

I had totally forgotten about the dance. I really did want to go, but I didn't know if Leto would want to take me. I didn't even know if we were still a *thing.* But Winnie, being the great friend that she is, encouraged me to go shopping with her and pick out a dress weeks ago.

She said that I could go with her and Kyle since Leto forgot I existed. I just don't know how you go from seeing someone every day, holding hands, making out, making plans, and then just nothing. And I know nothing crazy happened to him because, for sure, Miles or Ashley would have told me.

Maybe, I'll let you know. I don't really want to go as a third wheel.

And because I was hoping that Leto would take me, and I wouldn't have to tag along with Kyle and Winnie.

Leto texted me back before Winnie did.

I was thinking right now. I'm almost to your house.

Oh wow, I tried to force my stomach not to do a back flip without success. I hadn't told my mom about how involved Leto and I had become, so she didn't know how he'd been absent recently. I figured once I felt more secure about him, I would tell her. No use having her hate him if I wasn't ready to hate him yet.

I quickly ran up the stairs and jumped in the shower. I didn't bother to dry my hair. I brushed it out and left it long and wild. Putting on some jean shorts and a fitted t-shirt, I slipped on my patchwork boots. I skipped the makeup but put on perfume and mascara. I looked good, and smelled even better. I didn't really know what would happen, but I knew what I hoped would happen. Every time we touched, I felt a desire to be closer to him. There was a wall that I wanted to be on the other side of with him. Was there only one way to get there? I really hoped not. There were certain things I had promised to myself that I didn't want to compromise on. But what if he was worth it?

"Hey, I'm going to go have lunch with a friend. I'll be back before the dance!" I kissed my mom's cheek and ran out the front door. Not exactly a lie, but not the truth either. Luckily, she was distracted by work and the prospect of new suspects in Rosie's case; she didn't demand to know who I was going with.

Leto's truck sat idling a little way down my long

driveway. I pulled open the passenger door and hopped inside. Leto's golden eyes looked me over. I hadn't bothered to wear a bra on purpose. His eyes lingered just like I knew they would. He didn't look too bad himself. Freshly showered and in a clean blue shirt and cargo shorts.

"Hey, how's it going?" I buckled my seat belt and wanted to return his question with anger. But his relaxed voice took me off guard.

"Good?" I looked at him, confused.

"I'm glad." He smiled and put his hand on my bare thigh. "So, I was thinking that it was time you met my grandparents. My grandma made us lunch and is waiting for us now." My mouth felt dry. I was expecting a very different conversation. I thought he was going to do one of two things. Break up with me by telling me he had taken the week to think about us and decided it wasn't working. Or two, grovel and ask for my forgiveness for acting like a jerk with no expla- nation. I didn't foresee him just completely pretending that nothing happened. I couldn't even think of some- thing to say. So, I just sat there.

"Ray? Did you hear me?" He squeezed my leg, and I could feel a bead of sweat drip down my braless back. Was I the problem? Did he do nothing wrong? Was I overreacting? And should I risk starting a fight to find out? I don't know why, but I felt embarrassed.

"Umm, I'm confused." Honesty, I'll just try to be honest.

"About?" He tilts his head, and his eyebrows pull together in concern.

"Well, last time we spoke, you said you were going to pick me up for my soccer game. You didn't. And then haven't talked to me for a week. So, I'm not sure why you would want me to meet your family for lunch." I make it sound as non-accusatory as possible. But I see red creeping up his neck, and his palm starts to sweat on my leg.

"Oh. I guess I hadn't realized this was a situation where I am supposed to see and talk to you every single day, *or else.*" He pulls his hand back and places it on the steering wheel.

"So, you didn't feel like that was strange for you to do that? I'm not asking for constant contact, Leto. Just if you say you're going to be somewhere and then you're not, maybe give me a heads up. And if you aren't going to talk to me, maybe tell me why? I don't even know what we are, and your reaction to all of this makes me think we aren't anything." I self-consciously fold my arms over my chest. Fully regretting the no bra situation right about now.

"I literally saw you every other day for two months. I guess it didn't occur to me that you needed to know exactly what I would be doing at all times. Look, I don't want to fight. And I'm sorry that your feelings are hurt. But I told you I wanted to be with you. And I wanted you to meet my family today because I was going to ask you to be my girl-friend. I wasn't trying to ignore you; I was just busy hanging out with Damon and Miles. We went camping and didn't have service. I wasn't doing it on purpose."

I looked down at my legs. We were almost to his farmhouse, and I didn't know how to react. I know he wasn't camping with Miles because he hadn't missed a practice or our game this week. I could just let it slide.

He said sorry, kind of, and wants me to be his girl-friend. But on the other hand...

"Miles didn't go camping with you," I said in an even tone, trying not to sound emotional. Leto turns his head slowly towards me.

"So, I don't answer my phone, and you go straight to my best friend?" I hold his golden gaze.

"No, but I did see him at practice every day and our game this morning." He relaxed a little, but the red on his neck was creeping up his face.

"Yeah, he spent a little time with us camping, but didn't stay the night, I guess." So, he was really going all in on this no-service bit. My gut told me to tell him to take me home, to cut my losses and consider myself lucky that I only had to suffer for a week before I believed what people said about him. But I didn't say a word. I just sat there, all the way down to Sumner. When we turned onto Elm Street and bumped down his long driveway, he turned to me and put his hand back on my leg.

"So? Can we start over? Pretend this week never happened?"

I know what Winnie would say if she were here, something about knowing my worth. It's not that I didn't think I deserved to be wanted. I did. I just think that relationships are complicated and that maybe I should give people more than one chance. Maybe I could be the girl he settles down for? If I held him accountable? Like I just had.

"Okay, but if I'm going to be your girlfriend, I need to hear from you every day. That's part of being a good boyfriend. And if it's hard for you to *want* to hear from me everyday then we have no business being together."

He answered by unbuckling my seatbelt and pulling me onto his lap.

I melted into him, into his kiss, his chest. His hands were in my hair, and mine were under his shirt. I let myself wonder what it would be like to let him carry me up to the loft in the barn and do what people dating in their twenties typically do. But I needed more time. More trust. He doesn't try to go any further, but we lose track of time. I let out an involuntary scream when someone knocks on the window.

"Shit. Yup, that's my grandpa." He rolls down the window, and I am still fully in his lap. My hair is a feral mess twisted around both of us.

"Well, if you're done trying to swallow her whole. Your Gran is waiting in the kitchen." His grandpa was tall and slender. He didn't look very old, maybe in his fifties? He had on a button-up shirt and work pants. They were well-worn but clean. Not an outfit he had just been working in. Clothes that he had changed into for lunch. With me. My face burns with embarrassment, and I start to sweat again.

"Well, that was horrifying." I am sweating everywhere now and cursing myself to hell for choosing a tight gray shirt. Leto laughs and holds my hand as we walk to the front porch of his sprawling estate. I've never been here when it was daylight, or when so few cars graced the driveway. It looked even bigger under the sun.

"Hey, there's nothing to be worried about. Trust me, they have seen worse with Damon." He chuckles, and I realize Damon might be there. I hadn't thought about his out-of-the-blue behavior since the last time I was here.

"Is Damon having lunch with us, too?" I'm starting to regret every choice I've made since I picked up my phone today.

"Yeah, I'm sure the little rat bastard is, why?" He stops before turning the knob on the front door.

"Okay, well, I don't want you to hear it from someone else, so I'll just tell you. Damon kissed me at your party. Right before you walked up. I tried to push him away, and he wouldn't let go. Miles actually came up and threw him to the ground. I know he's your cousin, and I don't want to be rude, but he creeps me the hell out." Leto's mouth hangs open, and I wonder if it feels as fuzzy as mine does after kissing so long in his truck.

"Are you serious?"

"Yeah, I wasn't sure if you'd want to know or not." I'm searching his face for an answer.

"Yeah, I mean, I'm glad you told me, I just... I'm surprised. He's never tried to do anything with any of my girlfriends before. I'll talk to him."

I let out a breath I didn't realize I was holding. That went better than I thought it would. For some reason, I was half expecting myself to be blamed for that.

Leto led me through the grand entrance, where he had the party the night we first met. It looked perfectly put back together. We walked down a short hallway and into a dining room, but the big rectangular table wasn't set. He continued walking and showed me to the kitchen, where a small round table was set for lunch. His grandparents sat and sipped their drinks patiently.

"Ahh, you must be Ray." His grandma held out a

hand to me. She wore a button-up plaid shirt and form-fitting jeans. She didn't look much older than my mom. But she had mostly gray hair. It was pulled up into a neat bun. She was kinda pretty. But that could be the makeup. I could see a thick layer covering her face and neck. A stark contrast to my mom, who barely wore any makeup and still looked years younger than her age. There's nothing wrong with girls who wear makeup, but I never pictured someone who spent their life on a farm caring too much about it.

"I'm Pamela Lee, but most everyone calls me Gran." I take her hand, realizing I had just been staring at her face for way longer than I should have been.

"Nice to meet you, Pamela." I smile and take a seat opposite her.

"Oh, pardon my rudeness, I'm Dale Lee, Leto's grandpa. Everyone just calls me Dale." He doesn't reach his hand out, but does a little wave.

"Nice to meet you, too." I try not to blush, but I can feel my face grow hot. Dale winks at me like he knows I'm replaying him knocking on the window and catching me and his grandson making out in his driveway.

"Great, no Damon?" Leto sits next to me, across from Dale. I look to see there are only four place settings. In the middle of the table is a plate of tomato sandwiches. A pitcher of apple juice and sliced apples.

"No, he went to see what's taking the Berry Farm so long. They should have delivered the crates this morning." I sip out of the glass in front of me. It's full of crisp apple juice. I've never tasted anything sweeter or fresher. I actually closed my eyes when I swallowed it.

"It's good, huh?" I opened my eyes to see his grandma staring at me. "We sell it at all the local markets. Along with our berry apple butter, which I make right here in-house. But I won't make my distributors' deadlines if Damon doesn't come back with the crates today."

I set the glass down. "It's delicious, I would love to try some of that butter too. It sounds amazing." Leto gives my leg a squeeze under the table and puts a sandwich and apples onto my plate. Grandma smiles at me.

"You know, Leto hasn't ever asked us to have lunch with any of his girlfriends before."

I turn to Leto and smile.

"All we ever manage to see is the back of them scurrying out the front door in the morning."

My smile vanishes, and I can't help but feel gutted. By the look on her face, I think that's exactly what she intended. I couldn't help but think back to the night we met. He had never woken up in any one elses bed, but they had woken up in his. Leto sputters on his juice and starts to cough. Her eyes narrow at me in an almost cat-like stare.

"My wife loves to stir the pot, don't you, Pamela?" Leto's grandpa gives her a glare and takes a bite of his sandwich. "The truth is, Leto is a man I am very proud of. He hasn't had it easy growing up. He was a good boy. And he's a good man, and seems to feel some kind of way about you." I smile at his grandpa, pretending not to have been offended by his grandma's dig. She takes a nibble of an apple and rolls her eyes.

"That's enough, Gran." Leto challenges her.

She raises her hands and sighs. "How was I supposed to know she couldn't take a joke. You Luis girls are so sensitive." And then the mood in the room changed. Dale went stiff in his chair.

I knew what this was about. Sumner was a small town. Everyone knew the toll Rosie's disappearance had taken on my family. On my mom. They had moved away and sold their farm, their home. My Grandma Luis was never the same, nor was my mom. People were cruel about it. There was even a rumor that had started about my mom's parents being involved.

So yes, there were things they were sensitive about. That we were sensitive about. I knew what people had said, what they still say. The most common was that Rosie ran away. And that we should move on and accept it. But none of us did. And that was the truth. We hadn't moved on. And sometimes we couldn't take the jokes.

"It's okay, I am sensitive, and so is my mom. It was really painful for her to lose her sister. She was her best friend. And I guess there are some traits that trickle down through generations. Whether we mean them to or not."

I hold her gaze and take a big bite of my tomato sandwich. I choke it down with a smile. My two least favorite things to eat are tomatoes and mayo. But I'll be damned if I let her know that.

"I would say considering all that Ray's mom has gone through, they've done a really good job." I look at Leto gratefully. He smiles, and I feel a little piece of the wall around him crack.

Lunch carries on with just surface conversation

after that. What I want to major in, and where I want to transfer after I get my Associate's.

When lunch is over, Leto and I stand to leave the kitchen.

"Thank you for lunch, Mr. and Mrs. Lee." I smile, and Leto waves goodbye.

"Anytime, nice boots." Dale smiles, looks down at my feet, and then nods at Leto. I smile back and follow Leto through the hallway back to the foyer.

Instead of going out the front door, he takes my hand and leads me up the stairs. He opens the first door on the right. It's a big bedroom, with wood floors and a four-poster bed against the far wall. I'm surprised by how clean it is. And I recognize the blue bedspread as the one he brought to the cemetery. He locks the door behind me and lies down on top of the covers of his bed. I take my boots off and lie next to him.

He just stares at the ceiling for a while. "This used to be my parents' room. I slept in a crib in the corner over there. When they first left, I used to smell their clothes at night. Picturing them here with me. But I'd wake up alone and have to re-remember that they left. That they didn't want me. I think that's why..." He turns to look at me, and his eyes are glassy. "I think that's why I'm afraid to be with you. To let you in. Because what if you see me? And you don't want me either?" I scooted closer and kissed his lips.

"I guess you won't know until you try. It's not easy for me either. Why do you think I'm so careful? Why do you think I don't just sleep with anyone who wants to? My dad left me, too. I know it's hard. But give me a chance. Let me in." He kisses me back, and it's filled with such desperation I panic. Pulling away, I sit up.

"Are you sure I can trust you?" I look in his golden, dripped eyes. The ones he saves for me. The look that says, *believe me*.

"Yes. You belong to me. I will always take care of you. I love you, Ray." It was the words I needed to hear. I felt insecure about the things his grandma said at lunch. Sad about my aunt. About parts of my life, my absent dad. I wanted him to be the answer. I wanted what he said to be true.

So, I chose to believe him.

He could see it in my eyes and took off his shirt.

I couldn't go through with it. We lay there in silence for a few minutes. I had never been closer to crossing the line I had drawn in my head. Never had I even wanted to have sex before now. But with Leto, I wanted to. I felt like it was the one piece we were missing. The one thing I could do that would ensure he'd never ignore me for an entire week again.

But that's not a good enough reason.

When I made him stop, he said it was fine. But I felt panic start to creep up all around me.

"I guess you are a nun after all." I think he meant it as a joke, but he forgot to hide his disgust.

I can already feel my brain cursing my heart for not using emotional protection. I needed a distraction to keep from spiraling right in front of him, and I remembered the dance. It was only a few hours away, and I needed to tell Winnie if I was going or not.

"Hey, there's a dance tonight put on by the college.

It's on this big yacht on Puget Sound. It's supposed to be really fun. I was wondering if you wanted to go with me, Winnie, and Kyle?" He looks at me and doesn't smile.

"I don't really want to go. I am hanging out with some of the guys tonight, and I don't really have anything to wear to something like that anyway. Not all of us have moms working in the medical field." I tried to hide my hurt and disappointment. But he saw it.

"Why does it feel like all I do is disappoint you? Why can't you ever just be content?" He rounds on me, and now it's pretty clear that it was not *fine*.

"Oh, no, it's okay. Really. I think my mom wanted me to spend some time with her anyway. So, I'll probably just do that." I put on a forced smile.

"That may have been a little harsh, but you just had that look on your face like you were about to argue or something. Yeah, let Winnie and Kyle have their fun. I bet it would mean a lot to your mom if you spent the night with her anyway." Leto leaned over to his nightstand and checked his phone.

I sat up, still fully clothed, and put my boots on. Leto didn't notice. I'm glad I didn't have to explain to him how much I wished I hadn't followed him up here. For a moment, it felt like he had let me in. But even after I told him, he didn't even act like it was a big deal until I wanted to make actual plans to hang out with him.

And how easily I had forgotten how he liked to have his days with me and his nights free of me. Was this just another day where he passed the time with me, only to have a separate life when I wasn't around? When I had to be home for curfew?

On the way home, I couldn't stop thinking about what I wanted to do.

As soon as he dropped me off, he kissed me good-bye, and I couldn't get out of his truck fast enough. I showered and felt empty. A part of me did feel good. But did I make a mistake? He told me he loved me; shouldn't that have been enough? But it feels too vulnerable to let someone know you like that. But isn't that supposed to be the reward? To be able to share yourself and know that you are safe? Wanted? Loved? Cherished?

Why did I hope he would be thrilled to take me out and show me off at the very least?

And I don't know if he's even wrong for it. Maybe he was right. Maybe it was my inability to be *content* that left me so disappointed.

My mom had just left to run some errands, so I texted Winnie.

SOS. Come over now. Bring your dance stuff.

It only took her ten minutes to come bursting through the front door.

"What happened? Wait, is your mom here?" I shook my head.

"Okay, tell me everything." We move up the stairs together, and I shut and lock my door.

"Leto doesn't want to go to the dance with me. We had a weird lunch with his grandparents. Where they basically told me he has girls coming out of his room all the time. But he said he wasn't interested in going to the dance. He said he had plans." "And then he took me to his room...and told me he loved me."

"Tell me you didn't. Tell me, you marched your ass out of that room and straight home."

"I didn't...go home right away. But before anything really happened, I stopped it. And he took me home. But I could tell he was mad."

"Thank. The. Lord." Winnie clutched her chest dramatically. "Okay? And? What was his excuse for acting like a jackass this week?" Winnie's eyes are boring into mine.

"He was camping with his friends, and they didn't have service, I guess." Shrugging, I get out my dress that I picked out with Winnie earlier this week.

It was a light pink with a sweetheart neckline. The silk fabric was fitted and came to a V at the waist, then poofed out over the hips and hit my thighs well above my knees. It was strapless but tight enough to stay up on its own. Could I breathe? No. But did I feel amazing in it? Yes.

Winnie laid her own dress on my bed. It was perfect. Green and fitted with thousands of sequins cascading down to the floor. It was a round neck with small straps and a long slit up almost to her waist. I smiled at how her red hair stood out whenever she wore green.

"And you believed him?" She says slowly.

"I believe him. Plus, he asked me to be his girl-friend. And told me he would be better at communi-cating with me from now on." Her eyes went wide with my news.

"Leto Lee actually asked you to be his girlfriend? Why is that crazier than him saying I love you? Okay, maybe I believe him, too. But why wouldn't he want to take you to the dance?" I started to get my dress on, gesturing at Winnie to zip up the back.

"I don't know. But I do know I'm not going to be a third wheel. I may be Leto's girlfriend, but I'm not going to stay home and hang out with my mom when he has this entirely different social life every night after he drops me off. So, I'm calling Miles."

"What?! I mean, obviously I agree, but aren't you afraid Leto will freak out?" I zip Winnie into her gown.

"Yes, no, I'm not sure. But I don't care. I want someone to take me to the dance. I wanted *him* to take me, and he said no. So, I will go with someone who *does* want to take me." I may have been letting the rejection I felt cloud my better judgment.

But one thing I knew was that if I stayed home, my paranoia would eat me alive. What if Leto disappears again? What if he really has been sleeping with Ashley and...others? Stop. I push back the thoughts. Leto was sweet, gentle, and told me he would call me tomorrow. I told myself he was different after. He did want me. He told me he loved me. He *had* realized this meant we were serious. I'm only going with Miles as a friend.

I grab my phone, and instead of texting Miles, I call him. He only lets it ring once.

"Hey." His tone is flat. It makes me nervous. I mean, he has been acting differently ever since the barn party. What if he says no, too?

"Hey...I was wondering if you wanted to take me to the dance tonight? The one on the yacht... Winnie and Kyle are going together, and we could go with them? Also, it's in an hour..." My question is met with silence.

"Or not, I mean it's no big deal, I just thought it might be fun. But I get it if-"

"Why aren't you going with him?" We both knew who he was talking about. He didn't even have to say his name.

"Because he is busy tonight. He said it wasn't really something he was interested in doing."

"And he told you to go anyway? Or to ask someone else?"

Winnie mouths for me to put it on speaker. I press the button and hold my phone out.

"Not exactly, he told me to spend some time with my mom."

Miles starts laughing, and I can't help but smile.

"Well, in that case, absolutely, I will. What color is your dress this evening, Nutmeg?" I'm suspicious of the sudden change of attitude, but I don't question it.

"Pink," I say, grinning into the phone.

"Of course it is. And the boots? Will you be wearing those?"

"Yes." I wasn't planning on it, but might as well now.

"Perfect. I'll be there in thirty minutes."

Winnie starts jumping up and down.

"This is going to be awesome." Winnie squeals and twirls around in her dress.

We spend the next half hour doing each other's hair and makeup. Winnie helps me straighten my hair, and I dig out a pink rosebud headband that goes across my forehead.

Winnie's fiery curls are perfect. They frame her face and fall down her shoulders and back.

I open my phone to see a text from Leto, and my gut drops.

I'll miss you tonight. Try not to have too much fun with your mom, without me.

When we hear the knock at the door. I shut my phone, and we race down the stairs.

Miles and Kyle both step inside. I look Miles up and down; he's in a black suit with a pink tie—and cowboy boots.

"You look really hot." It comes out before I can stop it.

"You look really hot." He repeats to me and holds out his arm to lead me outside.

Kyle is in black slacks and a green shirt that matches Winnie's dress perfectly. He was all too willing to meet Winnie at my house instead of hers when she texted him the new plan.

Miles leads me over to his bike, and Kyle helps Winnie into his car.

My mom's car pulls up, and I stand there frozen, holding one of Mile's helmets.

"What do you think you're doing?" She's out of her car and has her hands on her hips. Winnie and Kyle leave before they can be stopped by my mom, too.

"I'm taking her to the dance, Miss Luis. I will have her home by eleven." He stands there with a stupid smile on his face.

"Please, Mom, I swear he will be careful."

"I suppose you are both old enough to be careful. And, you know what? As long as you stay together as a group, you don't have a curfew tonight." She looks at me, and I know the look in her eye. She must have gotten an update about Rosie. And it must be promising. She hugs me, and when we leave, she waves to us from the porch as we leave.

Miles's suit is soft on my arms. But I'm holding onto him as tight as I can, and my arms start to feel tired. We are cruising down Ruston Way. The sun is starting to set, and the water is a dark blue. There were sailboats still out. And a ferry heading to Vashon Island out on The Sound. The lights of the islands across the water were just starting to be visible.

I remember as a kid my grandpa taking me out on The Sound in his old fishing boat, we would eat pickled herring on crackers, and I'd listen to him tell me all about how old Tacoma used to look.

We arrived at the parking lot a little way down from the boat. All four of us show our IDs and are let onto the massive boat. The main deck was strung with twinkle lights and standing tables with white cloths draped over them. There are already people everywhere. The music is loud, and I can't help but feel the urge to dance. Miles gestures for me to go ahead, and I take his hand and pull it into the middle of the crowd of people already dancing. Miles starts to dance, and it makes all four of us burst into laughter. He is so tall and broad that he can barely move his arms without hitting everyone around him. I run into his elbows at least a dozen times.

And I felt good. Dancing with Miles, having Winnie there, so happy with Kyle. It felt right. Miles dark eyes found mine, and I wanted to kiss him. What is wrong with me? What kind of person can almost sleep with their boyfriend and then have the urge to kiss his best friend later that day? I need to stop. But he's not just Leto's best friend; he's Miles.

His gaze went over the crowd to the dock. I wondered who he was looking for. He looked at me and back to the dock; something like disappointment crossed his face.

It didn't take long for me to find out who he was looking at.

But I couldn't believe what I was seeing.

Leto.

THIRTY
RAY 2007
BASTARD

Dressed in a perfectly fitting gray suit and a black tie. Nothing about his demeanor said he didn't want to be here or that he was wearing someone else's clothes.

My heart leapt for half a second. Was he here for me? Did Miles orchestrate this? But then I saw what followed him. Damon, with Ashley on his arm. And a girl with long black hair on Leto's. She was in a purple strapless cocktail dress. Realization hits me like a hard slap. My eyes snap to Miles, who is watching me find out just what kind of a guy Leto was.

Leto and the rest of his group crowded around Damon; they were all drinking out of something from his jacket.

"Wait. Is that why you laughed? Did you know he planned on coming?" I pushed Miles away from me. He stumbled back. Winnie and Kyle were too busy in their own world to notice what was happening.

"No...well, yes...I just...I wanted you to see for yourself, Ray." I turn my back on him and make my way through the crowd up the stairs to the upper deck of the boat. There are a few couches, and luckily, no couples have found them yet. I turn around and bump into Miles, who has materialized at the top of the stairs.

"Why couldn't you have just told me? Why do all of this? Was it just to embarrass me? To make sure I felt even more shitty about what happened with him this morning than I already do?" I can tell by his face that this information didn't please him. Good. So maybe he doesn't know everything.

"Why would you...? So it's true?" He stumbles over his words and takes a step away from me.

"Oh, like you care, Miles. You ignored me this entire week. And then laid a trap for me to be made a fool of! You wanted me to be embarrassed? Good job. I am!" He looks at me like he's never seen me before, but rushes forward so we are a breath's distance away from each other.

"You want to know why? Why I could barely look at you? Talk to you? Because I had to watch you fall for him. Even when I knew what kind of a girl you were. You are good, beautiful, funny, talented. You are nothing like him or the girls he hangs out with. I had to watch him become obsessed with you. With trying to get you to cave to him. But I also had to watch him, just about every night, not get his way. It gave me hope that I was right. That you weren't going to fall for his shit. He doesn't deserve you, Ray. You want to know why you didn't hear from him this week?"

The sun has now fully set, and I want to jump off this boat into the black water. I would sink all the way to the bottom. And then I would suck in the salty liquid until it ruined me. That would be better than this.

But instead, I nod. I did want to know the truth about why Leto disappeared on me this week. There's a weird part of this that I can't get enough of.

I don't know why it's this way, but I've heard it told before. Seen it in movies, read it in books, listened to it in songs. Isn't love supposed to be hard? Isn't it supposed to hurt if it's worth anything? When you say ouch, doesn't that mean it wasn't just surface infatuation? Doesn't that mean it meant something?

So, I let him tell me. I gave him permission to hurt me.

"He spent this entire week on a drunk bender, sleeping with any girl who would have him. He's sloppy Ray. He doesn't give a shit about any girl. I was at his house when you called. I didn't even have to whisper. They were already plastered. He and Damon were getting ready to go, and their dates had just shown up. So, I thought I would finally have a chance to show you, to prove to you who he is. I didn't know I was already too late."

Too late? What is Miles talking about? I assumed Leto told him about saying he loved me. But this can't be why Miles is pissed at me.

He thinks I had sex with Leto. Miles reducing me to just another groupie who had sex with Leto is gutting. But so, what? Why *should* he care? What gives him the right to lure me here, just so I know Leto doesn't care about me?

"What makes you think that it's your job to police my relationships? You thought what? That I would see him here with another girl and come running to you?

That giving me tangible truth on how screwed up I am would make me suddenly over him?" My fists are so tightly clenched I can feel my nails cutting into my palms. I hadn't noticed that I was standing on my tiptoes, leaning into Miles.

"No. But I did want the chance to let you know that I would never tell lies about my friend to get a girl in bed with me." The way his shoulders slumped, I knew he meant it. "And that...that I would have let you be a nun for however long you wanted. It wouldn't have caused me to feel so insecure that I jumped into bed with anyone. Your hesitation, your patience, it would have made me fall in love with you."

I lean back on my heels, trying to physically get as far away from his words as possible. Nobody is actually that good, that wholesome. No one would have waited for me until I was ready.

My own dad didn't even wait with my mom till I was born. He fled at the mere thought of me. Plus, if what he was saying was true, then it was me who was insecure. Me, who didn't want to wait till I actually knew the guy. Me, the girl who has never been anything but self-assured a day in her life, crumble for one boy. But he didn't know that I never physically crumbled, only on the inside. But it's none of his business. If he thinks that's what happened, I don't care. I know what *didn't* happen, and that's all that matters.

"That's really easy for you to say now, isn't it?" My anger was gone. The only thing I felt now was sadness. I wanted to go home and just be with my mom. I was done with all of this.

"None of this has been easy." I barely hear his

response. I already pushed past him and am halfway down the stairs when Miles grabs my arm.

"Wait, Ray." His eyes are wild, desperate, guilty. "I have an idea. Look, I'm sorry. What you choose to do as an adult is not any of my business. And if this means we can't be friends anymore, fine. I get it. But, Ray, do you really want to run away? Do you really want him to see you upset? Or do you want to pretend to be having one hell of a time with his best friend?"

His proposal caught me entirely by surprise. It's not something a jealous boyfriend would do. It's something Winnie would do, something a best friend would do.

I don't rip my arm away. I relax. And slowly scan the crowd below me until I find what I'm looking for. Leto is grinding his date from behind. While managing to have his tongue down her throat. Classy. How could I pretend I was anything but devastated? How did I fall for all of his bullshit? How can I possibly do this?

I look back at Miles, who gives me a grin that shows his dimples on both cheeks. That's how.

"Okay. I'll try." Miles wastes no time and swoops his arm under my knees. I wrap my arms around his neck and let him carry me down the rest of the stairs like a bride to her suite.

I see Leto's massive frame freeze, out of the corner of my eye, when he sees Miles carrying me to the dance floor. Winnie and Kyle run over and, in a yell that was supposed to be a whisper, tell me, Leto is here with a girl.

"I know, which is why I am about to put on the performance of a lifetime." Winnie nods her head enthusiastically. She understood the grand re-entrance immediately. Even Kyle was on board.

The four of us started dancing like this was our own private club. And after a few songs, it starts to work. I start to feel less hopeless, less alone. Less like wanting to let myself drown in the Puget Sound. Miles wasn't grinding on me; he was actually dancing with me. Twirling me around, picking me up, and pretending like we had a choreographed dance. It was the most fun I had ever had dancing. When an upbeat country song came on, he grabbed my hand and pulled me to the middle of a line dance that had formed. He kept shouting, "They saw our boots! This song is for us!" and it was so stupid it made me howl with laughter.

A few songs later, they played a slow one. Miles pulled me in close and rested his chin on the top of my head. Even doing that, he tried to make me laugh. The song was sung by a woman, but he pretended to know the words, which he didn't, and acted like it was in his voice range, which it wasn't. When the melody grew slow, and the words stopped, we did too. I just stared at him. His deep brown eyes and tanned skin. Those stupid dimples. What if I had chosen him instead? What if I had asked myself what I really wanted and gone for it? But the reality is that I didn't. And now he doesn't want me. He thinks I slept with Leto. I open my mouth to tell Miles, but something stops me. An expression of annoyance on his face.

I felt him before I saw him.

Leto.

"Can we talk?" His hand was palm up, just waiting

for me to take it. I don't owe him anything. Not an explanation, not anything. But he owed me one.

"Sure." I left Miles and followed Leto a few feet away. We started slow dancing, and I waited for him to speak first.

"I'm so sorry. My friend Michelle had a really rough week. I wasn't planning on coming at all. It was just a last-minute decision. I would have called you, but I didn't want to feel guilty about not coming with you. I just figured I could take her and we would hang out tomorrow. But I should have just taken you. I should have been with you tonight."

He leans in to kiss me, and I turn my head. He's able to stop his face right before it hits the side of my head.

"Yeah, that doesn't explain why you were making out with her, though. Listen. You shouldn't have asked me to be your girlfriend, and you really shouldn't have told me you loved me. And you REALLY shouldn't have told anyone we had sex. Because we didn't. It's pretty clear that you have no idea what commitment means. In fact, I'm almost certain you say that to girls only so they'll sleep with you. And when I didn't, you got pissed." I don't break eye contact with him. I want to see his eyes when he tries to lie his way out of this.

"You're right. I'm just so sorry, Ray. I just didn't know how to handle someone like you. You've got me all mixed up. I feel like...I feel like I'm scared of how deeply I feel for you."

I can't be falling for this. But what if there was a chance he was sorry, if there was a chance that I didn't just waste an entire summer. Don't I owe it to myself to see if it's possible to fix this?

"So now what? What am I supposed to say to that? Do with that?" The song has now changed to an upbeat pop song. But we still stand there, slow dancing.

"So now, we can talk. Start over? As boyfriend and girlfriend? But no strings attached. We don't have to be sleeping together to date. I swear, I won't pressure you. I just want another chance. Please."

If it sounds too good to be true than it probably is. But my self-worth wanted to hang onto any shred of hope to make this better.

"What if I say yes to being boyfriend and girlfriend? But sex is off the table for now? Would you still want me? Or would you still go and sleep with whoever, whenever?" I could tell my question took him by surprise. He didn't know how much I knew. Trying to look indifferent, he leaned in and whispered in my ear.

"I will be whoever you need, as long as it gives me another chance. And I won't touch another girl."

Okay, what if he could take it slow? If we tried to mend what was broken. If we tried again. I could be okay with that. Miles will still be my friend, and Leto could become the person I always knew he could be.

"Okay."

He leads me off the dance floor and off the boat. We are walking down the dock towards the parking lot. I pull my phone out of my boot and text Winnie and Miles that I'm going with Leto. I didn't want them to worry. It was crappy of me to do this to Miles after he saved me. But he thought I was a lost cause anyway. Too late for him and me, I made my choice. Now I need to try and make the best of it.

. . .

I already knew he was taking me to his house. I wondered if he told his date that he was leaving? I guess she will have to go home with Damon and Ashley.

He parked his truck around back by the barn. I put my phone back in my boot and followed him to the old structure.

"I like you best all to myself anyway." He might have been reading my mind, or just my expression. I didn't see any lights on in the house, so his grandparents were surely asleep by now. I don't know why I felt nervous. I had been alone with him many times before. Something about tonight. I was already feeling like I couldn't trust myself. Worrying about being alone with Leto was unusual. I had let him take me to a graveyard once for hell's sake. And I don't remember feeling this uneasy. I suppose it could be because I know he's been drinking. But he wasn't acting drunk.

I laced his fingers in mine and let him walk me into the dark barn and up the squeaky stairs.

Leto turned on the lantern, and I looked around at the dimly lit hay around us. It muffled the sounds of the outside fairly well. No crickets chirping or frogs croaking.

In the summertime, you could hear it through your closed window at night. So many bodies of water around us in Pierce County, it was impossible to be rid of the noise. Unless the rain drowned it out, or you were surrounded by hay bales, apparently.

I sat down and lay my head back. Tonight, the sky outside was clear. It wasn't very often that it didn't rain through the night. Leto lay next to me and put his hands behind his head.

"It's the perfect night to see the moon." He smiled at me.

"Yeah, it looked so beautiful tonight." I agreed and smiled back.

"No, look up. It's only one night a month you can see it through the crescent cut out." He pointed directly above us, and sure enough, there in the old barn roof was the cutout of a moon. And it was perfectly visible.

"It has to be at just the right spot, and on a clear night to see it."

The moonlight shines through the hole and makes his eyes glow eerily. I hear myself agree with how cool it is when this feeling of deja vu hits me.

Why did it feel like I've been here before? Is it because I have been here with Leto before? At his party?

I thought it seemed familiar because it was the night I really fell for him. Really decided to give him a chance. But now I know why it feels so odd.

My breath starts to come out short and fast. A sheen of sweat covers my body. I haven't lived this before. But someone has. Rosie has.

"...*the moon. The third wheel on our trysts. I can see it staring at us through the perfect crescent cut out in the ceiling.*"

The words are in one of her journal entries. What are the odds it would be a different barn? After all, wasn't this farm next to hers? On Elm Street?

"Who made it?" I did my best impression of someone unfazed and in love.

"Oh, I'm not sure, someone in my family from way back. It's been here as long as the barn has been here. So at least one hundred years."

I felt like I was going to be sick. Rosie, she had been warning me all along. Unknowingly laying the breadcrumbs for me not to end up like her. What did she write about? What she thought was love but was instead manipulation and abuse? And then no one heard from her ever again. I need to get out of here. Just as I think it, the gold leaves Leto's eyes, and all I see is black.

THIRTY-ONE
RAY 2007

RUN

I pull out my phone when Leto is distracted with loosening his tie. Turning the volume all the way down, I hit redial. Without shutting the phone, I slide it back into my boot. So the light is covered up.

"Oh shoot, that was my mom, she wants me to come home apparently." Silently, I thanked God that I didn't tell Leto about not having a curfew tonight.

"Miss Dotty is so overprotective, isn't she?" His tone startled me. And the way he said her name. I swallowed my urge to shudder.

"Yes, and if I don't go, she knows where to find me." Faking a little chuckle, trying to keep things light.

"She won't miss you if you're only ten minutes or so late? Plus, I'm feeling really tired suddenly. I think I need your help to wake me up."

I start to inch my way backwards towards the lantern. He puts a strong hand on my thigh, stopping me from moving.

"That's okay if you're too tired to drive me. I'm sure she wouldn't mind picking me up, if you want."

"That's not what I want." No. I knew what he wanted. He wanted what he promised he could wait for. What he told me we wouldn't do. He wanted what I wasn't ready to give him. He intended now to take it.

"I know, but you said we could take it slow. You said we were starting over. Remember? So, please? Leto, take me home?" He sat up and stared at me. His hand still gripping my thigh.

I don't know if it was the shift in the moonlight or his soul, but the black in his eyes got darker. A shadow crossed his face. I need to be stronger or faster than him, but I was neither. Maybe, just maybe, I could be smarter than him.

It was like time was moving in slow motion. Leto, the guy I had been drawn to from the moment I met him. The guy I chose to give another chance to, because I thought I loved him.

Love.

I thought I was in *love*. I only use that word because it was a feeling I never felt before. I mean, sure, I knew what it felt like to be loved. But *in* love? That was different, but so was this. It was painful, but I didn't know any better. The pain made the peace, the times when we would chat, kiss, laugh, so addicting. Enthralling, overwhelming, underwhelming, and a lot of times, lonely. But one thing was for sure: if anyone was going to find out what happened to Rosie, it was going to be me. She had been missing and forgotten for too long. And the realization that I would rather put myself in danger, be privy to the most gruesome insights in people's minds, and possibly go missing myself, than stay in this relationship for one second longer was all the confirmation I needed.

One by one, somehow, I need to unhook the cat claws of Leto, stuck to my soul.

And if I was going to find those answers, then I was going to have to play nice. And get out of here.

"I'm not saying never, I'm just saying not tonight. It's not something I want to rush. And you know my mom. She will have no problem tracking me down at your house." I make sure to say that last part loudly. Leto turns his head to the side and thinks for a moment.

"Please let go of me Leto. I know you care about me. I care about you too."

I start to hatch a plan. Because if a girl is saying *no,* and a guy has to contemplate whether or not he accepts it, it's really time for me to go.

"No, I don't think that's what you want. I think you want to stay here with me. And I think you want to show me, just how much you care about me."

I smile and tell my heart to stop beating so fast. If this is going to work, then he needs to think he's right and to believe that I do want him.

"I mean, I guess ten minutes wouldn't cause her to freak out right away. But I want to freshen up. Can I use your bathroom? It'll be quick."

I can tell he's glad that I am finally giving in and going to give him what he wants. He takes his hand off my leg and shoots it out to the side.

"Be my guest, the side door should be unlocked. And then straight down the hallway."

I stand up slowly and make my way back through the maze. I fight my instinct to sprint, not wanting to alert him that anything is wrong. Down the creaky stairs, and out the barn doors. Stopping to listen for the sound of his footsteps following me. When I don't hear anything, I take off running towards the road.

When I'm a good way away from his driveway, I reach down and grab my phone. But I don't even have to look down to see if my call worked. Roaring down the road is Miles on his bike. He stops two feet away from me and doesn't bother to get out his extra helmet. He takes off his own and shoves it on my head.

We are gone in a matter of seconds. Racing up the winding road to Edgewood. My tears fall freely and are collecting in the fabric of Miles' helmet at my chin.

Miles blew through every stop sign until we pulled up to my porch. When I removed his helmet, he took it from me and set it on the seat of his bike, and just stood there. Staring at me. He's still in his suit and boots. He must have left the dance moments after I did.

Looking at his face, I can't even guess what he's thinking. Does he wish he left me there? Does he regret ever meeting me? Does he think I'm more trouble than it's worth? Does he think I'm worth anything?

"Why did you call *me*?" He's looking me up and down, and I think maybe he's trying to figure out if I had other intentions besides *get me the hell out of there*. And I think he's wondering why I didn't call Winnie or my mom.

"Because I knew you'd come."

He lets out a cynical laugh.

"I guess that's what I get. For always being the nice

guy. Never the guy on the other end of the call about to sleep with the girl. Just the guy she calls when she's bit off a shit more than she can chew."

I meant it as an endearing statement. I called him because I knew I could count on him. I knew he would never put me in any of the situations that Leto had. But Miles was right. He was the guy all the girls called when they were in trouble. Because he was the guy at all the parties making sure he wasn't too drunk to drive. The one who would take out a girl and her best friend just to make another guy jealous. The guy who, even after getting his heart broke told the girl who broke it he would help her not feel so embarrassed about her boyfriend lying and cheating on her.

Then what was it about Leto? Because so far, he was none of the things that Miles was. So far, Leto was just the guy all the girls were drawn to, and I had fallen for it. The way people wanted him made me want him even against my better judgment and actual experiences with him.

And I should have said all of this out loud to Miles, but as I was going through it all in my mind, something took over. I remembered why I fled Leto's barn. It wasn't only because I didn't want him to take from me something I didn't want to give.

It was also because Rosie had been there. I know it. And Miles isn't just the kind of guy who would stand up for your virtue. He's the kind of guy who would be committed to helping me find out what happened to my aunt. All I had to do was ask.

"Miles, someone has been following me. They have been leaving notes for me and my mom to find. And I know you already know that. But recently they left her whole notebook. The one that went missing just days after she died. And my mom made copies, and I read all the entries." Miles eyes narrow, he's definitely wondering why the hell I'm telling him this.

"Listen, while I was in Leto's barn. I had already decided I wasn't going to sleep with him. And in case you didn't catch on, I didn't sleep with him this morning or ever. He had promised we could start over and go as slow as I wanted. That's the only reason I gave him another chance. But as I was lying there, I looked up and saw something Rosie described in her journal."

My tears had tried, but my voice was cracking out of frustration.

"People couldn't prove it, but speculated that she was seeing someone other than Harvey. Yes, Harvey is the guy who went to jail." I tell him when his brows pull together. "That's who I think she was with the night she most likely died. I looked up and saw the mo-" Miles interrupts me.

"Moon-shaped hole in the roof. Yeah, it's been there since we were kids. Leto said it's been there for a hundred years or something stupid."

"Yes, exactly. Well, my mom's wheat farm growing up was neighbors with their apple orchard. They both lived on Elm Street. Harvey said the last time he saw Rosie was when they parted ways...on Elm Street."

I could see goosebumps below Miles pushed up sleeves.

"And you're not just bullshitting me, so I'll stop being mad about you and Leto?" I shake my head slowly.

"You can be mad at me the rest of your life if you

want, but the bottom line is I made a choice. At the time, I thought I was giving Leto the benefit of the doubt. Now I see it for what it really was. So I'll make you a deal. Once I forgive myself, I'll let you know, and then you can start the process of forgiving me, too." You could have cut my thick sarcasm with a knife.

He looks at me again. So intense, I think he might start shouting. But closes his eyes instead.

"Deal." He surprises me by relaxing and giving me a wink.

"So, what now? Do we go to the cops? Or your mom? Or who?"

I look out over our tree-filled property and try to think what the best avenue would be.

"I need to have a reason, or a theory, before we tell anyone, I think." Standing there, I get an idea.

"Okay, wait here for a sec." I run inside and find my mom in the den. She is up reading the copies of the journal. I need to act just right for this to work.

"Hi, sweetie! How was it? Did you guys kiss?" I lean down to hug her, and she stifles a yawn.

"What? No, I didn't kiss him, Mom. But I did have such a good time. I am super tired, though. Is there anything I can get you before I go to bed?" I yawn to really sell it.

"No, I don't think so, honey. I'll be up in a bit."

Walking up the stairs, I pull out my phone.

I just need to wait for my mom to go to sleep. Then I'm going to sneak you upstairs.

I have never snuck anyone into my house before. I don't know if it will even work. Miles is massive. Does he even know how to tiptoe?

Okay.

Okay, with a period? So, he's still mad. I don't blame him. I have been so stupid. But I can't think about that right now.

I changed out of my dress and boots, throwing on a t-shirt and boxer shorts. I wash my face and make sure my mom sees me ready for bed when she finally retires to her own room.

"Goodnight mom!" I call out to her after she shuts her door. I only need to wait five minutes to hear her deep breathing when I put my ear to her door.

As slowly as possible, I walk down the staircase. The house is cloaked in darkness, but I still make sure to skip the stairs that creak. Opening the front door with laser focus, I almost scream when I see Miles about an inch away from my face. I open the door just enough for him to step through it sideways. I look down and see that he's in socks. He must have ditched his boots by his bike. I smile to myself at his readiness.

We walk up the stairs, and he steps only in the places I point him to. Finally crossing the threshold to my room, I lock the door behind us. Putting a finger to my lips, I wait to hear if my mom stayed asleep. Standing there, we both decided the coast was clear. I exhale a large breath I was holding. Miles looks at me and mouths, "Now what?"

I make a gesture for him to sit on my bed, and he

does, but also takes off his jacket, tie, and white shirt. Underneath is a white undershirt that is arguably the hottest thing I've ever seen. His broad chest pulls the t-shirt tight around him. I blink and realize I'm open-mouthed, staring. I've seen him without his shirt on at practice and haven't acted this juvenile. But I've never seen him in my room. Or any man in my room, for that matter.

"Okay, I'm going to give you all the facts I know. And we need to work it out. I need another person who's not as close to the situation to see what I'm not seeing."

Miles grins and starts to throw to himself a pair of balled-up socks he finds on my bed.

"Cui bono." Miles stares at me, still throwing and catching the socks.

"Excuse me?" I look at him stupidly.

"To whom is it a benefit?" Miles quietly explains. "Who had the motive to want her gone? Something about Leto's family's estate is that they have hired help there. In fact, they chose to sell off a few parcels of their land just to be able to keep affording the help. After Leto and Damon's parents were such a disap-pointment, they needed even more help than they planned. So the chances of it being a drifter who was passing through are high."

"A drifter? I had never even thought of that..." I start to pace, thinking about any clues from the diary pages. Anything that could have given evidence of her being in love with a farm hand.

"I can't think of anything from her diary that would support that, besides her talking about running away a lot. Running away with him. What if they? What if Rosie and some transient ran away after all?"

"It's possible, but if that's the case, who would have reason to steal the diary? It wouldn't have mattered if she had been alive. Once she was eighteen, she could have just said, I've started a new life."

"Right, and she wasn't the type to just never talk to her family again or to never show back up anywhere."

"So, you think it wasn't Harvey. But what if it still was? Did he have a reason to do it?"

"Well, sure he did. Rosie broke up with him. And Harvey used to hurt women. He beat up Winnie's mom around the same time my aunt went missing, and he tried to kill my mom...that's where her scar is from. And why he went to jail. But he died before I started being followed, and before we got the journal."

"Oh...I'm sorry, I didn't know about your mom. That's messed up."

"Thanks, and I just barely found out myself. One of the downsides to having your mom's sister go missing is how much trauma she tried to hide from me."

"Yeah, but she's making strides. Remember? No curfew tonight?" I smiled at his attempt to lighten my mood.

"She has been a lot more hopeful since she sent the journal in for DNA testing. The case has been cold for so long, she can't believe they reopened it." I watch him throw the balled-up socks to himself, up and down, up and down.

"And my aunt going missing isn't the only thing that happened. It was my dad who helped my mom through it all. Up until the day he left, he was obsessed with finding out what happened. My mom told me that the day she told him she was pregnant with me, he said he had a surprise for her. But the surprise was that he left. Never came back. After a while, there was evidence of him living in another state, so that was that."

"Oh wow, no wonder your mom is so...protective of you. I would be too."

"You are. Thank you for coming to get me tonight. And for being like, my best friend."

"Whoa, be careful, I wouldn't want Winnie to kick my ass for that." Miles is grinning, but I can see he's still on edge and wondering what exactly we are doing here. Can he tell that my choice to call him was convenient, yes, but that there was more to it? I stop thinking about my other reasons; I need to focus on only one thing at a time.

"I promise I won't tell her. So, Harvey had a lot of motive and certainly the personality for it. But something in me isn't buying it. So, who else could she have been in that barn with?" I look at the floor and ask slowly, because I have a realization while I'm saying it.

"But she does talk about him like...like he has commitment issues. Like he couldn't decide if it was worth it to be with her or not...the only men who I have had experience with that can't commit are the ones who feel like they have more than one option."

Miles stops throwing the makeshift ball up in the air and lets it fall to the bed.

"Or someone who has a girlfriend, or is...married."

I feel like I've been punched in the gut. The tomato sandwich that I ate at the Lee house earlier today somehow feels like it's still in my stomach now, twisting into putrid acid. "But...she didn't even know the Lee's. She...she is way too young. They are old...I mean, ancient-looking. There's no way."

"They are younger than they look, only about six years older than your mom, even. The years, their kids, their grandkids, just haven't been good to them. They spend their days in the sun, too."

I walk over to the bed and sit on top of my bedspread next to Miles. Our legs are touching. He doesn't pull away, something in me hoped he wouldn't.

"Mr. Lee just sat there. I mean, we had lunch, and he just sat there, looking at me. He seemed so... boring. Just old and unassuming. His wife, though, was a kind of a bitch. She told me Leto had girls in his room all the time... or maybe she was just being honest with me. Trying to warn me?"

Maybe I actually liked her. Maybe his grandpa was like his grandson. Charismatic, crafty, and uncaring about the women who love him. Maybe he was the one from whom Leto learned it?

Was it really only this morning that I almost gave to him what I'd promised to save? Why has this day felt like an eternity and only seconds all at once? I'm still trying not to think about what could have happened. Still doing my best to put it out of my mind forever, what might have happened if I hadn't run away from the crescent cutout ceiling of that barn.

Miles looks at me, and I can tell he knows what I'm thinking about. It keeps crashing into me in waves. Rosie, her story, it's the distraction I need.

Miles puts his arm around me and squeezes me into him. And just looks at me.

"Miles...I...I needed to try. The thought that I

almost so carelessly threw that part of me away to someone who cared so little for me...I needed to make sure I couldn't make it right. I wanted so badly for him to be the person I thought he was. I'm just not the kind of girl to give up. And I needed to see it through. No matter how much I wished I could have been with someone like his best friend in the first place."

Miles smells so good. Despite all his dancing and riding his bike, he gives off a wind-blown, leathery smell. We are both sitting against my headboard, and he slides his arm down around my waist. I lay my head on his shoulder.

"I'm not going to try to understand why you would trust Leto. But it isn't fair of me to judge you too harshly. I spent so much time trying not to come off as the jealous friend that I wasted too much time not telling you what I really knew about him. I just thought you would see through him. I thought you would be done with him when you got sick of him pulling you in, just to cut you off. I just never thought you'd fall for it. If I had been a better friend to you, then you wouldn't even be in this situation."

My eyes feel heavy. I'm feeling more at peace than I have since I met Leto. My stomach was in constant knots with him. But I thought that's what love was supposed to be. It was supposed to make you feel... right?

"Leto tried to date my older sister, you know. Or, well, maybe you don't. Not sure how you would, it was a year before we met you. Anyway, he was close to actually getting her to well...get more serious, and then she went off to school. It wasn't until I called her after you left the dance to ask her what really went down that I found out what happened. I don't know what made me call her, but after Leto and my sister were a thing, she just never has been the same towards me. Then she finally told me what happened. He told her he loved her and wanted to be her boyfriend. She told him she was going to school, and she didn't want to do long distance. So she broke up with him. But he showed up to campus a week after classes started and tried to convince her otherwise. His need to be accepted is nothing I have ever seen before. She denied him, and her roommate came home and found him shaking her shoulders, yelling in her face. After that, she deleted his number and never said a word about it to anyone until I called her. I was so close to riding right past you tonight and confronting him in the barn. To answer for my sister and for what I heard him say to you. You were so obviously not interested. And he didn't even care. The only reason I didn't was because of the look in your eye when I got there. You looked...terrified. And I realized your need to be safe was greater than my need to beat the shit out of him. And you can't even imagine how happy I am to know that Leto still didn't get what he wanted with you."

"And I may owe you for the rest of my life for that." I tilted my head up so that I was breathing onto his neck and into his ear. I wanted him to hear what I was about to say. I wanted him to be the first person to hear out loud what I had been feeling for some time.

"Something tells me I would have been Rosie; her story would have been my story had I not run, had you not been there, Miles. It's why...I need to find out who hurt her."

THIRTY-THREE
RAY 2007
BIG ROCK

I don't know when we fell asleep, but the crick in my neck tells me it was hours ago. His steady breathing calms me, even before my eyes are open. I wonder how many girls have been lucky enough to open their eyes to someone like him in the morning. Someone who might stick around.

The memories of all that had happened yesterday flitter across my mind in a rush. I hadn't moved, but my change in anxiety levels must have alerted Miles.

"Whoa! Hey, sorry. I...where?...Oh...right. Oh shit! It's morning. I'd better..."

His broken and panicked sentences force me to smile. Grabbing my phone out of the toe of my boot, I see that it's six in the morning. Good. My mom won't be awake yet.

"Relax, it's Sunday. The one day that my mom actually sleeps in. Plus, I'm pretty sure we fell asleep mid-sentence last night. Or maybe we hatched a plan, and I was too tired to remember?"

I really want to go brush my teeth and comb what

I'm sure are feral tangles in my hair, but I don't want to leave the room and wake up my mom. So instead, I stay standing a few feet away from my bed and start to pace. I try to brush my fingers through the ratted mess.

"No, we never said what we should do about what we've found out. But I was wondering if you remember hearing anything about when Rosie went missing. Has your mom ever mentioned anyone searching the Lee orchards?"

"Not that I can recall, but they would have been stupid not to. My mom's childhood home shared a backyard with them, basically. I mean, not really, their lands touched. But that's acres and acres."

Miles gets off my bed and puts on his white shirt. He shoves his tie in his pocket and doesn't bother to button anything. He looks at me, running my hands through my hair. He walks over and puts his own hand in my hair, so he's holding the back of my neck. It forces me to tilt my face up to his.

"I love that you wore my helmet, and it messed up your hair. You wouldn't believe how hard it's been to not have my hands in your hair."

I blink, and a dizzy feeling of heat goes through my body.

"I.." I start to stammer, but he cuts me off.

"Well, I know you're not going to like this...but it's time to wake up your mom. She was there, and she needs our help, and we need hers. Give me an hour or so to go get washed up. I'll be back here as soon as I can. I may have to take care of some things at home. But go ahead and talk to your mom. Tell her everything."

I knew what he meant by that. He meant to tell her all about Leto and what I had been going through, and about Rosie. I nodded and closed my eyes when he took his time removing his hand from my neck and softly grazing my cheek with his fingers. Then I watched him turn my doorknob. Before he steps over the threshold, he turns and looks at me.

"I could have sworn that was locked. Hey, please don't do anything without me. Do not leave this house. You promise?" I nod again, only slower. There is something I wanted to check on while I waited for him. But I was also certain that the door had been locked.

I didn't even hear his bike rev when he left. He must have rolled it down my driveway a ways before starting it up.

I showered, got dressed in my jean shorts, and a fitted short-sleeve white V-neck. I slid on my boots and left my hair long and wild.

Taking the stairs two at a time, I rushed past the kitchen and almost didn't notice the white piece of paper on the table. Doubling back, I pick it up, and I recognize my mom's handwriting.

Rayel, I had to go to downtown Seattle. Cops think they got a hit on one of the prints from the journal. I peeked into your room and saw Miles. Glad you both were clothed...and sitting straight up. We will definitely be talking about you sneaking him into the house when I get back. But listen, don't let Miles leave until I get back. I woke up today, and something just feels off.

Love you,

Mom

Chills trickled from the top of my head down to

the bottom of my feet. My mom had never begged for a guy to stay here with me while she was gone. I had planned to get on the internet and check out the county's land records. I wanted to know about the property lines back in 1972.

Flipping open my phone, I dial Miles, and it goes straight to voicemail. His phone was probably dead from not having it on the charger last night. I looked at mine, and it was dangerously low too. Running upstairs, I plug it in quickly, but turn the ringer on full volume.

Then I check all the doors and make sure they are locked. If my mom is nervous enough to warn me, then I would at least be smart enough to lock the doors.

Booting up the computer took a few minutes, but once I was in, it was easy to find what I was looking for. The State archives had birds-eye maps of the property lines from 1972 in Sumner, Washington.

Sure enough, I saw my mom's house on Elm Street. Their land went back quite a ways, and then the outskirts of the berry farm started to the east. And the apple orchard to the west. The entrance of the Lee family's driveway was just a stone's throw away from my mom's house on Elm Street. But the sprawling farmhouse was set a few acres from the road. There was one farm towards the south, tulips maybe? I couldn't remember what my grandpa had said about it, and I'm not sure that it mattered here. I printed the map out and set it beside me.

Then I searched for the current 2007 property maps for Sumner. Almost all of my mom's childhood farm had been sold and turned into apartments. The handful of times I had driven past it this summer, the yard and trees were so overgrown that I could barely see the house itself. The tulip farm and berry farm hadn't changed at all. But the Lee's orchard had gotten smaller. To the west, near where you drive up the hill to Edgewood, they had sold off about five acres or so. It was technically in Edgewood and not Sumner. Construction hadn't started, but there was supposed to be a park-and-ride going in. It's right near the train station that takes commuters to Seattle.

I guess it was easier for them to sell that land because of how up-and-coming the city of Edgewood was. And if there was something to be found on that part of the land, the chances of it being discovered were slim. There is very minimal digging to put in parking lots. In fact, anything buried deep enough-would most likely be hidden forever.

I roll up the two maps and look at the clock; it's half past eight in the morning, and I didn't hear my phone ring. Where could Miles be? A feeling of dread was trying to take root in my stomach. I pushed it away and ran upstairs to call Winnie.

It rang and rang, but there was no answer. She would be sleeping in too. I wonder if Miles went home and just fell asleep without plugging his phone in. Neither of us got very good sleep. I hang up and call my mom's cell phone. My dread starts to creep back in when I hear her cell phone going off somewhere downstairs.

I don't want to wait anymore.

Snatching my keys, I sprint down the stairs with the maps under my arm. I'm driving down the hill to Sumner two minutes later. This isn't privately owned property, I tell myself as I'm slowing down just on the edge of town. I won't get into trouble by looking around a little bit.

Weirdly enough, I end up parking close to the cemetery. The edge of the Lee's old property line is just a few blocks away. You wouldn't know it, though, the trees get so thick on the side of the hill. It's hard to imagine there's anything besides woods beyond this point. I pull out the map from 1972, and lay it on my lap. I place the new map over it. Perfect, the corner of their estate that's now publicly owned is close enough to walk to. I startled as the horn of a train blew. I'm so close to the train tracks that my car rattles even though I can't see the train.

It reminds me that this may be one of the only opportunities I have to check out my hunch. Once they pave over the dirt, there won't be any easy way to look. Memorizing the map, I decide to leave it in my front seat. The fewer things I have to carry, the better.

I sit there for a moment and remember that no one knows I've come here. I should call someone and at least leave a message. Reaching for the cupholder, which usually always has my phone, my fingers hit a round, empty plastic bottom. Shit. I left it plugged in, charging. I take a deep, annoyed breath. It's not like they are going to make it a parking lot today. I really don't need to rush into this. Is what I should have been telling myself. But instead, Leto looking at me like he was going to get exactly what he wanted regardless of what I was saying. And looking up to see the moon through the ceiling, just like Rosie wrote about, my thoughts were only going to allow me to go forward.

Get out of the car. Walk to the old Lee property. Find Rosie. My brain knew it wouldn't be that easy, but my heart was trying to tell me otherwise. My heart wasn't the one I should have been trusting, though. My heart almost told me to climb into bed with Leto to feel something. Loved. Wanted. Sought after? My brain was the one now cleaning up the mess and asking all of the questions. Why didn't he want me like I wanted him?

I hadn't even realized that I was halfway down the narrow shoulder where I parked. I looked around and inhaled the fresh air; the sun was covered by clouds today. But the humidity was brutal. A bead of sweat rolled down my back and hit the back waistband of my shorts. I guess my heart had decided to go while my brain was busy. Because there's no denying that this was stupid.

But I kept walking anyway.

I rounded the corner of the tiny road and almost tripped over a rock the size of my head. It looked like a jagged piece of black and white speckled granite. I stumbled but righted myself. To the left was a clearing. There was the pine needle-covered road, a deep ditch, an old rust-covered barbed wire fence, and acres of uncut tall cream and green grass. This section on the map kind of made an upside-down teardrop. The narrowest part is closest to the main road, and the wider part is near the Lees' white farmhouse and apple trees.

It stuck out because there were no apple trees on it in the 70's or today. It's totally flat, perfect for a parking lot. No tree roots would be coming up to ruin the pavement.

Ducking down, I step one leg over part of the fence and go underneath the sharp wire sideways. Cursing myself for not wearing long pants, one of the barbs scratches my legs, and a trickle of blood runs down my thigh. Once I get onto the other side, the ground drops down a bit, making the grass feel even taller. It came all the way up to my shoulders. Not even sure what I was looking for, I kept my head down. Scanning the ground for...well, anything, I guess.

I stop moving when I hear something. A faint rustling, like a bird walking on the ground. Or a cat weaving through the grass. Or a person, trying to sneak up on someone. I crouch down and hold my breath. The sound is getting closer. And then I hear it, someone humming or whistling. It's far away, so I can't tell where it's coming from or recognize the tune. I pivot, and all I see is grass all around me, and then trees in the distance beyond that. I could start running, but I can't tell where I'm going, so I might run right into them.

Then, from the right, a small squirrel scurries past me. I let out a long sigh of relief.

Standing back up, I keep walking, hoping to reach something that will give me a better idea of where I am. I suppose it's either towards the farmhouse and apple trees, towards the other farms, or towards the road. Either way, I feel so exposed not knowing exactly which one.

I start to pick up the pace a little when the first raindrop hits my forehead. This was stupid. I don't even know what I'm looking for. I start to walk so fast that it turns into a slow jog on the uneven, soft earth.

The ground was always soft and wet where we lived. I was looking at my feet and totally missed the massive rock I ran headfirst into. Bouncing back and slamming to the ground on my butt. The rock looks like another piece of granite, but it's bigger than me. Rubbing the top of my head, I felt a little bump start to form. At least there wasn't any blood this time.

I put my hands on the rock and hoisted myself up. Now I could finally see where I was. Standing on the top, I can see that I'm at the widest part of the teardrop. I can see the Lees' house, their trees, the corner of the berry farm, a sliver of the rows of tulips, and just past a small apartment building, the back of a little blue house and an old tree swing. There wasn't anyone on it now, but I knew whose it used to be.

A searing pain split my thoughts. I heard a crack and felt something pouring out of my head. And then everything went black.

THIRTY-FOUR
RAY 2007

JEALOUS

"What the hell?!" I try to sit up, only to find that my arms and legs are hog-tied together behind me. I woke up screaming in complete darkness. The floor is hard beneath me, but I can smell hay. My arms and legs are asleep. I wonder how long I've been unconscious. Lying on my side, I try to look up. To my horror, I'm exactly where I feared I was. Seeing that crescent cut out in the ceiling filled with stars told me where I was and who brought me here. Well, maybe I don't know exactly who brought me here, but the list is getting shorter and shorter.

My head feels like it has its own heartbeat, but I don't feel anything hot or wet dripping down, so the blood must have clotted. Once my eyes adjust to the night, I look down at my white shirt and see it covered in something dark and stiff. I must have stopped bleeding sometime ago. I hope that's a good sign that my wound wasn't too serious. But the pain that was throbbing told me it wasn't going to be an aspirin and a band-aid kind of recovery.

I look around, trying to see if there was anything I could use to get out of these ropes. I stretched and saw the unlit lantern on the hay bale against the wall. The blanket that I had lain on only last night was nowhere to be found, though. My wrists and ankles are so swollen there's no way I can wiggle my way out of my restraints. Rolling over onto my stomach, trying to get gravity to help get the swelling down. I lay there for a while, I might have been minutes or hours. I'm not exactly sure. I still feel like I'm slipping in and out of consciousness. I try to move my hands and find that I can. Not enough to get free, but it's giving me hope.

I press my ear to the floor and can hear two people talking. It sounded like a man and a woman. My stomach turns thinking of who it might be. The barn door opens beneath me, and someone leaves. Whoever stays starts making their way up the creaking stairs.

I make my breathing as quiet as possible and close my eyes. I hear them making their way through the maze of hay bales. Their footsteps stop right in front of me. They bend down to my face. I assume it's to check if I'm still breathing. They smell like dirty hair and rotten apples.

"You don't have to pretend you're still asleep, you little whore. We both heard you wake up screaming." It was her. The skinny and tall farmer's, wife.

Slowly, I open my eyes and look up. Pamela Lee, with her long, white, and silver, stringy hair and waxy old skin. No makeup or perfume to hide her ugliness.

Just sheer hate radiating from her dark eyes. She leans over me and turns on the lantern.

She only looks worse in the dull light. Every hateful wrinkle is magnified by the light. Something tells me to play dumb. I know she's most certainly covering for Dale, the tall, sinister farmer.

"Is this about last night? I'm not going to tell anyone. Leto didn't do anything wrong. He's my friend. I would never want to make trouble for him."

Her head cocks to the side almost violently.

"Leto? My poor, innocent Leto? Oh no, I saw you fleeing like the whore that you are. I'm sure you got exactly what you Luis girls have always asked for. Much like your aunt. She deserved everything she got. And my Dale, so like my Leto. Never the wiser. Always suspected but never man enough to ask." While she was talking, I made the smallest movements to get my wrists free. Making the tiniest bit of progress, I had to keep her distracted.

"What are you talking about? Rosie never knew you or your husband. She was in high school, a child." I double over in pain when she kicks me in the stomach.

"Don't you think I knew that? The disgust it caused me to know that he was seeing her behind my back? In this very barn! So what if she was almost eighteen? He was an adult. And she was a child! My husband! They both thought that they were so clever sneaking around. So I took care of it. I took care of this farm, of our family's legacy and reputation. Me. But Rosie, dear Rosie, never left, did she?"

I'm trying to concentrate on my breathing and my hands. I have them twisting and turning, trying every position possible to break free. When she kicked me, it gave me an excuse to roll slightly and hide my hands and legs behind me a little.

"Every turn, I can feel her judgy little eyes on me. When it took me years to conceive, I just knew she was watching, laughing. Oh, so pleased. Because she knew my husband preferred her in every way. And then when I finally had kids, they were the trash that I bet Rosie always thought they would be. Rosie, with her long brown hair. Piercing blue eyes. Sometimes I look out and still see those eyes staring back at me. She's there, standing on that damn rock staring at me. The way I used to stand and stare at her, plot to end her, all the while she dreamed about moving onto my farm, into my house! It infuriated me to see her slut of a sister on that swing looking my way, too. I guess your family's apples really don't fall far from the tree."

The farmer's wife stands there staring at me with her head still bent to the side. If I didn't know she was real, I would be convinced that she was a demon. My hand is seconds away from being free when she pulls out a long kitchen knife from underneath her tattered, long brown sweater. It was serrated and typically used to cut bread. I started to shiver when I thought of her cutting into me like the crust off those tomato sandwiches. I was able to get one of my hands free, and then the other. I kept my legs bent up so she wouldn't realize that I was free. I need to keep her distracted so I can get past her and out of here.

"So, it was you? You took Rosie's journal? You're the one who's been following me? Haunting my mom and me?"

To my horror, her face splits into a wide grin. I see

no teeth in the darkness but a black pit where her mouth should be. The pain from being restrained and then free is staggering. All the blood rushing back into my extremities is causing me to see stars.

"Yes, I've read her journal many times over the years. I first saw her writing in it while she sat on her swing. After she wasn't a problem anymore, I knew I had to find it. She wasn't too clever, your aunt. She and Dale always thought they were alone. But I was always there. Always listening. I knew he was always going to be one foot in and one foot out. He would never fully be with her. But of course, he wouldn't ever have told her that. And I think he knew, because he was older and smarter, that she would always come back. Never be able to stay away, not fully anyway. So I took it. And everything I had already heard confirmed it. Rosie was a good-for-nothing tramp. And I saved my marriage, and this orchard by ending her."

From behind me, someone steps out of the shadows. A tall figure, too tall to be anyone here to help me, I realize with dread.

Leto.

"Hey, Ray." For a small moment, I think he might come to me anyway. Help me, save me. But then I see his face is dark. There's a shadow across it. Did he know? Did he want me, just to hurt me?

"You shouldn't be here. I thought I told you to leave." Pamela croaks out with surprising force.

"Had to see for myself. Damon mentioned you found someone snooping. I'm elated to see you back here, so soon, Ray. I thought the way you ran from me last night meant you didn't like me anymore." He fakes a frown that makes me want to laugh. At him, his cowardice, he desperateness. What a joke. I know I'm the one injured and on the ground, but somehow I'm still not the most pathetic thing here. They are.

"Well, you can have what's left of her. Someone's going to pay for Dale. And it's going to be her. Now, best leave so you don't have to see the unpleasantness." Leto walks by me and puts his hands up, like he might catch something from me. I turn my head and spit on his shoes.

"Your entire dumb hick family are pieces of shit. I hope you all rot in hell." I yell, as a tear rolls down my face at Leto's last ever rejection of me. He ignores my outburst and disappears behind the hay.

Could he see through me? Through my spitting rage? Does he know why my dad never wanted me either? The idea of me caused him to disappear. Is it the same reason Leto didn't want me either? Why, sometimes I don't even want me? Is that why he thought that when I said no, he would turn it into yes, regardless of what I wanted?

I didn't say anything, as we both listened for Leto's footsteps to tell us he was all the way down the stairs. I feel more resolved as I hear the barn door open and then close behind him. I didn't let another tear escape. Not for him. I won't let my last moments be for him. I feel strength, but I don't know the source. I've been bleeding, beaten, and passed out. And yet, I feel brave.

"What do you mean? Pay for Dale?" I whisper, try to talk around the lump in my throat.

"So nosey, just like your mama. They came and arrested him tonight. They think he's the one who killed Rosie."

Isn't he? I'm confused, and she knows it.

"Do you want to know what it feels like to take the life of the one person keeping you from happiness? It feels like taking a deep breath after drowning. I was content that she was dead, even if I didn't feel she was totally gone. Until I saw you. That night at the slaughterhouse. I like to roam, and I find myself there from time to time. It's a quiet place for me to fantasize. Imagine my astonishment when you showed up in her boots. Looking so much like her. And then you set your eyes on my Leto. He's not like me, you know. Doesn't quite have the stomach for it like Damon. Damon is much more like his gran. I had to stop him several times from taking that poor Ashley girl up here a time or two. But he wasn't ready. He would have been caught before I could finally put an end to the curse of the Luis girls. I had such a good time getting into your heads. Leaving you confused and scared. What luck that you should show up, alone, just for us today. He should be here by now, though. I wonder what's taking him? Dale won't be able to ignore what I've done for us this time. He will get to have a front row seat."

She turns towards the entrance of the hay maze, and I throw my ropes out and lunge to get past her.

With surprising speed, she turns around and thrusts the knife's blade towards me; she slashes, and it makes a cut horizontally. Gasping and slipping in my fresh, falling blood. I bulldoze over her and weave through the hay until I find the stairs. Taking three at a time, I fly down and run out the barn door. I don't bother to look behind me. I just sprint towards the road. Just like I did last night. But this time, in much more pain, and running from a much worse situation. I have one hand around my middle, keeping everything inside. And one hand pumping through the air as I try my best to keep running down the long driveway. My head is pounding from the gash in the back of my head. I reached up only briefly to try and find out how exactly I was hit off that rock. Apparently, by something sharp and long.

All I need is to flag down a car. I just need one car, and then I'm free. I keep repeating this to myself, but as I take my first steps onto Elm Street, my vision starts to get murky.

There are no cars in sight. All I hear are the crickets and frogs from the nearby ponds. So loud, I wish I could cover my ears. And then I hear it. The low familiar melody.

I hit the asphalt with my knees. Then I fell to my side. Now clutching my stomach with both hands. The night is still warm, but I start to shiver. My vision starts to blur even more.

And I think, if death is the door, then love is the catalyst. The love I thought I had for Leto, the love I know I had for my mom, for Winnie, even Miles, maybe. My soul would have splintered a thousand times for Leto. I would die to learn the truth for my mom. And for my friends, I would die, so they wouldn't have to.

But my mind turns to Leto again, being with him felt like being with a poet.

What a strange thought to have. I must be losing more blood than I had hoped. But it's true, being with him felt like being with someone important. With Leto, there was desire, even in the pain.

Everything was something, and even the smallest

something meant I wasn't alone. That even if it hurt, it was a feeling. Made just for me, by him. He somehow got to curate each and every emotion I was, and wasn't, allowed to have. Was my knowing I was going to die the one he picked for me now? Did he pluck it off his shelf of torture for me? With the hands that said he loved me? As I lie here in a pool of my own blood, I wonder if anyone is going to see that I died right here on Elm Street. I hope they know my heart broke first, and then my body.

I black out but don't know how long for. When I come to, the strange thoughts keep coming.

A delusional part of me felt like finally, finally, a physical manifestation of the inside pain I felt. Of the deep hurt and abandonment, I had already been acquainted with, at least now everyone else can see it.

Why didn't I listen to Rosie? Why did I secretly long for her passion? Her adventures. Her escapes.

But it was nothing like I thought it would be. Rosie, help me. How do I not end up like you?

Just as I thought it, I see a woman's shape out of the corner of my eye. I wonder if my prayers are answered. Did my mom come home and find me missing? Did Winnie pick up Miles and figure out where I was? I make a move to try to go towards the figure. I've rolled myself onto my stomach. Please don't be *her*.

Still doing my best to clutch my wounds with one hand, I barely manage to drag and pull myself in their direction. The woman comes into full view, and my stomach drops once again. I'm reminded of the nightmare I had of the old woman in my bedroom. Only it wasn't a nightmare. It was her. At the slaughterhouse.

Under that hood. A waxy, old, crinkled face. She had been in my house, while I slept, she watched me. The apple farmer's wife. The grandmother who raised Damon and Leto. Raised them to hate women. The wretch who stabbed me. She has found me again.

She looks at me, half dead, crawling towards her, and she laughs, a cackle that runs a chill through my core. Her wild gray hair flows behind her with her long brown sweater and sweat-stained plaid dress. It's like I was only seeing half of her lunacy in the barn. Out here, she bared it all.

"I have always wanted to see those boots covered in Luis whore blood." She takes a step towards me. "But little slut Rosie didn't wear them the night she came over to see my Dale. Nope, she wore torn-up tennis shoes and those jean shorts of hers. I was the one who caught them, you know. They had no idea I was ever there."

She is starting to repeat herself, and it warns me that she's more dangerous, more wild.

"I had a feeling when he started taking care of himself, shaving, showering more, going into town. Making trades with the Berry Farm. I watched them for months until one night, when she thought she was meeting Dale. She was actually meeting me. I left one little note for her to find, and she was so easily tricked. It wasn't quick for her. No, I made her suffer. Like I suffered."

I'm still trying to slow the flow of my blood. Breathing shallow and trying to stay awake. But I know if I don't get help soon, I will die right here on Elm Street. The street my mom and aunt had so many fond memories of...until they didn't.

She goes on with only my blood to prompt her.

"And when I was finished, I buried her. But you may have guessed that. She wasn't totally dead when I put her in that hole. I wanted her to lie there, under the dirt. And under that rock, thinking about what she did to cause this. I still go and stand on that rock thinking of the girl on the swing who was now underneath it. I knew the moment I saw you dancing at my dear Leto's party. I knew you were just like your aunt. Whore boots and all. Damon did assure me you deserved it. That you were a tease. A bully. That you thought you were better than everyone, just like Rosie."

She stops to hobble closer to me. I can't help it, I have to ask.

"What about Leto? Did he know about Rosie?"

"No, you dumb bitch, haven't you been listening? It's Damon and me. We are the ones who are alike. Leto is a nasty thing, but his games stay in the psychological department. Damon's games are like mine. Much more hands-on. We didn't want Leto in the way, but you know he knows now. Didn't seem to care any." She laughs her layered cackle again.

I walked right into their unholy coven, praying the whole time to understand any of the crumbs that Leto left for me.

I am determined to keep my emotions in. She doesn't deserve to see my sadness. My feelings of betrayal. I save my energy to hold my middle together.

"You look like you're nearly there. So I'll leave you with one last thing before I get my grandsons to bury you with your dear aunt." I'm just as shocked as her that I'm not dead yet, so I turn and listen to what she has to say. If not only to keep my mind off the pain. I had nothing left. No more plans to survive anyway.

"Rodger, your mom's stupid, stupid husband." I immediately perk up. My dad. She's talking about my dad.

"He figured it out. About twenty or so years ago. Oh, it was just my luck showing up at the Berry Farm for my regular crates. I overheard him talking to the owner. Back then, she was just a girl, but of course, your aunt and Dale weren't as careful as they thought. The girl saw them together in his truck one day. I don't know what made him think to ask her about it. But she was sure who Rosie was with. And the next day, he came around snooping. Sneaking through the trees, trying to find clues of some kind, I suppose. I knew all he had to do was tell the police, and it would have been over. So fortunate that I found him. He tried to confront me when I saw him. But I got him good with my hatchet, and he didn't get too far. Found him under a tree and buried him next to his sister-in-law. Such justice. And no one was the wiser. I suppose he might be your dad? But knowing Dotty, she most likely doesn't know who your daddy is."

It was like the last piece of the puzzle had fallen into place. The last thing that I had never been able to make sense of. Rodger was so excited at the thought of me that he couldn't wait one more moment to figure out what happened to Rosie. That's what the surprise was going to be for my mom. He not only wanted my mom, but he wanted me. He used his dying breath to keep his promise to my mom. And now, so will I.

I can't help but smile. The most important thing I

got from my dad. We both were smart enough to figure it out.

"What the hell do you have to be smiling about you-"

But she never gets to finish her sentence. Because out of the darkness came a tall flash of white. From behind a giant oak tree, someone is barreling toward her and shouts. "NUTMEG!"

I hear flesh on flesh, and then flesh on pavement. One tackle and she was out cold.

"Eww, I think some of her teeth came out." I hear Miles say, as he is scooping me up and running with me into the night.

"Ray, Ray, stay with me, okay? Stay awake, Ray! Your mom is waiting for you. She is going to be so happy you're okay. I'm so happy you're okay." We are bouncing up and down, and I am going to be sick.

"I'm not okay," I whisper into the air. "I'm not going to make it."

"YES YOU ARE. I CALLED YOUR MOM. SHE IS ALMOST HERE." He speeds up, and we finally get to his bike.

"Rosie is under the granite rock on the tear drop, and so is my dad." It takes all that's left to tell him that. When I see his bike, I know I won't get to tell him later. Because everything goes black.

THIRTY-FIVE
MILES 2007
PROMISED

S he should have been here. I told her to wait for me. She promised she wouldn't do anything without me. And what does she do? Everything apparently. Because she is nowhere to be found.

Once my phone was charged, I called her like twenty times. I missed one of her calls, and she just leaves?! And who forgets their phone in a situation like this?

I'm still looking through Ray's house, trying to find anything that might tell me where she went. I called Winnie, no luck. I even called Ashley, but nothing. And then there was the note her mom left in the kitchen. I shouldn't have even left this morning. What if something happened to her?

I walk past the den and see that there is a laptop that's open on the couch.

On the screen are the property maps for Elm Street in the 70's and Elm Street now. So, she was looking into the Lees' property line...But there's no way she would have gone there alone. Not after what

Leto almost did to her last night. And who we suspect is behind her aunt's disappearance, and where the hell is Dot?

Just as I think it, I hear someone walk onto the front porch. Shit, I'm going to scare the shit out of her.

I step out of the den to make myself known, but it's not Dot or Ray that I see. It's Damon. He's peaking through the windows with cupped hands. I step back behind the den's door and see him walking around the outside of the house, looking into all the windows.

What the hell is he doing here? Ray must not be at his house, because if she is, then he wouldn't be here looking for her, right?

He walks around for over an hour looking around. But never coming inside. I look out the glass of the front door and see him running through the woods. He didn't even drive here. I wonder if he saw my bike.

And then, to my relief, I see Dot's car pulling up the driveway to the house. I come out on the porch and wave. She barely puts her car into park and runs to meet me. Only she doesn't look surprised to see me. She looks relieved.

"Oh, thank heavens!" She throws her arms around me, and I'm too confused to hug her back.

"I left my phone here when I went to Seattle. You guys didn't answer the house phone, so I couldn't tell you what was going on. The prints, the DNA, it all led back to the Lees', those apple farmers. They picked up Dale Lee earlier, but his grandson got away. Damon, I think his name was? They are working on getting a warrant to search the farm. But I was so worried

Damon would make it here before I did. Where's Ray? I've got to tell her!"

She pushes past me and goes inside, calling for Ray. I feel like I am about to tell someone their loved one is dead. Please be okay, Ray.

"Okay, don't freak out. She isn't here. I went home to shower and charge my phone, and I told her not to leave. I had to do a few things at home, and before I knew it...I don't know. Time just went by or something. And when I got here, she was gone. I took a lot longer than I thought I would; she promised me she would wait." I showed her the laptop and filled her in on what her daughter and I spoke about the night before. She looked right through me. Like I had told her, the one thing she had dreaded to hear. That Rosie was dead, and her daughter was missing. I felt like a piece of shit for not staying with Ray.

"Listen, Dot, I'm going to go find her. I'm sure she's just snooping around, and I've got these maps, so I'm pretty sure I know which side of the property to start on. Here is my number." I write down my number on a scrap of paper and give it to her. I open my phone and have her give me her number, too.

"I am going to find her and then call you right away. You stay here in case she comes back. And if she does, please call me." She flinches when I say that. But as soon as I'm done writing my number down, I jump on my bike and speed towards the side of the property I know they sold off.

It's in the shape of a teardrop turned sideways. I find her car and see the maps on her seat through the window. I follow the road till I find an opening to the property. I walk over to the fence and see that there is some torn fabric and a small amount of blood on the fence. So she definitely went this way.

I wander around for an hour in the grass until it's dark. I come to a giant granite rock. One side is covered in what I can only assume is blood; it's dry but not very old. The rust colored stain brings bile to my throat. Please don't be her blood.

My body starts to panic. No, no, no, no. I'm going to find you.

I run back from where I came and call the cops. I tell them everything and ride my bike around to the other side of the property. Once my bike is stashed out of sight, I wait there to see if I can hear any cops. Why did I leave her? I'm cursing myself.

I'll never forget the first time I saw her. Sitting in that circle playing that stupid game. Her eyes looked at me, and I just knew. There was nothing that would keep me from being around her. The way she spun and laughed and danced like she owned the place. I couldn't even focus on who was talking to me. I just kept watching her dance in those boots.

I leave my bike and jog down the road closer to the entrance of their driveway.

I have no weapons, just me. I start to sneak through the trees and see Leto's grandma hobbling in the opposite direction, going towards the road. I'm too far away to see what's going on, and so I creep over as quietly as possible.

Then I see it, her, Ray curled up on the ground, and the old woman standing over her holding something.

They are talking, and it's clear Ray isn't doing well. I decide to take a chance. I get as close as I can.

It's Leto's gran. She is talking about killing Rosie. And how she's going to kill Ray, too. And Ray's dad. She killed him, too. Holy shit, Leto's gran?

I look at Ray and realize she is not doing well at all. I need to do something. The glint of the silver only gives me the slightest pause. I don't want to freak Ray out even more, but I need to act now.

Tackling the old woman as I yell *Nutmeg!* to make sure Ray knows it's me.

I smash into the old lady, and I hear a crunch as her teeth go scattering across the pavement.

I pick her up and see that her insides are almost falling out.

Please don't die, please don't die.

"Ray, Ray, stay with me, okay? Stay awake, Ray! Your mom is waiting for you. She is going to be so happy you're okay. I'm so happy you're okay." I can't face her mom if she dies. I won't be able to face myself if she dies. My cheeks are wet with tears, mixed with her blood.

"I'm not okay," she whispers.

"I'm not going to make it."

"YES YOU ARE. I CALLED YOUR MOM. SHE IS ALMOST HERE." I run as fast as I can. I am so glad I called her mom on my way to this side of the property. It would only take her seven minutes, tops, to get here. And we finally get to my bike. Ray is mumbling something.

"Rosie is under the granite rock on the tear drop, and so is my dad."

Even though those words seem like nonsense. I know exactly what they mean.

She is covered from the top of her head to the toe

of her boots in her own blood. Her white shirt is soaking, and now mine is too.

Why did I never tell her how I felt? The first time I saw her dancing in those boots, she took a little piece of my heart with her. And every day since.

Please don't die, please don't die. Her eyes closed as soon as I heard the sirens. I could tell she was still breathing, but barely. Lifting her to my mouth, I kissed her lips and felt that she was still warm. I knew as the paramedics grabbed her from me, as her mom rushed to be at her side, I knew that no matter where she went from here on out, I would follow.

I can't believe it. It wasn't just that Rosie's body was recovered. Or that Pamela, Damon, Leto, and Dale will all do time for their parts in what happened to my sister. The unbelievable part is that Rodger, my Rodger, was every bit the man I had always hoped he was.

She tried, that skinny farmer's wife tried to make it look like he ran off, and I fell for it. But the day I told him about being pregnant, he had wanted to surprise me with what he found. He had been working so hard on tracking down people we hadn't thought to follow up with.

He found the girl who gave us the pink silk ribbon from all those years ago. He thought to ask her a few more questions, and it led him to the apple orchards. And then his own daughter figured it out.

Rosie would have loved my Rayel. Rosie did love my Rayel. After learning all that went on between Leto and Ray, it was hard for me not to believe that Rosie wasn't there beside Ray. Helping her not to end up meeting the same fate. My sister, even in death, was my person. Was my best friend. We kept dad's promise to you, Rosie. We never stopped.

Over the next few months, watching Miles care for my Ray was like having a glimpse into the past. A reminder of where I had started, shattered, I thought beyond repair. The way Rodger would show up for me in every single capacity was how I survived it. The hurt, the fear, the Rosie-sized hole in my heart. Over time, it was Rodger who had helped me patch it. Rodger, who had helped me feel worthy of happiness again. And when I looked at Ray after all she went through, she was so full of betrayal. Not sure why one man, whom she pledged her love to, could so easily discard her, in every way imaginable. While another man can take hold and cradle all the broken pieces of her, and see her as being whole. That not one part of her is too much for him. And I can see that she is starting to believe him. Realizing that Miles is right. She is deserving of all the love life has to offer.

ACKNOWLEDGMENTS

I couldn't have written, *When Edgewood Met Elm Street,* without the support of my family, especially my husband and three kids. Thank you to everyone who read and supported my first Novel. It gave me the confidence to keep writing. I hope to continue entertaining you all with my stories.

ABOUT THE AUTHOR

Bree Keller was born and raised in a small town in the Pacific Northwest. Dense forests, fog, and all the secrets they can so easily hide, shaped her insatiable curiosity. Although she has since moved out of her drizzly Seattle town, she still finds excitement in remembering all the spooky encounters that helped cultivate her love for all things macabre. Telling scary stories has been Bree's favorite pastime since she can remember. She is married, has three kids, and never misses an opportunity to share a chilling tale. So come on in, and keep your wits about you for another spine-tingling thriller.

ALSO BY BREE KELLER

Dark Del-Look for this spine-tingling romance thriller.